FOREST WOLVES

RISE OF THE IMMORTAL

DAVID W. CROPPER

CAT MAN PUBLUSHING

Forest Wolves -Rise of the Immoral

Copyright © 2024 by David W. Cropper

Catmanpublishing@gmail.com.

This novel is entirely a work of fiction. The names, characters, and incidents portrayed in it are a work of the author's imagination. Any resemblance to actual persons, alive or dead, events or localities is entirely coincidental.

Cover Illustration: Miblart

ISBN: 979-8-9890530-5-6 (E-book)
ISBN: 979-8-9890530-3-2 (Hardcover)
ISBN: 979-8-9890530-4-9 (Paperback)

Library of Congress Control Number: 2024914018

CAT MAN PUBLISHING

To my Lucky, a special cat who will always be in my heart. Thank you, my little Lucky Monster, for saving me.

This book is also dedicated to all those who feel unworthy. I want you to know that even if others doubt you, I believe in you. Let go of the past and focus on creating a better tomorrow for yourself.

CONTENTS

CHAPTER ONE

A NEW THREAT

"By the power of earth, wind, fire, and spirit, I send thee into darkness. Be gone from this place, vanish from sight, forever into the night you shall stay."

What becomes of the departed souls who do not pass into the next realm, our ultimate destination, after our time on this earth is done? Death is not a finality but a gateway to a new existence where we take on a new form. But if we resist crossing over or are prevented from doing so, we may endure an eternity of suffering at the hands of something evil.

Crox settled into his favorite chair on the back deck, his feet resting on the railing as he waited for the sun to rise over the dense forest surrounding his property.

The peaceful sounds of birds singing and leaves rustling filled his ears as he pondered the tasks ahead of him for the day. He took a slow, satisfying sip from his coffee mug, which was infused with a splash of Bailey's, in an attempt to shake off the restless night he had just endured.

The howls piercing through the forest behind his home kept him awake, a sense of unease creeping over him. These weren't the normal sounds of coyotes or wild dogs that were common in this part of Virginia; they were different and unfamiliar.

Fredericksburg, Virginia, was conveniently situated between two major cities: Richmond, the state's capital to the south, and Washington, D.C., the nation's capital to the north, both about fifty miles away. The eerie howling echoed throughout the property despite being in an urban area.

Crox couldn't shake off the feeling that something more sinister was behind it than just a pack of wild dogs. The intensity of the sound, which still rang in his consciousness even now, made his heart race and his mind wander.

Jax, Crox's loyal feline familiar, sat faithfully by his human's feet. The typically self-assured black cat appeared anxious, fear evident in his expression. His emerald green eyes were wide and dilated, giving him a disturbing appearance.

Crox Andrews, a middle-aged man with a happy spirit and weak knees, owned and operated Crox Home Sales Inc. in downtown Fredericksburg.

He had a colorful history, marked by a transformation from his wild and careless youth, which was the reason for the weak knees, to becoming a well-respected community leader as both a business owner and an advocate for making his hometown a brighter place to live.

The vibrant red hair that once adorned his head had faded to a distinguished shade of gray, and the wrinkles around his eyes told the story of his life's journey and experiences. The physical toll of his battles and triumphs was evident in the slight limp that accompanied his every step, a reminder of the struggles he had faced and overcome throughout the years.

Crox's few alluring qualities remained unchanged despite his physical limitations—his piercing green eyes and carefree attitude toward life. He couldn't resist dancing when a lively tune played on the radio. His warm smile and kind words brightened the day for anyone he encountered.

It also didn't hurt that he was born into a family of witches, from whom he inherited a few special skills. One was the ability to see earthbound spirits who had not crossed over. The other was his ability to cast minor spells from his mother's grimoire, *"Death is the Beginning,"* a powerful book of magick written by his mother using spells she had gathered from other practitioners of the mystical arts.

Crox's feline companion, Jax, also had a few extraordinary abilities. He could communicate with Crox through telepathy and see the spirits of the dead, and he had been human once. In his human form, Jax was known as Jaxson Diamond, Crox's half-brother. But after being killed, his soul was reborn into the body of a cat. Jax made it his mission to protect Crox from all natural or supernatural threats.

Crox and Jax lived on twenty acres in Stafford County, Virginia. The property was surrounded by a thick forest on three sides, well hidden from the main road. His home had once been a commune for an occult group called the Circle of the Eternal Shadow, which his mother and Jaxson had led. The coven was now disbanded, and its members were scattered throughout the Fredericksburg region and worldwide.

Jaxson was the property's original owner, but after his brother's passing, Crox inherited it. He settled in a year ago and immediately started clearing out the old single-wide trailers and rundown outbuildings that dotted the land, turning it into his home.

Crox had constructed a grand white house in the classic Georgian style, complete with two welcoming front porches and all the necessary modern luxuries for a comfortable life. The spacious home boasted five bedrooms, three bathrooms, a private office, and a fully finished basement, perfect for hosting guests.

It may have been more room than one person and a cat needed, but Crox felt that such an elegant property deserved a touch of Southern charm. He even had plans to add additional outbuildings, a pool, and a cabana in the future.

Crox relished this part of the day, observing the sun's transformation from a warm orange to a vibrant yellow, accentuating the clear blue sky. Jax lounged on the deck railing, stretching his back and emitting a soft, cautious growl. His gaze remained fixated on the thick grove of trees enveloping their land. Suddenly, Crox's ears picked up the distant sound of howling from the forest's depths.

Rising from his seat, Crox snatched his thick black jacket off the hook by the back door and ventured out into the hazy morning. Jax trailed close behind. They stood side by side in the middle of the backyard, examining the dense woods beyond, trying to pinpoint where the howling was coming from. Suddenly, a piercing howl pierced through the air, originating from the western edge of their land. Jax startled at the sound, his fur standing on end as if shocked.

Crox cautiously took a step backward, his heart pounding in his chest. The strange noise that filled the air was unlike anything he had ever heard, causing the hairs on the back of his neck to stand up and his legs to tremble. He couldn't help but wish he had brought his gun for protection.

From the dense treeline, an enormous wolf stepped out from the shadows into the early morning light. The large animal stood on its hind legs; it must have been at least eight feet tall, and its thick black and white fur flowed over its sleek, powerful build. The animal had an aura of authority around it. The wolf looked at Crox and howled loudly. The sound sent shivers down his spine. Jax stood his ground, baring his fangs, and hissed in return.

Another of its kind soon joined the giant wolf. This one was smaller, and its fur was primarily gray, with just a streak of white on the top of its head. It stood protectively in front of the larger one. The two animals stood at attention, staring intently at Crox as if sizing him up.

Crox's heart pounded intensely as he watched the two imposing animals, not quite believing what he saw. These creatures did not look like ordinary wolves, and their presence in this part of Virginia was nothing short of unnatural.

Over the years, he had been in those woods multiple times and had seen many things, but nothing that even compared to the animals that now looked at him as if he were breakfast.

In his mind, a faint whisper echoed. It was Jax communicating telepathically. "They are from the other realm," the cat's voice trembled. The Shadow has released them from the dark realm and into the forest.

"What? I think you are mistaken. We defeated the Shadow," Crox spoke out loud to the cat. "I think it must be wild dogs or something. I'll call animal control and have them look into it." In his heart, Crox knew his words were a lie, but his mind couldn't fathom another battle with the supernatural.

Just twelve months prior, Crox and Jax had fought fiercely against an evil known only as the Shadow. This evil entity had emerged from an alternate dimension, and it was up to Crox to close the portal that allowed it access to their world. With the help of his mother's coven, they had managed to place a protective spell over his homestead, hopefully shielding them from further mystical dangers.

Jax gazed at Crox with a mixture of shock and disappointment. After everything that happened the year before, Jax couldn't believe Crox was ignoring his warning. Crox needed to set aside his fear because if this were the work of the Shadow, they would have to revive the coven Circle of Eternal Shadow. Ever since the occult group disbanded, the protective spell over the forest surrounding their home had weakened.

Crox stepped back into the house and closed the door behind him, heading straight for his home office. He settled into his red leather chair with gold rivets at the large maple desk and pulled out a bottle of bourbon. Without hesitation, he poured himself a generous four-finger portion and downed it in one swift gulp.

The memory of the Shadow's attack was still fresh in his mind; he refused to consider anything related to witchcraft. Since that fateful battle, he had consciously tried to lead a mundane life of normalcy.

Shaking off the fear that had overtaken him, with the help of the bourbon flowing through his veins, he called the Sheriff's Department and got through to animal control, to whom he reported wild dogs in the woods off of Ramouth Church Road. He thought to himself, "Let them deal with it. I have no reason to go back into that forest again."

After the call to animal control, Crox came into the family room and saw Jax sitting in the cat's favorite place, an antique Paul Bunyan rocking chair, looking at Crox with disappointment. The cat could sense the unavoidable danger, and the sooner Crox understood this, the faster they could deal with it, hopefully before someone died. They were dealing with something more than wild dogs in the woods. Something sinister was afoot.

Glancing out the kitchen window, Crox saw the two wolves standing on the forest's edge, staring intently at his house. Their presence felt threatening, as if they were waiting for him to make a move. He reached for the .38 special pistol on his side table and tucked it into his waistband. Taking a cautious sip of bourbon, he thought it was better to be safe than sorry.

Jax leaped onto the windowsill, fixated on the two wolves outside the house. It was as if they could sense his presence, and they gazed directly at him before unleashing a loud howl in unison. Jax couldn't contain his fear and began hissing and baring his tiny fangs. The whole scene felt surreal, almost like a scene out of a cheesy B movie horror flick.

Crox couldn't shake the feeling of impending danger. The howling from the forest persisted, and the presence of those two wolves gnawed at the edges of his soul. In his heart, he knew these were not merely wild dogs. Jax's ominous warnings couldn't be dismissed any longer.

He decided to explore his mother's grimoire, *"Death is the Beginning,"* which she had left him as her final gift after her death.

Maybe something within its pages could provide insight into these wolves. The old book, bound in worn leather, contained a wealth of information on dark spells, rituals, and supernatural entities that existed beyond the mortal world. He went to his floor safe and retrieved the grimoire. Carefully opening the potentially dangerous book.

As he began to read, the room grew colder as he poured over the pages. He remembered this sensation well from his fight with the Shadow when he had used the spells from this book to push back an evil that sought to claim his very soul. The words on the pages started to shift, rearranging themselves, forming new spells before his eyes.

Crox followed the newly formed text and began to chant the words, invoking a spell of his mother's making to create a connection to the spirit world. The room darkened as the spell took effect. Suddenly, his form was transported to the woods beyond his property. He found himself standing at the forest's edge, the wolves' howls resonating in his ears.

Crox could sense the presence of the Shadow, that evil entity from the past. It was still here, lurking deep within the woods. The Shadow had grown stronger, feeding on the lingering darkness of the past, and it had summoned these wolves to do its bidding. In his mind, he heard the Shadow say, "You will be mine, and I will be free; you were promised to me."

Jax jumped onto the desk and pushed the grimoire onto the floor, which caused the vision of the woods to disappear.

Jax then telepathically told Crox, "You are not strong enough to use this power alone. Put this book back in the safe now." Crox was taken aback, but he knew the cat was right deep down, so he did as he was told. He had no business playing with powers he could not control.

He closed the spell book and locked it securely in the floor safe. The room returned to normal. The Shadow's message was clear; he may have to face it again, and the thought of dealing with the Shadow again turned Crox's stomach.

Crox looked at the clock; it was now 8:30 a.m. It was too early for this craziness, he thought. He had always been able to compartmentalize his emotions, and now would be no different, he thought to himself as he went into his bedroom and crawled back into bed.

Perhaps this had all been a dream, he thought to himself as he pulled the covers over his head. In response to Crox ignoring the obvious, Jax hacked up a moist hairball, a reminder of who the boss was in this house. As he lay in bed, Crox attempted to dismiss the eerie events of the morning as mere figments of his imagination.

The sun had continued its ascent, filling the room with a welcoming warmth and light. Crox closed his eyes, trying to convince himself that the howling wolves were just a figment of his exhausted mind. But deep down, he couldn't shake off the sense of unease. He knew something was wrong, a darkness lurking just beyond this reality, and it filled him with fear, knowing that something horrible was approaching.

CHAPTER TWO

DO NOT ENTER

Mary Brynes, a middle-aged woman from Fredericksburg, was determined to end the suffering of feral cats in her community.

She volunteered at Operation Help, a non-profit organization specializing in trapping, spaying/neutering, and releasing stray cats back into their natural habitat. Mary has devoted her life to caring for these vulnerable creatures by providing food, shelter, vaccinations, and sterilization procedures to break the cycle of unwanted litter. She also collaborates with local animal shelters to find permanent homes for these cats.

After hearing about the increase in stray cats on Ramouth Church Road, Mary couldn't longer ignore the situation.

Despite the forest's known dangers—where people had gone missing or died—Mary was determined to help these cats. She gathered her supplies this morning and entered the dark forest to set traps and rescue the abandoned cats.

Her destination was an old, rundown shack off Ramouth Church Road. The driveway was barely visible from the overgrown vegetation surrounding it, indicating that no one had lived there for quite some time. Weeds and small trees had overtaken the area, almost obscuring any traces of human presence.

A do-not-enter sign tied between two trees on a cable chain blocked the driveway leading up to the rundown house. Additional signs were scattered about every five hundred feet on the property. Despite knowing she was technically breaking the law by entering without permission and risking trespassing charges, Mary believed her mission was justified and would deal with any consequences.

Mary had heard rumors of a nearby abandoned commune and supposed witchcraft in these woods, but her desire to save the feral cats outweighed any fears or superstition. Mary ducked under the chain and ventured into the darkness of the forest. Setting up traps every few feet, she hoped to rescue as many cats as possible and give them a better life.

As she ventured further into the forest, a feeling of being watched crept over her. The haunting sound of howling echoed through the trees, reminding her of the potential danger lurking in this unfamiliar terrain. Other than feral cats, what other wild animals roamed these woods?

The thick trees and shadows of the forest felt like they were pressing in on her. Fear overcame Mary, causing her to drop her bag filled with food for the traps. She quickly turned and sprinted towards her car.

The sense of being watched was overwhelming, and she knew deep down that something unseen was chasing her as she darted through the trees back to her car. She had to escape, and she had to do it quickly.

Just as Mary was about to retreat to the safety of her vehicle, she was confronted by a pair of glowing green eyes in the darkness. They belonged to a small gray wolf with a white patch on its head. The wild animal stared at her with an intense, predatory focus. Frozen in fear, Mary could not move; she lost control over her bodily functions and felt the wetness running down her right leg.

Out of the shadows appeared another wolf, one larger and with sleek black and white fur. It stood beside the smaller wolf, effectively cutting off any escape route for Mary. As the smaller wolf circled behind her in a predatory fashion, Mary could sense the intelligence in its eyes and the glint of sharp teeth illuminated by the morning sun peeking through the trees. A chill ran down her spine at the sight of these two figures, emanating an aura of pure wickedness before her.

The forest's silence was shattered by a deafening, spine-chilling howl that sent shivers down Mary's spine. She stumbled backward, her feet tripping over the gnarled roots as she tried to escape the approaching wolves. The darkness of the trees seemed to swallow her whole as the wolves' hungry snarls grew closer and closer. With Mary now on the ground, the smaller wolf attacked. With each snap of its jaws, Mary's screams of agony was soon drowned out until all that remained was the sound of the wolf's ravenous feeding. Her flesh was torn apart, revealing her still-beating heart, which they devoured by the wild beast with gusto. The Shadow had demanded a sacrifice and claimed its first victim in a gruesome display of blood and terror.

Crox awoke in a state of distress, drenched in sweat. In his dream, he had heard the piercing screams of a woman in utter terror, and the sound still echoed in his mind even as he woke up. He lay there trembling, unable to fully remember the details of the dream, only knowing that something terrible had happened to someone close to him.

Crox's dreams held more significance than just random images; they were a channel for him to communicate with his spirit guides and receive visions from the past, present, or future.

The fact that he couldn't recall the specifics of this particular dream troubled him deeply - it almost felt like something was deliberately blocking his memory of what he had dreamt.

Feeling a sense of heaviness in his chest, Crox got out of bed and went through his morning routine of showering, shaving, and dressing. Jax, his loyal guardian, followed him to the kitchen, where he made a strong pot of coffee.

As he waited for it to brew, the landline phone suddenly rang, a rare occurrence since everyone usually contacted him on his cell phone. Crox hesitated before picking up, unsure who could be calling from an unknown number. However, against his usual instincts, he answered the call. A hesitant voice on the other end asked for Mr. Crox Andrews. Still unsettled by his dream, Crox asked, "May I know who's calling?"

Officer Laura Burrows of the Stafford Sheriff's Department introduced herself to Crox as she spoke. She informed him they found his contact information in Mary Byrnes' abandoned car, located on a section of his property. Crox's heart skipped a beat at the mention of Mary Byrnes' name. He explained that he knew her only in passing, and he couldn't understand why her car would be on his property. His stomach dropped with a sense of dread as he asked if something was wrong.

Officer Burrows explained, "We're still in the process of investigating. Her son reported her missing, stating that she had planned to go into the woods on your property a few days ago to set traps for feral cats. However, she has not been seen since then. We discovered her vehicle, but there was no sign of her or the traps. Her family is worried about her. According to her son, it's not like her to not let them know where she is."

Crox couldn't shake off the shiver that ran down his spine as he listened to the officer's words. His mind jumbled with fragments from his dream and the eerie coincidence of this situation. After briefly pausing, he replied, "I haven't seen Mary in months. Mary never mentioned coming by to trap feral cats on my property. It's private land, and I have posted clear do-not-enter signs.

I did call Animal Control about some wild dogs I spotted in the forest yesterday. I hope nothing happened to Mary."

The officer sighed heavily and explained, "We're assembling a team to search the surrounding woods. We will need to search your property as well. Please inform us if you remember anything or hear from Mary Byrnes."

Crox responded, "Of course, feel free to search wherever you need to. If there's any way I can help, please don't hesitate to ask. I'll keep an eye out for her as well."

After hanging up the phone, Crox felt dread fill Him as he lowered himself into a chair at the kitchen table. He stared blankly at his cup of hot coffee, lost in thought.

Jax nuzzled against Crox's leg, breaking him out of his thoughts. The cat emitted a strange noise between a growl and a purr. Crox bent down to stroke the cat, finding solace in the simple act. He finished his coffee and stood up from the table. Despite his gut feeling that Mary was not alive, he remained determined to discover the truth behind her disappearance.

Crox phoned Sheriff Relda Michealson, his good friend who had played a crucial role in saving him from the Shadow's grasp last year. He had been introduced to Relda through her ex-girl-friend Vonda, a mutual friend of Crox and his mother, Pittapat. Vonda had once been a member of the Circle of the Eternal Shadow, further highlighting Fredericksburg's smallness despite its growing population.

Relda was a tall, no-nonsense woman with a close-cropped hairstyle and curves that accentuated her police uniform perfect-ly. She was known as Stafford County's youngest and first black female sheriff and an expert marksman. Beyond her impressive credentials, Relda had also become a dear friend to Crox and Jax.

After finally getting past the gatekeepers at the Sheriff's office, Crox reached Relda on the phone. He explained the details of his call with Officer Burrows about Mary's disappearance and his encounter with wolves in the forest. Knowing that Relda was an expert in law enforcement and supernatural matters, he asked for her help.

Relda agreed to meet with him after her shift ended that night to discuss the situation. With some time to kill before their meeting, Crox decided to walk around his property.

As Crox put on his coat and put the Smith & Wesson .38 pistol in his pocket, he heard Jax say telepathically, "You are not leaving without me."

Crox smiled and answered, "Of course not. I wouldn't have it any other way than to have you by my side."

Crox and Jax leisurely strolled down the man-made path behind the house, basking in the warm afternoon sunlight. Suddenly, an eerie quiet descended upon the forest, with no chirping birds or buzzing insects to be heard.

The sun began to set, and the moon started to rise above the horizon; Crox couldn't shake off the chill that seemed to penetrate his skin down to his bones. He glanced at Jax, whose eyes were wide with fear.

The cat could sense something nearby. A piercing howl shattered the silence, reverberating through the woods. Despite feeling unnerved, Crox's curiosity pushed him forward. He and Jax ventured deeper into the trees.

In a clearing, he saw the massive black-and-white wolf from before, watching them intently but not making a single move. After a moment, it turned and disappeared into the forest's darkness before the wolves noticed them.

Crox and Jax swiftly turned and sprinted back to the house. Jax had to slow down his pace to match Crox's, who was only blessed with two legs instead of the cat's four. They reached the house's safety, and Crox quickly secured the door behind them.

As the sun set and darkness descended, Crox nervously sat and waited for Sheriff Relda to arrive, occasionally getting up to pace around the living room with Jax following closely behind.

The Sheriff's knock on the door relieved Crox, and he eagerly opened it to see his friend. Relda's expression hinted at mischievousness as she entered, her first words to him being, "So, what's happening at Crazy Catman Manor, Sunshine?"

Crox recounted all the unsettling events that had occurred recently - Officer Burrows's call about Mary disappearing.

Crox also told his friend about his strange dreams and the unnerving encounters with wolves on the property. Relda informed him that she had spoken to Officer Burrows and knew all about Mary's disappearance. Crox reminded her that Mary was someone he knew personally from charity work and not just a random person.

Crox advised he didn't want any trouble from the police if she had gone missing on his property. Relda listened attentively, and her brow furrowed in thought. She then explained that she would thoroughly search the woods and surrounding area the next day, ensuring to cover every inch of the property. She also wanted to know if Crox thought something supernatural had returned to the forest. As if on cue, Jax let out a piercing yowl as if to say, "Damn right, there is; you better recognize." Relda ignored the cat, as she could not understand the feline the way Crox could.

As the night grew darker and the moon illuminated the room, Relda and Crox sat at the kitchen table, surrounded by the warm glow of candles. Jax perched on the windowsill, his eyes reflecting the flickering light as he watched over the two humans. Crox took out a bottle of bourbon and poured drinks for himself and Relda to ease the tension in the room.

The bourbon helped relax them as they discussed their plans for the next day. Meanwhile, Jax remained fixated on something outside, occasionally letting out a low growl. It seemed as though the cat could sense an unseen presence watching them.

Relda, feeling a bit drowsy and maybe even tipsy, said goodnight to Crox and made her way out. He wished her a safe journey back home as Jax watched with disinterest. They were both exhausted; it had been a long day and would only get longer. Crox headed to his bedroom, Jax following behind him, and they both prepared for bed.

Crox settled under the covers and drifted off to sleep. He thought he heard a woman's voice speaking to him in his mind.

Crox slowly opened his eyes and saw a faint silhouette illuminated by the moonlight at his bedroom window. A woman appeared to be in distress, frantically waving her arms and mouthing words that he couldn't hear.

Crox tried to move, to go to her and provide assistance, but something held him back. A jolt of primal fear shot through his body, causing him to freeze in bed, unable to break free from its grasp. He could only stare in terror as the same word repeated over and over in his mind like a broken record - "Death." The figure at the window seemed to grow denser, its shape morphing and shifting, emanating a sense of pure malice.

Suddenly, the mysterious figure disappeared into the air, leaving behind a lingering stillness. Sleep or the bourbon took hold of him, and Crox passed out. The following morning, he briefly questioned whether what he had witnessed was reality or a figment of his imagination from a bad dream. But deep down, he knew the truth: a supernatural entity had indeed returned to the woods.

CHAPTER THREE

THE PACKAGE

Crox's nightmare was more than just a mere dream; it felt like a warning of things to come. In the strange realm of his unconscious mind, he found himself lost in a vast forest. The bright moon hung low in the sky, casting an eerie silver glow that filtered through the treetops. Stumbling through the thick underbrush, he couldn't shake off feeling entirely alone and in danger. Every step seemed to reverberate through the silence of the night, and his heartbeat pounded loudly in his ears.

In the distance, a chilling howl shattered the stillness, sending shivers down Crox's spine. With a growing sense of dread, he quickened his pace, trying to get away from whatever was out there in the darkness. Shadows danced among the gnarled trees, and the moonlight played tricks on his mind.

The deeper he went into the forest, the more it felt like something was closing in on him - as if the shadows themselves were alive and had their own sinister intentions for him. Then came another howl, closer this time. Panic surged through him as he realized that he was being hunted.

The trees seemed to move and twist menacingly, their branches reaching out like bony fingers to capture him. He stumbled over exposed roots and moss-covered rocks falling to the ground, his breath coming in ragged gasps.

He was then stunned at the sight of numerous glimmering eyes peering at him from within the shadowy thicket ahead. A pair of wolves materialized from the darkness of the trees. Their sharp teeth gleamed in the moon's luminous glow, and their eyes displayed an uncanny human-like awareness.

These were no ordinary wolves; they were beings with the minds of men, their piercing stare exuding a calculated ferocity and their howls resonating with an eerie intelligence.

With synchronized movements that seemed orchestrated by some unseen force and propelled by a shared purpose, the wolves began to converge upon Crox. Every step mirrored his own as if anticipating his actions, a relentless pursuit driven by an insatiable hunger for something beyond mere flesh. Their howls rang out as one, almost as if communicating through a telepathic link.

Crox frantically weaved between the trees, his heart pounding as he tried to outrun his pursuers. But the wolves were relentless and seemed to predict his every move. Every escape attempt turned into a treacherous dance through the dark forest.

Crox soon came upon a clearing filled with scattered rocks. In the center stood a circle of stones, with a large pentagram burned into the ground. An ominous feeling crept over him—he had been to this place in the past, where darkness reigned supreme and evil dwelled. A lone wolf whose eyes held a glimmer of recognition as if it were a human emerged into the clearing, followed by the smaller wolf. Crox stood in the center of the rock circle upon the pentagram as the two wolves encircled him, their piercing stares locked onto their prey.

The leader wolf emanated an undeniable aura of power, and its human voice rang out with a mixture of reason and feralness that sent shivers down Crox's spine as it spoke. "You can't run from us. We are creatures of the night, summoned by the Shadow from the dark realm. Our purpose is to eradicate you and your coven."

Crox woke up suddenly, drenched in fear and warm wetness. He realized he had wet the bed and shivered from the embarrassment of pissing the bed. He dragged himself out of bed and changed the sheets before putting them in the laundry. Jax watched from a corner with a pensive expression.

They both made their way to the kitchen for breakfast, but not before noticing an envelope on the floor near the front door. It must have been slipped through the mail slot in the front door. Crox opened it and found a photo of Mary Byrnes and a small crystal pendant hanging on a black velvet rope.

At the bottom of the image was a handwritten note in a foreign language that vaguely resembled Latin, though Crox couldn't understand it.

Crox placed the photo gently on the table, his heart heavy as he thought about Mary. He didn't need to look at it to know she was no longer in the living world. He then picked up the crystal pendant, and Jax, his familiar, sprang into action. The cat jumped up and swatted the pendant out of his hand.

Crox crouched down to pick it up but was met with a loud hiss from Jax, who backed away in fear. Something about the crystal clearly spooked the feline. Crox quickly picked it up, pocketed it, and called Relda to tell her about the photo and pendant. Relda listened intently before asking who might have sent it and what it could mean. "I have no idea," Crox replied absentmindedly.

Relda agreed to come over and see the mysterious package before going to work. As Crox waited, he couldn't shake off the lingering unease from his nightmare. The details of the dream replayed in his head, and the sinister presence of the wolves, particularly their leader.

Crox wondered if there was any connection between his dream and the disturbing package. When she arrived, Relda thoroughly examined the photo and crystal necklace. Her expression grew more serious as she analyzed the photo. "This note," she said, squinting at the foreign writing. "Do you know what it says?"

Crox shook his head. "No." He suggested taking it to Galinda the Good Witch: Books, Curiosities and Notions, an occult shop nearby. Sun-Moon, the owner, might be able to provide some insight into the writing and the crystal.

Relda promised to pick him up the next day for a trip to the downtown Fredericksburg shop. Today, she had a lot going on and needed to leave right away. She kissed Crox goodbye and headed toward the door, where Jax was waiting for her to get out, as she had nothing to add and, in his view, was wasting their time. As soon as Relda left, Crox heard Jax's telepathic voice say, "Do you really want to bring that crazy bitch Sun-Moon back into your life?"

Sun-Moon had once been a devoted follower of his mother's cult, the Circle of the Eternal Shadow. Crox didn't respond to Jax's question out loud, but he couldn't hide his thoughts from his feline familiar, who responded with an eye-roll of disgust. The cat was correct; Sun-Moon had been involved in his mother's wicked cult. However, she had also helped him defeat the Shadow - the powerful entity his mother and her coven controlled.

The following morning, Relda arrived to pick up Crox and take him to Galinda, the Good Witch's occult store. Crox still felt the unease that had settled upon him since his nightmare. Relda noticed his discomfort and tried to reassure him.

"Don't worry, we'll figure this out. Sun-Moon is crazy as hell but knowledgeable in occult matters, and she might be able to decode that note and shed light on the crystal pendant. It looks like some occult artifact.

Yes, she may be eccentric and untrustworthy, but she could potentially help us," Relda said, keeping her eyes on the road.

They crossed over the Falmouth bridge, leaving Stafford County and entering the City of Fredericksburg by crossing the Rappahannock River. Crox felt a knot form in his stomach at the thought of seeing Sun-Moon again; it would surely be an unpleasant experience. Sun-Moon was the type who would have worked as a double agent for the Union and Confederate troops during the Civil War, two-faced to the core.

They slowly made their way down Caroline Street; the sounds of the highway faded away as they approached the quaint occult shop in Fredericksburg's historic district. The one-way streets and centuries-old buildings created an atmosphere of traditional values and old money, but this coexisted with the presence of progressive youth and working-class individuals.

While parking the car a block from the occult store on Sophia Street, Crox couldn't help but wonder how this store had managed to survive and how its owner evaded damnation for openly practicing her unconventional beliefs. When they entered the shop, the air was thick with the smell of incense, making Crox's eyes water and his head begin to ache. Sitting on a stool and wearing an extra large bright orange mumu, Sun-Moon greeted them.

"Ah, Crox, my dear, it's been far too long since we've seen each other," Sun-Moon purred, her voice low and sultry. Relda greeted the heavy-set woman with a forced smile, trying to hide her suspicion and disdain. She explained the strange package Crox had received and watched as Sun-Moon's eyes lit up with interest.

Sun-Moon examined the photograph and crystal pendant, slowly turning them over with her portly fingers, her gaze intense and calculating. "Dark energies surround this," she murmured, tracing the edges of the note with a fingernail painted black as night. The language is ancient; this appears to be a spell that calls upon the power of the dark forces. Whether it is a warning or a threat, I am not sure. Deciphering its true meaning will take time."

Crox couldn't help but shift uncomfortably as memories of his mother's cult flooded back to him.

Crox could feel the presence of his mother around them as Sun-Moon continued, "And this crystal pendant looks to be a conduit for energy fueled by a desire for revenge. Someone has purposely infused it with dark magic, using it as a tool for their nefarious plans." Sun-Moon stated.

Relda, always practical, inquired, "Really? Can you give us any more details, like who sent it?"

Sun-Moon's expression turned cold as she locked eyes with Relda. Her vibrant, bright pink hair seemed to take on a darker hue, reflecting her changing mood. After moments of tense silence, she finally spoke, "I recognize the handwriting; it belongs to one of my clients, Hazel East. She owns Simply You Salon on Amaret Street. Perhaps you should visit her and waste her time?"

Relda disregarded Sun-Moon's sarcastic tone and, in an overly sweet voice, said, "Bless your heart, dear; thanks for what little help you have provided." Which basically meant, go fuck yourself in southern speak.

Crox said nothing as he left the occult shop, not bothering to bid farewell. On the sidewalk, he and Relda exchanged meaningful looks, both visibly relieved to have left Sun-Moon behind. They hopped into the car and headed towards Amaret Street. As they drove, Relda asked, "Do you think this hairdresser, Hazel East, has any information about Mary Byrne's disappearance or who sent this pendant through your mail slot?" "The only way to find out is by talking to her and observing her reactions," Crox replied.

Relda pulled the car into a parking spot outside Hazel East's hair salon on Amaret Street. The neon sign above the entrance flickered, giving the place an old-school charm.

As soon as they stepped out of the car, the scent of hairspray wafted through the parking lot. Upon entering, they were greeted by a young blonde girl, no older than five, who announced their presence.

A woman Crox assumed was around seventy with vibrant black hair streaked with red and purple, wearing tight jeans and a blue halter top, looked up from attending to a client's hair and welcomed them.

Hazel asked them to sit and said she would be with them shortly. Another stylist emerged from the back room and escorted the little girl out of the shop, leaving just the four of them inside.

Crox and Relda sat on the hard, uncomfortable Ikea chairs, patiently waiting for Hazel to finish with an elderly woman getting an old-fashioned perm. Crox's eyes wandered around the salon, taking in its eccentric decorations. The walls were adorned with strange paintings covered in occult symbols—some of which Crox recognized from his mother's grimoire. Hazel East's salon appeared to have a dual purpose: hairstyling and serving as a hub for paranormal believers.

After assisting her elderly client to her car, Hazel returned to Crox and Relda. Her violet eyes glinted with a sharp intensity as she addressed them. "What can I do for you today?" She asked politely, though an undertone of annoyance could be heard in her tone.

Crox took a deep breath and got straight to the point. "I received a package with a photo of a missing woman, Mary Byrnes, and this crystal pendant in my mail slot. Sun-Moon from the occult shop on Caroline Street suggested you might have some information about it."

Hazel's expression didn't change, but there was a flicker of amusement in her eyes. "Ah yes, a little present I sent Mary. She was quite the nuisance, poking around where she shouldn't have been. The crystal carries a mild curse, just a bit of payback for her meddling."

Crox's temper flared, but Relda quickly grabbed his arm to keep him from acting rashly.

"What do you mean by meddling? What did Mary do?" Relda demanded

Hazel's laughter was like nails on a chalkboard, causing Crox to shiver involuntarily. "Mary stumbled upon something she shouldn't have, and I'll leave it at that."

"Why did you come onto my property and put this through my mail slot? I barely even knew Mary, let alone you!"

Hazel's face could not hide the shock of this; she stuttered, "Whaaat are you talking about? I left this for Mary at her house a week ago. I have no idea how you got it."

A dark expression crossed Hazel's face, betraying her thoughts. Even at her advanced age, Crox could sense that she could be dangerous.

Hazel glanced at Relda and spoke in a dry, sarcastic tone. "Sheriff, if you're going to arrest me for something, just do it. Otherwise, kindly get the hell out of my salon. I have nothing else to say to you."

Relda and Crox exchanged a knowing look, realizing they were at a pivotal point. The tension in the room was palpable as Hazel stared them down. Holding his breath, Crox spoke calmly.

"We have no intention of causing trouble. We want to understand what happened to Mary; she's disappeared. If you didn't put it in my mailbox, then who did?" Crox's gaze remained fixed on Hazel's.

Hazel strode over to the door, opened it, and motioned for them to leave. As they exited, she closed the door firmly behind them, and the sound of the bolt locking echoed in Crox's ears.

Crox furrowed his brow and asked, "So, what's our next move?"

"I'm still figuring that out," Relda admitted. "I can't just arrest the old woman based on her claiming to have cursed a necklace. I'm heading back to the sheriff's office to follow up on the case of Mary Brynes and check if Officer Burrows found anything during her search of your property. I'll let you know if I come across any new leads."

CHAPTER FOUR

ANOTHER GIFT

Despite his appearance, Jax was not an ordinary telepathic feline familiar. He had not always roamed the streets as a feline. This sleek, muscular cat with piercing green eyes use to be a man named Jaxson. Unfortunately, he fell victim to the Shadow and had his soul imprisoned by the evil entity. But now, in cat form, taking the name Jax, he managed to break free from the Shadow's grasp and aided Crox in banishing it back to its dimension.

Not only was Jaxson a powerful witch in his human life, but he also could communicate with spirits and manipulate weak minds. Along with their mother, Pittapat, and Jaxson's girlfriend, Analee Morgan, the three were leaders of their coven, the Circle of the Eternal Shadow.

It was founded over a hundred years ago by a witch from Kentucky named Victoria Parham, a woman hell-bent on revenge.

The family had been forced out of Kentucky for practicing dark magick. Victoria, along with her husband and four children. They settled in Stafford County, Virginia. After starting her coven, Victoria brought the Shadow to our world, trapping it in the forest with the help of her fellow occult members.

Decades later, Jaxson and his mother, Pittapat, lost their lives while attempting to control the Shadow creature and keep it confined within the forest on Ramouth Church Road. This was all on the twenty-acre land that now belonged to Crox, who inherited it after Jaxson's horrific death.

Through the use of powerful dark magick, Victoria Parham summoned the Shadow into our realm. She harnessed its deadly abilities to eliminate her enemies and maintain control over her coven as their high priestess. After Victoria's demise, one of her loyal followers took over the coven.

The Shadow remained confined to the forest thanks to the occult group, unnoticed by the unsuspecting community; if the residents had known of the deadly evil in their backyard, the coven members might have been put to death.

Decades later, after Victoria's passing, Crox's mother, Pittapat, took on the role of high priestess within the coven. Together with Jaxson and Analee, they attempted to safeguard the Fredericksburg area from the evil forces of the Shadow. However, as time went on, Pittapat became drawn to the tempting power of the Shadow and began dabbling in dark magic herself.

The Shadow demanded a sacrifice in exchange for its services in giving Pittapat spells to control the coven. It started with smaller offerings but eventually demanded someone from Pittapat's bloodline.

Aside from Jaxson and his daughter, Crox was the only remaining blood member of Pittapat's family. With his two older brothers deceased, it seemed inevitable that Starleena would inherit the role of high priestess when she came of age.

That left Pittapat with no choice but to select her son, Crox, as the sacrificial offering for their deity.

Crox's magical abilities were subpar, and he was not a Circle of the Eternal Shadow member. To appease the Shadow and gain the power she desired, Pittapat saw him as the perfect sacrifice to offer in death.

Despite his mother's plan, Jaxson refused to let Crox perish and instead offered himself as an alternative to appease the Shadow. He ventured into the forest alone to confront the Shadow and offer his life.

The Shadow, however, had no intentions of letting go of the soul it was promised. He would have both brothers. So the entity took Jaxson's life, trapping his soul while waiting to do the same to Crox.

Jaxson bargained with the Shadow to get it to release his soul back into the land of the living; in doing so, his soul was reincarnated into a cat's body.

Since they were linked by blood and Jaxson was still a witch, he could communicate with his brother telepathically. Jaxson then took on the name Jax, becoming a familiar and helping Crox defeat the Shadow.

With the assistance of Jax and a few other witches, Crox successfully banished the Shadow back to its dark realm. As a result, those who had been held captive by the Shadow were released, and their souls were reincarnated as cats, who now serve as guardians of the forest.

Once the intense battle was over, the foreboding forest near Ramouth Church Road transformed into a peaceful sanctuary watched over by the spirits of those who had fallen victim to the Shadow. A variety of cats with emerald green eyes now roamed the woods, protecting it from any future darkness that may try to invade the living realm.

After Jax became a feline familiar, he became the leader of their newfound mission to protect and maintain the balance between the magical and mortal worlds.

Despite their different forms, Jax's bond with Crox remained strong as they worked together from their home in Stafford, Virginia. While running his real estate brokerage, Crox Home Sales Inc.,

Crox dedicated his life to preserving the natural harmony of the woods and safeguarding its hidden secrets.

He was guided by the spirits of his ancestors, who watched and supported him in his endeavors.

Using his mother's powerful book of magick, "*Death is the Beginning*," Crox continued to hone and reinforce his magical abilities, aided by his telepathic familiar, Jax.

Along with the army of guardian cats, they ensured that the Shadow remained banished and unable to breach the mystical barrier surrounding the forest. However, as he soon discovered, this may not have been enough to keep its dark influence at bay.

Crox sat in his home office in the evening, scrolling through real estate listings, trying to shake off the unsettling feeling that the nightmare he had a few days ago and the strange package he had received were somehow connected.

He couldn't make sense of it or determine who could have sent it to him. The unease weighed on him like a heavy stone resting on his brain, causing his head to ache. Meanwhile, Mary Byrnes was still missing despite multiple searches of the surrounding forest that yielded no clues or leads.

Sitting on the windowsill, Jax noticed Crox's unease and communicated telepathically. "The forest is agitated," he said, "and the cats who live there are reporting strange happenings near the hidden cavern."

The cavern was deep within the forest and difficult to find. It was also where the Shadow had been summoned from over a hundred years ago, and then, with the help of the Circle of the Eternal Shadow, Crox had sealed it away in its realm.

Crox's brow furrowed as he realized his nightmares may have been a warning. "We must stop whatever is causing this before more people go missing. Perhaps I can gather the remaining members of the Circle and seek their aid."

Jax looked concerned. "The protection spell around our home is weakening. We must reinforce first before doing anything else."

Crox nodded, determined to find a way to fortify their spell and contact the other members of the coven. "Let's go see Sun Moon," he suggested.

Jax gave him a skeptical look and countered, "I don't trust her; let's call Vonda instead."

The mention of Vonda's name sent a shiver down Crox's spine. It had been over a year since they last spoke. He couldn't forget how she had betrayed him, working with his mother to sacrifice him to the Shadow. And to think, she had only befriended him to gather information for his mother.

Vonda was not a witch or gifted with any supernatural abilities, but she held great influence over the Circle of the Eternal Shadow members that they were all once part of. Her estate, named "Honey Suckle Hill," sat on a large hill in Stafford County, just a short distance from Crox's home.

Crox's friend and Sheriff of Stafford County, Relda, had been in a relationship with Vonda at different times, so he and Relda were frequent visitors to Honey Suckle Hill. Vonda was known for throwing extravagant parties, reserved only for adults, that were the talk of the town. Her lively personality and anything-goes attitude were contagious.

Crox had given her the nickname "The Vonderful Vonda," as she was sixty-nine but had the energy and spirit of someone half her age. With her long white hair and piercing blue eyes, Vonda was a stunning beauty who used her looks to her advantage. Although Crox wasn't sure if he was ready to forgive and make amends with Vonda, he had agreed to Jax's suggestion of reaching out to her. He had no choice; Vonda still held power over those who served in the Circle of the Eternal Shadow.

After a brief pause, Crox gathered his courage and dialed Vonda's cell number. As he waited for her to answer, he couldn't help but wonder if she would even pick up. To his surprise, she responded immediately.

"Crox, my dear! What brings me the pleasure of your unexpected call?" Vonda's voice came through the phone, infused with her mischievous nature.

Crox took a deep breath, attempting to control his emotions. "Vonda, I need your assistance. Something strange is happening in the forest, and I fear the Shadow may be trying to return.

A local woman and friend of mine, Mary Byrnes, has gone missing in the forest, and I had a dream that feels like a warning of more deaths to come."

There was a moment of silence before Vonda responded with a serious tone. "The Shadow? Not again! I'll be right there. We can discuss this face-to-face."

After hanging up, Crox was left with a jumble of emotions. He had been trying to forget and move on from Vonda's past involvement with his mother's evil deeds, but if he wanted to stop the looming threat in the forest, he needed all the help he could get.

Not long after, Vonda arrived at Crox's house, her confident stride and charismatic presence filling the room. Jax, perched on the windowsill, eyed her with caution.

"Crox, my dear, you look like you've just seen a ghost. Don't worry, it's only me," The Vonderful Vonda said with a playful smile.

Crox paused before speaking, "Vonda, I need your assistance reinforcing the protective barrier around my home. Can you contact the remaining Circle of the Eternal Shadow members who possess magical abilities? Wolves are lurking in the nearby forest that I believe were sent by the Shadow."

Vonda's tone turned serious, "The Circle has a purpose of confining that evil being, and if the Shadow is stirring again, we can't ignore it. I will contact those living in this area and ask them to strengthen the protection spell. I am more than willing to do my part."

Vonda informed Crox that she kept in touch with most of the cult members, many of whom had joined another church dedicated to the occult. However, they were still searching for their spiritual path and had not found it.

Vonda assured him that she would gather those with magical powers to come and reinforce his home's protection spell. She made it clear that she did not want to enter the forest herself, as she did not wish to encounter whatever lurked within its depths.

In just under two hours, Vonda managed to gather a diverse group of individuals at Crox's house.

The seven members, aged thirty to eighty, consisted of two men and five women. Of the two men, both were white; two women were also white, while two were black, and one was Hispanic. Initially hesitant, Crox eventually accepted Vonda's decision that these individuals could help protect him and Jax.

With Vonda leading the way, the nine began the ritual to strengthen the protection barrier surrounding the house. As they chanted the incantation, a powerful electric energy filled the air, fueled by their collective voices.

"Calling upon the powers of earth, wind, fire, water, and spirit, we declare this home to be a sanctuary protected from harm. We invoke the spirits of our ancestors to envelop this house in light and shield it from darkness."

As the group chanted the incantation, a faint purple aura surrounded the property, creating an invisible barrier to protect against any dark forces attempting to enter. Using his telepathic abilities, Jax focused on connecting with the guardian cats in the nearby forest, ensuring they remained vigilant against the encroaching darkness.

With the shield now in place, Crox thanked Vonda for her assistance. Despite their underlying tensions, the urgency forced them to put their differences aside - at least temporarily. He also expressed gratitude to the others for their help and promised to consider reviving the Circle of the Eternal Shadow.

Crox was grateful that the spell would protect them if they stayed inside the house and away from the dark woods. The supernatural shield was powerful enough to ward off any harm.

After everyone left and he and Jax were alone, Crox prepared dinner. They enjoyed a delicious meal of homemade Mac' n Cheese with pasta shells, chicken, and broccoli baked into it.

Afterward, Crox and Jax snuggled up and watched Bridgerton on Netflix until it was time for bed.

As Crox drifted off to sleep, a calmness settled over him like a warm blanket. The stillness of the night enveloped him in a gentle embrace, lulling him into a sense of tranquility.

Little did he know, this peaceful slumber would soon be shattered by unforeseen events to come.

The next day, Crox woke up feeling refreshed and content. Jax was also in high spirits. After breakfast, Crox suggested they go into town to meet Relda for some coffee.

As they walked down the main hallway towards the kitchen, Crox casually hummed a tune. Suddenly, he caught sight of something glimmering near the front door. A shiver ran down his spine as he approached and saw what had been pushed through his mail slot.

On the floor rested a ring, shining with brilliance. It was made of white gold and featured a princess-cut diamond surrounded by smaller diamonds. However, its beauty was overshadowed by the gruesome image it was attached to: the ring was looped around the severed finger of its owner.

CHAPTER FIVE

BYE BYE BIRDIE

Crox's heart pounded in his chest as he stared at the severed finger lying before him; the diamonds in the engagement ring sparkled in the morning light shining through the window. The sight was gruesome and disturbing, causing a knot to form in his stomach. The gruesome sight made him feel queasy.

He fought back the urge to vomit as the wave of nausea overwhelmed him. Jax heard Crox retching and hurried into the front hall to investigate. Seeing the severed finger, Jax felt an inexplicable desire to eat it.

"What kind of twisted shit is this?" Crox cried out, stumbling backward as his head spun.

After regaining his composure, he reached for his cell phone in his back pocket. His hands were shaking as he dialed the sheriff's department to report the severed finger. He left a message for Sheriff Relda Michaelson to come and see for herself.

Relda and her two officers arrived at Crox's house with their sirens blaring within twenty minutes. The officers searched every inch of the property, looking for clues about who had sent the finger or if there were any other body parts. Unfortunately, they found nothing.

While Relda had one of her officers gather fingerprints from the door and mail slot, Crox and Jax stood outside, waiting for the police to finish their search. After three long hours, the officers finished investigating the house and property. They took Crox's statement before leaving.

"What do we do now?" Crox asked Relda, who had stayed behind after the other police officers had left.

"I'll send the finger to the FBI in Quantico. They have a department that analyzes latent fingerprints. Hopefully, they can identify the owner. I'm assuming it belongs to Mary Byrnes. I will also check the engagement ring for any identification markings; most jewelry stores keep records of their customers," she replied.

"Do you think it's Mary's finger? How awful."

"I want to know who put it in your mail slot. Do you have any enemies or suspects I should be aware of?" Relda asked in a flat tone.

"No, I can't think of anyone who would do this," Crox whispered.

Relda promised to update him on any progress regarding the severed finger and Mary Byrnes. She said her goodbyes and left to return to her office.

Crox watched Relda pull out of the driveway, then returned inside the house and stood in his family room, unsure what to do next. The horrifying discovery haunted him and took him to a dark place mentally. Memories of the past, the Circle of the Eternal Shadow, and the supernatural battles in the forest resurfaced.

Now, a missing woman who was possibly killed on his land. Sensing his distress, Jax stayed close, offering silent support through their telepathic connection.

"Did the protection spell not work?" Crox asked his feline familiar.

"Nothing evil can cross the barrier," Jax said flatly.

"Then how did that nasty Finger get in my house!" Crox yelled at the cat.

Looking offended, Jax stuck his tail up and walked away.

While Crox was dealing with body parts being delivered to his home, Sun-Moon was being visited by Hazel East, the elderly but precarious hair stylist. As she entered the occult shop, Hazel went right to the point, disregarding any Southern platitudes.

"Your wicked charm killed someone. You have blood on your hands, bitch." Hazel said, glaring at Sun-Moon.

With an air of superiority towards the visitor, Sun-Moon sarcastically replied, "Pish Bosh, what are you talking about, you old witch? I suggest you watch your mouth if you want to remain standing."

"How dare you threaten me? Do you realize Mary Byrnes is dead because of your little hex charm? Hell, they can't even find her body. Why in the hell did you send that damn real estate agent and his friend, the dyke Sheriff, to my shop?"

Sun-Moon didn't respond but only smiled slyly at her hysterical visitor.

"You are an evil bitch!" Hazel screamed, her voice cracking with rage. Her face flushed crimson as she clenched her fists, trembling with fury. She spun on her heel and stormed out of the store, the bell above the door jingling violently as she slammed it behind her.

Sun-Moon laughed while she walked behind the sales counter, pulling out a notebook from under the cash register.

She opened it, showing a list of names; just under Mary Byrnes's crossed-out name was Hazel East's name. With a red pen, Sun-Moon crossed out her visitor's name.

She murmured to herself, "Just one more to go."

While Hazel was causing a commotion at the occult store, Crox took some time to shop downtown, unaware of what was going on a few blocks away.

Instead of getting into arguments with local witches, he was at Ace Hardware on the other side of the Rappahannock River across from the City of Fredericksburg, in the historic part of Falmouth, the birthplace of George Washington, our nation's first president.

Crox gathered lights and cameras, determined to discover the source of the disturbances on his property. Despite a protective spell surrounding his home, something was still breaking through, and he was determined to put a stop to it. After purchasing additional lights and cameras, Crox set to work installing them along the perimeter of his home. Jax observed silently from nearby, allowing Crox to focus on his task undisturbed.

With the cameras in place, Crox connected them to a central monitoring system inside his home. This way, he could constantly watch the area and hopefully catch any unwanted intruders or supernatural beings attempting to breach the protective barrier.

Using their telepathic connection, Jax communicated with Crox. "The forest is tense, brother. There's an uneasy energy, and even the guardian cats can feel it. We should stay near the house."

After setting up cameras for added security, Crox cooked dinner for himself and Jax. They both sat down to watch a few episodes of Supernatural on Netflix before going to bed, feeling slightly more at ease.

While Crox and Jax took a brief break from the chaos, Sheriff Relda Michaelson focused on her investigation of the missing Mary Byrnes. The FBI had been sent the severed finger for analysis, and Relda was also in contact with local jewelers to trace the source of the engagement ring. The town was abuzz with theories about Mary Byrnes' disappearance, including rumors that her unfaithful husband may have played a role.

The following morning, Crox awoke feeling watched. He sat up in bed and scanned the bedroom. Jax was sleeping peacefully at his feet, and no one else was in the room.

Crox noticed the curtains on the window were pulled back, allowing light to filter into the room.

Curious, Crox approached the door from the bedroom leading to the upstairs porch and stepped outside.

In the hazy morning mist, he noticed small paw prints scattered across the second-floor balcony. It seemed that a visitor had come by during the night, watching him as he slept. Even if it was just a cat from the nearby woods, Crox couldn't shake off the feeling of unease.

Crox playfully climbed onto the bed, rousing Jax from his slumber. "Did you notice someone watching us through the window last night?" Crox inquired, stroking the cat's fur as he stretched and yawned.

Jax glanced at Crox and then turned to look out the window, a flicker of uneasiness crossing his features. Without a word, he hopped off the bed and hurried downstairs.

Crox followed suit and started brewing a pot of coffee. He poured himself a bowl of cereal and gave Jax his morning meal of kibble. As they ate, the sound of something being placed through the front door's mail slot made them both jump.

"Oh sweet Jesus, What the hell now?" Crox thought.

As he made his way to the front of the house, he braced himself for yet another shocking discovery. But instead of a severed finger or a weird charm, his eyes fell upon a red cardinal. The bird was clearly distressed, perhaps attacked by some wild animal. Crox quickly unlocked the door and scanned the area, but no sign of anyone could have forcefully shoved the injured creature through his mail slot. His legs trembled with fear as he gazed into the surrounding forest, searching for potential threats.

The bird was still alive. Hurriedly, Crox retrieved an old Amazon box from his attached garage and carefully placed the wounded animal inside, cushioned by a few kitchen towels.

"I have to get him to the emergency vet," Crox advised Jax.

The black cat licked his lips and said, "I think you should let me have it. It looks delicious."

The comment made Crox's stomach turn as he looked at the cat distastefully.

"I will be back later, you nasty thing," Crox mumbled as he got into his truck and drove off to the vet.

After several hours of running tests and examinations at Saint Frances Animal Hospital, the veterinarian assured Crox that the bird he found was in good health and had no significant injuries. They handed the bird back to Crox along with a whopping $700 bill.

Uncertain of what to do with the bird now, Crox hesitated to bring it home with Jax lurking around. He remembered a local wild bird feed store on Caroline Street and figured the owner might have some advice on caring for the injured bird. With this idea in mind, Crox drove to Wren and Sparrow and noticed it was only a few doors down from Galinda the Good Witch: Books Curiosities and Notions, the occult shop. He marveled again at the diverse community of Fredericksburg. However, as he pulled up, he saw that the bird shop was closed for the day. He would have to return tomorrow.

Unable to bring the bird home because of Jax, he took it to his Crox Home Sales Inc. office. He planned to leave the bird with his office manager, Armand, and ask him to care for it for the next twenty-four hours.

Crox arrived at his real estate office, taking a deep breath before entering. He was still the owner but had left the day-to-day operations to Armand, a middle-aged man with white hair and a relaxed demeanor. The agents who worked at the brokerage enjoyed working with him. Crox, however, was not a big fan of Armand after discovering that he used to be a member of his mother's cult, the Circle of the Eternal Shadow. Unbeknownst to Crox, his mother had sent Armand to watch over him a few years ago when she planned to sacrifice him to the Shadow.

When Crox found out, he fired Armand. However, after Armand helped him fight against the Shadow last year (using his limited witchcraft skills), Crox rehired him for his usefulness.

Armand was back working at the real estate brokerage under Crox's supervision despite their past.

As Crox entered his real estate office, Armand looked up from his desk with a strained smile. "Hey, Crox! What brings you here?" he greeted.

Crox sighed, glancing at the box containing the injured cardinal. "Long story. I need a favor. Can you take care of this bird for me? It needs some attention, and I'll pick it up tomorrow."

Armand raised an eyebrow, curious but not prying. "Sure thing, Crox. I'll find a cozy spot for our feathered friend. Is there anything else going on?"

"Nothing that concerns you," Crox said without emotion as he left the office, got in his truck, and returned home.

"What a dumb Ass," Armand said after he saw the truck leaving the parking lot, knowing Crox was out of earshot.

Crox drove in silence, trying not to dwell on the strange occurrences happening around him. His thoughts drifted back to his late mother's grimoire, and he wondered if it held any clues about the mysterious gifts being left at his door.

When he finally arrived home, Crox found Jax waiting for him in his office, perched on the desk.

"Hey there, little guy. I have good news for you - the cardinal survived and is doing well," Crox said with a smile.

Jax licked his lips again, and Crox heard his telepathic voice say, "I would have been happier if you let me eat that bird for dinner."

"Eww, gross," Crox replied.

Just then, his phone began to ring. It was Relda on the other end.

"Hey buddy, we got some information from Quantico. The severed finger belongs to Mary Byrnes. We also discovered that her husband Harry has been having an affair with Hazel East."

"What?!" Crox exclaimed in disbelief.

"That's what I've heard. Apparently, the old woman has something special that Harry can't resist. They've been seeing each other for a while now, meeting on a regular at the no-tell motel Relax in on Princess Anne Street."

"Are they going to be charged with Mary's disappearance? She must be involved somehow." Crox asked.

"We don't have enough evidence to charge them yet. But I'm bringing them in for questioning. I'll update you later." With that, Relda ended the call.

"Well, that could be one piece of the mystery solved," Crox muttered.

"No, it's not. Something else killed that woman, and it's coming after you," Jax warned ominously.

"I think I might agree with you. And that worries me," Crox replied as he walked out onto the back deck, staring out into the forest—Jax trailed behind, providing comforting purrs along the way.

CHAPTER SIX

UNDER SUSPICION

Crox closed his eyes and inhaled the fresh grassy scent of the meadow. The soft blades tickled his bare feet as he walked, making him smile. He paused under a towering maple tree, its leaves rustling gently in the warm breeze. Suddenly, his cousin Danny appeared before him, but something was wrong. Danny's mouth moved rapidly as if trying to convey an urgent message, but no sound came out. Crox strained to listen, suddenly aware that he couldn't hear anything. In this dream state, he was mute.

Crox shifted uncomfortably as his cousin Danny's frustration radiated from him like a bomb ready to explode. The tension between them thickened with each passing second.

Danny raged on, attempting to tell his cousin something meaningful. His voice booming but falling on deaf ears, Danny clenched his fists, ready to knock some sense into his cousin, who looked at him like an idiot.

Crox felt frozen, unable to move or utter a single word to calm Danny's frustration.

Crox felt like he was sinking deeper into a thick fog, unable to break through and communicate with his cousin. Suddenly, the scene changed, and Crox was standing alone in the dark forest, with multiple trees looming over him and an eerie stillness hanging in the air. His heart raced as he realized he was lost and alone.

As the moon rose high in the sky, a black-and-white wolf stepped out from behind a giant oak tree. Its thick fur gleamed under the silver light, and its piercing green eyes seemed to hold otherworldly wisdom as it stared at Crox. To his astonishment, the wolf opened its mouth and spoke in a soft but commanding tone as if it were one with the wind that rustled through the forest.

"I am Amara. The Shadow has sent me to find you. My master demands your soul, and I will not rest until my mission is complete."

The shrill ringing phone startled Crox awake, and he flailed in the darkness, tumbling off his bed with a loud thud. He checked the time on his alarm clock – 7:30 am – and cursed whoever was calling him at this ungodly hour. Struggling to untangle himself from his sheets, he finally grabbed the phone and answered gruffly, "Who the hell is this?"

"Good morning," came the cheery voice of someone who had obviously already had their morning coffee.

"Who is calling this damn early," Crox asked hoarsely.

"My, somebody isn't a morning person. It's Lola Knight, your old near in Fredericksburg, came the chippy reply.

"Hey, Lola, sorry. I didn't mean to sound so rude. I'm just waking up. To what do I owe the honor of your call his fine morning."

"Sorry to have awakened you, but you know me. I am up with the morning frogs. I haven't seen you since you moved to Stafford, and I wanted to get together.

If you are free for lunch today, I would love to take you out to Foode if you are up to coming downtown. The chef just won another competition and is now considered a *Top Chef*."

Crox responded, "Sure, I have to go downtown today. I found an injured bird and wanted to talk with Melisa and Emily at Wren and Sparrow to see if they could take it off my hands. How about we meet at noon?"

"That sounds like a plan. I will arrive a little earlier to get a table since the place is usually packed. I can not wait to get their chicken and waffles. See you in a few," Lola said before hanging up.

Crox lay in bed, still trying to wake up fully. He thought Lola's call was odd. He had not spoken with her since he moved a year ago, but he did not dwell on it. He got up and made his way to the kitchen. A strong pot of coffee was calling his name.

Jax was already in the kitchen waiting to be fed. He stared at Crox, waiting for him to do the right thing and feed him before attempting to do anything else. The cat was a bit of a prima donna.

After he and Jax were fed, Crox shit, showered and shaved. Ready to sparkle. He advised Jax not to tear up the house and that he would be home later. The cat could not come with him. Jax, though offended, did not say anything as the human can opener walked out of the house.

Crox headed to his office; he planned on picking up the bird and hopefully ridding himself of the obligation by dumping it on Melisa and Emily at the bird shop. The two women were avid wild bird lovers, so he was sure they would comply without making too much of a fuss.

Crox arrived at Crox Home Sales Inc. and found the place deserted. Armand had placed the bird in the conference room with food and water. The red cardinal looked in good shape, though it wasn't flying. The vet said there had been no damage to its wings, so Crox wasn't sure why the bird couldn't fly. He figured he would leave it to the bird ladies to figure out.

Crox gently scooped the wild bird into a cardboard box and carried it to his truck.

The tiny creature didn't resist or flutter in fear as if it sensed Crox meant no harm.

Crox drove down Princess Anne Street, turned onto William Street, and found a parking space conveniently located between Wren and Sparrow, the bird shop on Caroline Street, and Foode, the restaurant where he was meeting Lola on Amelia Street.

Crox walked the two blocks to Wren and Sparrow. As he entered the shop, Melisa, one of the owners, greeted him. "Hey, Cracker Jacks, what's shaking? Long time no see. Do you need some hot birdseed to keep the squirrels at bay?" She asked

"Hello, sunshine," Crox said, smiling. "I have a little gift I need to dump on you."

Melisa looked puzzled as she looked in the box and saw the small bird. Crox explained how the animal somehow got through his mail slot and looked like it had been attacked, but the vet said no major injuries occurred.

The bird lady promised she would take care of the cardinal. Just then, a gay couple Crox knew walked in. Will and Willy Williamson. The two were also friends with Melisa and had stopped in to buy a *Birds of Virginia* book.

Crox had known the couple, Will and Willy, for a few years, but he hadn't seen them since he started building his new house in Stafford. Will stood at 6'2" with a neatly trimmed beard and glasses perched on his nose.

Will worked as an anthropologist and preferred quiet nights at home playing board games with small groups of friends. On the other hand, Willy was a vibrant 5'4" retired Latino man. He dyed his hair different colors, refusing to accept his natural gray. Unlike Will, Willy loved being the center of attention wherever he went. Despite their differences, both men were devoted to one another and fiercely loyal to those they cared about.

"Hey bitch, how's it hanging? Where the hell have you been?" Willy said, addressing Crox.

"Hey, slut puppy," was Crox's response.

Crox wrapped his arms around the two men, giving each one a bear hug, and shared with the couple his reason for being there – to discuss the bird – but kept quiet about the strange events surrounding it.

After a few minutes of chatting, Crox bid the group farewell, telling them he had a scheduled lunch meeting but assured them he would be in touch soon.

As Crox walked out the door, Willy turned to his husband Will with a concerned look. "Did you see how worn out Crox looked? Do you think he's okay?" Will grabbed a book and a bag of birdseed from the shelves. "I'm sure he's fine, but we can check on him next week if you'd like." Willy rolled his eyes and playfully tugged on Will's arm. "Yes, master, whatever you say," he muttered sarcastically as they headed towards the register.

Crox made his way through the bustling streets of downtown Fredericksburg, dodging tourists and street performers. He finally reached Foode, a trendy restaurant known for its award-winning owner and mouthwatering dishes. As he approached, he saw a long line snaking out the door. But just as he was about to turn away, a familiar face appeared in the window and waved him over. Lola had snagged a prime table near the front, using her charm (and maybe a few bribes) to secure it before the lunch rush.

When Crox took a seat, the efficient waitress had their order and drinks on the table in just a few minutes. Their renowned chicken and waffles dish was delicious, made with locally sourced ingredients from nearby farms. To complement the meal, he also requested a bottle of Odeimin, a strawberry wine produced by a local winery called Mattaponi.

Crox couldn't help but be captivated by Lola's stunning appearance as they savored their meal and glasses of wine. Her deep, flawless complexion accentuated her shapely figure and ample bosom, catching the eyes of every man in the establishment, regardless of their sexual preference. But it wasn't just her physical beauty that drew attention; her large, expressive eyes, laid-back personality, and sharp mind added to her appeal. As he got to know her better, Crox learned that Lola was a high-ranking member of the FBI, recently promoted to head the fingerprint identification division.

After taking a long sip of her wine, Lola's gaze sharpened as she focused on Crox. "What is happening at your house? I was the one who processed the latent fingerprint from that severed finger you found. And guess whose finger it belonged to - Mary Byrnes, who used to live in our neighborhood while you were still my neighbor. I had no choice but to inform the investigating officer, and now the FBI is involved. Did you play a part in Mary's disappearance?"

Crox's jaw dropped in shock as Lola posed her question. "Why would you even ask me that, Lola?" he exclaimed incredulously. "Is this why you called me here? To accuse me of murder? That's absurd."

Lola leaned back in her chair, studying Crox's face intently, her eyes narrowing.

No, I don't believe you killed Mary," she stated firmly. "But strange things have been happening around you, and I need to know if there's something you're not telling the police. Your property was the last place she was seen before she went missing."

Crox shifted uncomfortably, unsure of how to answer. He couldn't reveal the truth about the portal to another realm in his forest or his encounter with the wolves. He definitely couldn't tell her about his mother's grimoire and its dark magic. How could anyone understand the dark secrets of Ramouth Church Road and its sinister history? She saw him as just a regular real estate agent, unaware of his true origins as a descendant of witches. Little did she know that he could communicate telepathically with his cat and even have an entity from another realm in his backyard, capable of killing anyone who entered his property.

Crox responded with a monotone voice, "I have no idea what's happening. Someone shoved the finger through my mail slot, and I can't even begin to guess who or what might have been responsible for Mary's disappearance. The only peculiar occurrence is the delivery of these strange gifts through my mail slot."

"What kind of gifts?" inquired Lola, her eyes piercing with suspicion.

Crox felt uneasy answering this question, but he replied anyway. "First, there was a small charm along with Mary's picture, then the finger, and finally an injured bird." He hoped this would satisfy her curiosity and not lead to more probing questions

Lola's voice was filled with suspicion as she asked, "Do you have any idea who could be leaving these strange gifts? The finger had bite marks on it from a cat."

"I honestly don't know," Crox replied. "Relda from the Stafford Sheriff's Department is looking into it."

He couldn't reveal anything about Jax or their encounters with supernatural forces. He couldn't risk being taken away by his former neighbor and locked up in a mental hospital or, even worse, jail.

Lola sipped her wine and finally relented, "Okay, I believe you. But be cautious. The FBI is now looking into this. If they discover any connection to you, it could spell trouble." Crox nodded in agreement but remained silent as he finished his meal, feeling uneasy about the situation.

As they exited the restaurant, Lola hugged Crox and promised to stay in touch. But Crox couldn't shake off the feeling that she still had concerns about him. He felt like he had been set up during the lunch meeting.

All he wanted was to go home. As he walked back to his truck, Crox couldn't help but feel that both Lola and the Stafford Sheriff's Department were closely monitoring him, suspecting him of something.

Crox drove home with Lola trailing behind him in her blue Toyota Highlander. She had a soft spot for Crox and didn't want to believe he was involved in Mary Byrnes' disappearance and possible death, but the evidence couldn't be ignored.

After all, the severed finger was found on his property. As much as Lola didn't want it to be true, she had to investigate Crox because if he did commit the crime and she helped crack the case, it could boost her career.

Unaware of Lola's presence, Crox pulled into his driveway while she drove past it and parked a few hundred feet away.

Lola parked her cart on the side of the road and went through the trees to the edge of Crox's backyard. From this vantage point, Lola kept a close eye on Crox using high-powered binoculars for a couple of hours, waiting to see if anyone came by or if Crox exhibited any suspicious behavior that could incriminate him for murder.

Crox stepped into his home and immediately felt watched. He glanced outside and noticed the blue indicator light on his security system was flashing, alerting him that it had been activated while he was away. Curiosity getting the better of him, he checked the cameras but found nothing unusual, just an orange cat darting through his backyard toward the nearby woods.

Ignoring his growing unease, Crox headed to the living room for a much-needed nap, hoping to alleviate the pounding headache that had plagued him all day. As he drifted off into sleep, he couldn't shake off the image of the wolf from his dream, whispering menacingly, "I am coming for you, and the Shadow will have your soul."

CHAPTER SEVEN

LOVELY NIGHT TO DIE

Relda's determination to solve the mystery of Mary Byrnes' disappearance had hit a dead end. The only piece of evidence she had was the severed finger, which wasn't enough to prove if Mary was still alive or not. She could have been the victim of a random animal attack or had an unfortunate accident but still be alive.

In her search for answers, Relda spoke to Mary's husband, Harry Byrnes, who revealed that they were going through a separation and he had no knowledge of her whereabouts. The district attorney's office couldn't charge Harry with anything without solid proof. The photo and charm sent to Crox were deemed insufficient for a search warrant or to bring him in for questioning.

Despite the ongoing investigation, Crox tried his best to maintain a semblance of normalcy.

With the strange gifts no longer appearing in his mail slot, Crox shifted his focus to his daily routine and occasional visits to his office at Crox Home Sales. The real estate firm thrived thanks to his efficient office manager, Armand. Despite things going well, Crox couldn't shake off the feeling of being watched, which lingered each day. It was a constant reminder that his peaceful existence could be shattered at any moment; he felt like he was walking on thin ice.

One evening, while sitting on his back deck and enjoying the serene forest surrounding him, Crox's calm was suddenly interrupted by rustling in the bushes beyond the backyard at the forest's edge. Jax, who was sitting beside him, immediately perked up and stood on high alert, fur bristling and claws extended as he gazed into the darkness. Crox strained his ears, trying to pinpoint the source of the noise. Even the forest seemed to have fallen silent in anticipation.

A low, deep growl echoed throughout the thick undergrowth as a massive wolf emerged from the shadows, looming at the edge of the tree line. Crox's heart raced in his chest. The wolf's intense green eyes were fixed on him.

"Do not fear. It cannot break through the barrier spell. It is still holding strong," reassured Jax.

"Why is it staring at me?" whispered Crox aloud, more to himself than to Jax.

As the large wolf continued to observe Crox, Will and Willy Williamson were planning a romantic evening. Earlier that day, Willy had been in a sour mood, and Will was determined to turn things around. Will had gifted Willy with a high-end camera for his birthday, and he couldn't wait to use it.

"On our way, Let's swing by Crox's place. He has a stunning wooded area around his home. I want to capture some shots of those tall trees and maybe even capture a picture of the elusive northern mockingbird.

Melisa mentioned the bird only comes out at night. After we finish with our photography, we can visit Crox, have a glass of wine, and catch up."

Will let out a small sigh as he watched Willy become fixated on the idea of a nighttime walk through the woods. His husband could be a real pain in the ass.

"Did you already contact Crox to see if we can visit him?" Willy asked eagerly, anxious to get started. The sooner they got started, the sooner they could return home.

"No way. Let's surprise him. It's been ages since the bastard invited us over for dinner in his fancy new house." Willy replied.

"Fine, let's do it. And I must admit, it's a beautiful evening for a stroll through the woods." Will conceded defeat, knowing he had lost the argument.

Will and Willy loaded their camera equipment into Willy's small Mini Cooper, eagerly anticipating the opportunity to capture the stunning night landscape and visit Crox. As they drove toward Crox's estate, Willy proposed they park at the beginning of his long driveway and explore the nearby woods before going to the house afterward.

Before reaching Crox's driveway, Willy parked his car on the side of the road, leaving enough space for other vehicles to pass by and for Crox to exit if he needed to leave. They grabbed their equipment and set off into the woods, following a path leading back to the road.

The moonlight filtered through the thick canopy overhead, casting an eerie glow on the twisted branches and foliage. As they ventured deeper into the woods, the men became disoriented in the darkness. Will suggested they find their way back to the road before it was too late, not wanting to risk getting lost in the unfamiliar woods. Will kept his fear of what may be lurking in the shadows hidden from his husband.

Their heavy breaths created visible clouds of mist in the chilly night air as they pushed through the dense underbrush, desperately searching for any signs of the road.

Every rustle of leaves and snap of twigs seemed to send shivers down their spines as they imagined what potential dangers were lurking in the darkness.

As the couple strolled down the path, they were unaware of the two hungry wolves trailing them. The predators moved silently, their eyes glinting in the darkness. The men's instincts warned them of an unknown danger and urged them to pick up their pace. Fear coursed through their bodies as they quickened their steps.

Suddenly, the forest erupted into a cacophony of menacing howls. The once-hidden wolves emerged, closing in on their prey at a terrifying speed. The men were now being hunted. Willy became overwhelmed with fear as he felt the warm liquid trickle down his left leg. The smell of urine filled the air, causing the wolves to attack.

The larger wolf leaped forward, swiftly closing the gap between them. Its sharp teeth snapped shut with a sickening crack as they sank into Willy's right leg. His agonizing screams pierced through the stillness of the night, echoing through the trees and shaking the entire forest. The intensity of the pain was overwhelming, causing him to lose control of his bowls and soil himself, ruining his new shorts.

The smaller wolf moved with a graceful yet menacing swagger; its eyes fixated on Willy's vulnerable neck. It circled him, ready to eat its prey, baring its sharp teeth in anticipation.

Then, in one swift and brutal movement, it leaped forward. The wolf's sharp fangs sang into Willy's soft neck, tearing out his vocal cords with savage force. The sound of his screams was drowned out by the gush of blood that erupted from his throat, resembling the powerful geyser at Yellowstone National Park.

The larger wolf joined in on the attack, sinking its teeth into Willy's chest, and viciously tore the skin from the bone. With an insatiable hunger, the wolf ripped out Willy's still-beating heart and devoured it greedily. Frozen with fear from the horror he was witnessing, Will was unable to move as his husband's body thrashed on the ground in excruciating agony.

The wolves continued their victorious attack, ripping into the man's body with relentless fierceness.

The forest floor was drenched in blood, and the metallic scent of death, mixed with the involuntary release of Willy's bodily fluids, hung heavily in the air.

Will's survival instincts finally kicked in. He stepped back, trying to distance himself from the relentless predators. The wolves had already claimed their first victim and turned their attention to the last remaining prey. Will was alone in the forest, knowing that no one would hear his cries for help and uncertain of what fate awaited him at the mercy of these ravenous creatures.

Out of nowhere, the forest was filled with a chorus of tiny growls that made the wolves stop in their tracks. A pack of cats emerged from the shadows, each a different size and color. At least thirty or forty of them formed a barrier between Will and the two wolves.

The sight of the standoff between the felines and wolves under the bright moonlight was unsettling. Will was still in shock as the cats hissed and snarled at the wolves, their fur bristling and tails puffed up like bottle brushes in defense of their territory. The narrow slits of their eyes glinted in defiance, reflecting the moonlight.

The larger of the two wolves, undeterred by the sudden appearance of the feline army, bared its teeth in response. It let out a low, guttural growl, its eyes locked onto the nearest cat, an orange tubby tabby. The wolf's teeth, sharp and glistening with saliva, caught the moonlight, making them appear even more menacing. It stepped forward, muscles rippling under its coarse fur, ready to kill the small felines that dared to challenge it.

The cats, however, did not waver. The orange tabby stood its ground, arching its back and letting out a fierce hiss echoed by its companions.

The forest was silent except for the low growls and hisses of the opposing sides. Will could feel his heart pounding in his chest as he watched the scene unfold.

Out of the darkness, a figure emerged into the moonlight. Lola, the FBI agent who had been discreetly surveilling Crox's property, stepped into the clearing with her gun drawn.

She had silently trailed the two men through the woods after spotting them parked near Crox's home.

Lola looked at Will and whispered, "Walk over to me slowly." She waved her .357 magnum from the larger wolf back to the smaller one. Will slowly approached the black woman with the big gun, his mind a blank; he had no idea where he was or what was happening.

"Get behind me now!" Lola shouted. The urgency in her voice snapped Will out of his daze, and he quickly moved to position himself behind her.

The larger wolf looked at Lola and bared its teeth, but it seemed to know the danger of the gun. It looked at the smaller one and then back at Lola. She could have sworn they were having a conversation without speaking. The two all of a sudden took off into the woods, leaving behind the bloody remains of Will's husband.

Lola kept her gun trained on the retreating wolves until they disappeared into trees. The forest fell eerily silent. The only sounds were Will's labored breaths and the distant hooting of an owl.

"Are you alright? What's your name?" Lola asked, her voice softer now as she turned to face Will.

Will could only nod, shock and grief written across his face. The reality of what had just transpired began to sink in as he stared at the ghastly scene that was once his husband.

"I'm Lola. Let me help you back to my car and call for an ambulance."

"Ambulance, are you kidding!" Will screamed, "We need a fucking hearse! My husband has just been torn to pieces by those wild animals."

Lola took the hysterical man by the arm and led him back to her car, calling 911 as they walked. As the two humans retreated from the death scene, the orange tabby cat emerged, prowling around Willy's body.

The cat slowly and meticulously began pawing at the dead man's back pockets. Soon, the orange feline thief had Willy's wallet in its teeth and darted back into the darkness of the woods.

The wolves hadn't entirely run away; they lingered just out of sight, watching the fat cat steal the dead man's wallet. The larger wolf howled, prompting the smaller one to join in. Their howls echoed loudly through the night, sending birds and other woodland creatures fleeing in fear.

The haunting sound of the wolves lingered in the air as Lola guided the still-shaken Will back to her car. The forest seemed to close in around them, the darkness bearing silent witness to the gruesome event that had just unfolded. Lola's sharp instincts told her there was more to this than a simple animal attack.

After a short wait, the Stafford County volunteer Rescue Squad showed up and took Will to Mary Washington Hospital. Lola could see that he didn't have any physical injuries, but emotionally, he was deeply wounded.

Lola watched as the ambulance disappeared from view, then made her way to see Crox. He had to be aware of the wild animals that roamed his property; he could potentially face consequences for the death she had just witnessed.

Lola noticed a faint glow from within as she approached the house. It seemed he was home, unaware of the tragic events that had unfolded just moments ago.

Heart pounding, Lola knocked on Crox's door, realizing at that moment that she was also in a state of shock. The door slowly swung open, revealing Crox's perplexed expression as he saw her standing on his doorstep.

"Lola, what the hell? It's 10:00 pm. What are you doing here?" Crox asked.

Lola's chest heaved as she took a deep, shuddering breath. She began to recount the horrific events that had taken place in the woods, holding nothing back. With each word, Crox's face grew paler, and his eyes widened in shock at the news of Willy's tragic death.

When she finished her story, Lola made her way to the kitchen and settled down at the table while Crox continued to pace back and forth, his mind reeling from the news, his footsteps reverberating on the polished wooden floor. Why were Will and Willy lurking around his property at night? The revelation of Willy's death was like a blow from a sledgehammer.

Two people he knew were now gone, both meeting their end on his land. And despite Mary's body not being found, deep down, Crox felt it was only a matter of time before they found her dead body.

"Did you know there were wild wolves on your property?" Lola asked.

"I was aware of what I believed to be stray dogs roaming around back there. I did call animal control about it," Crox replied.

"A lot of good they did," Lola stated absently.

She decided to verify Crox's story with animal control in the morning to be safe. Maybe he honestly had nothing to do with Mary Byrnes' disappearance. Perhaps she was a victim of the wild animals in the forest. But where was her body? Lola scrutinized Crox, sensing that he was somehow involved.

Lola bid Crox farewell as she departed, suggesting he contact the local police department—they might want to take his statement. As she settled into her car, she couldn't help but think what a lovely evening it had been. It was a shame it had to end the way it did.

After Lola's car disappeared from view, Jax entered the living room and leaped onto the couch beside his human. In Crox's mind, he heard the cat say telepathically, "More deaths will occur if you do not bring back the Circle of the Eternal Shadow."

Crox stepped out onto the back porch, lighting a cigar. As he watched the smoke swirl into the night air, a thought crossed his mind: "What a lovely night to die."

CHAPTER EIGHT

ANOTHER DEATH

In his dream, Crox stood in a circle of jagged rocks deep in the dark forest. A large pentagram was burnt into the ground, and the smell of smoke filled the humid night air. Despite the warmth, goosebumps formed on his bare skin as strange whispers and echoes surrounded him.

As he frantically searched for a way out, Crox noticed he wasn't alone. Unseen spirits watched him from the shadows, their eyes glowing with an otherworldly light. Above him, the full moon shone brightly, casting its eerie glow on everything below.

Suddenly, the rocks surrounding Crox began to emit a pulsating purple light, creating a barrier around him.

He was trapped within the circle, unable to escape. The ground beneath him started to tremble, and just outside the ring of rocks, a wolf emerged from a gaping hole in the earth. Its piercing green eyes seemed to hold a sinister intelligence. The animal stared at Crox with satisfaction before slowly circling him. Each step it took sent shivers down his spine, and for a moment, he thought he saw a twisted smile on its dog-like face.

Crox's heart pounded in his chest as he stared at the wolf, unable to process what was happening. He had thought it was a mere animal, but now it stood on its hind legs and spoke in a deep, chilling human voice. "The Shadow has released me back into this realm to fulfill the agreement with your mother." Fear and anger surged through Crox as he demanded, "Why am I here?" After a menacing howl, Amara replied, "Your soul belongs to the Shadow."

Crox's eyes widened in disbelief as he digested the wolf's words. He was aware that this was only a dream. However, it felt real. He frantically looked around, searching for an exit from the circle of light that held him captive, but the barrier remained impenetrable. Amara observed her prisoner's struggle and declared, "You belong to me. There is no escape from me."

The pentagram glow started changing from purple to lime green and no longer encircled Crox. Amara stepped back and snarled in anger. The lime green light gradually took on the form of a woman. Crox thought he recognized her but couldn't recall who she was. Suddenly, the wolf lunged forward, ready to attack him.

Abruptly, Crox woke up from his deep sleep, his pajamas and bed drenched in sweat. He trembled from the cold wetness, and the terror of the dream lingered in his mind.

Jax was perched on the edge of the nightstand, his green eyes wide with concern. Crox sat up in bed, rubbing at the ache in his head. He knew it wasn't just a dream this time. The Shadow's power was seeping into his mind despite the protective spell. Jax purred softly as Crox stroked his soft fur, seeking solace in his feline familiar's comforting presence.

Crox's hands shook as he gripped the edge of his bed. "Jax, what's happening to me?" he pleaded, fear lacing his voice.

Jax blinked slowly, his eyes glinting with hesitation. He wasn't entirely sure how to explain Crox's newfound ability to tap into the dark realm through his dreams.

"Your dreams are no longer just dreams," Jax finally replied, his deep voice almost a whisper. "They are a gateway to the other side. And you must protect yourself in both your physical and dream states."

Crox let out a frustrated sigh and rubbed his temples. "It was just a fucking dream," he muttered, feeling overwhelmed by the weight of Jax's words.

With a heavy sigh, Crox dragged himself out of bed and went to the bathroom. His muscles ached from the restless night, and his head was foggy with remnants of the dream. He stepped into the shower, letting the hot water soothe away the tension in his body.

After he had taken a long shower and dried off, he went to the kitchen to make a pot of coffee. He didn't notice Sun-Moon's car pulling out of his driveway. She had been parked there since dawn, just out of sight from the house. Crox was unaware of the hex bag beside her, allowing Sun-Moon to control Crox's dreams.

Sun-Moon was headed back to her occult store. She sped around a sharp curve on the winding backcountry road. Her small white Kia couldn't handle the turn and swerved off the pavement, heading straight for a deep ditch. She braced herself as the car slammed into a towering oak tree trunk. The sound of metal crunching against nature's strength echoed through the forest.

Sun-Moon's hands shook as she unbuckled her seatbelt and pushed open the car door. The acrid smell of burning rubber filled her nostrils, and she stumbled out onto the pavement, disoriented and in shock from the collision. Her face was throbbing with pain, and her back felt like it had been slammed against a concrete wall.

She took a few steps back to survey the damage to her crumpled car when a loud rumbling caught her attention. Before she could react, a Tesla Cypertruck barreled around the bend, colliding with her body and sending the witch through the air.

Sun-Moon's last thought was of her little white dog Tessie before her body crashed down onto the hard pavement with a sickening thud.

Her head split open on impact, mixing blood and brain matter with the dirt and oil on the road. In an instant, she lost consciousness.

The electric truck came to a halt, and its panicked driver stumbled out, hastily dialing 911 as he gaped at the lifeless form of the woman he had struck, which was sprawled on the pavement. In the distance, two wolves watched with intrigued fascination at the gruesome scene. The smaller wolf licked its lips hungrily, eager for its next meal.

Sirens blared as the ambulance raced toward Mary Washington Hospital, swerving around cars and pedestrians. The victim, barely clinging to life, lay motionless on the stretcher as paramedics worked frantically to stabilize her.

Meanwhile, at the accident scene, Sheriff's Deputy Shelly Eye questioned the truck driver, Tom Hughes. Hughes passed a sobriety test and remained calm, though he looked visibly shaken.

Deputy Eye examined the skid marks on the road and conducted a preliminary investigation. Excessive speed was not a factor in the crash. She released Hughes but warned him that Sheriff Relda Michaelson may follow up with further inquiries.

As Hughes climbed back into his Cybertruck and headed east on Ramouth Church Road, the sheriff's officers drove west toward town. The winding back road took on an eerie atmosphere, causing Hughes to grip the steering wheel tighter."

Tom, a former marine with a strong physical and emotional constitution, was not easily intimidated. But as the dense woods seemed to envelop the electric Cyper truck, he couldn't shake the feeling of being watched. He retrieved his semi-automatic 9mm pistol from the glovebox and placed it on the passenger seat, ready for action. He stepped on the gas, eager to leave this road and the sight of the woman's brains all over the road behind. In hindsight, he regretted taking this shortcut instead of staying on Route One to avoid traffic.

Not only had he hit a woman standing in the middle of the road, but now he also had to deal with the police and could face charges of assault. It could also worsen if the weird old woman with the multi-colored hair died. The thought of going to jail made him even more nervous than a teenage girl running through the woods in high heels, knowing that a monster was hot on her heels.

Tom had barely gone two miles down the winding road when his electric truck suddenly lost power, causing the vehicle to shut down. Tom was confused, as the truck had over two hundred miles of charge on the battery just a few miles back, and there should be no reason for the battery loss. He attempted to restart the Cypertruck to no avail. Finally, he had to get out and push it to the side of the road, hoping another car wouldn't come spending around the bend.

He took out his cell phone and, to his disappointment, realized that the battery was completely drained. Stranded on a dark back road with no means of calling for help, he had no choice but to walk down the winding road, hoping to find Route 1 and a nearby convenience store where he could call for a tow truck.

While locking up the vehicle, Tom grabbed his 9mm pistol. He wasn't expecting any trouble, but it was always better to be prepared. Tom strolled along the center of the road, looking for other vehicles. He didn't want to get hit by a car. If only that careless woman had been as cautious, maybe he wouldn't be in this mess now.

Tom continued along the deserted road. His thoughts drifted back to the moments leading up to this solitary journey. The memory of the collision, which had altered the course of his evening, lingered in its presence, a constant reminder of the fragility of existence.

He tightened his grip on the pistol, a silent gesture of resolve in the face of uncertainty. Though the night air held no tangible threat, he understood that danger often wore the cloak of invisibility, lurking in the shadows of the night, waiting to pounce upon the unsuspecting.

Within a short time, the tiny hairs on Tom's neck stood at attention, and a sudden chill swept over him.

Having served in combat for his country, Tom was not easily frightened. He tried to rely on his military training, but fear quickly crept over him. With a steady hand, he retrieved his gun and stood poised, straining his ears to see what was causing this unsettling feeling within him.

The thick foliage of the forest seemed to swallow him whole, making Tom feel trapped and disoriented. As he strained his ears to hear what was watching him, the darkness seemed to play tricks on his senses. He was about to give up when a chilling howl tore through the stillness, causing him to freeze in place.

While the sun began to rise above the tree lines, two wolves emerged from the shadows of the trees. Their eyes were illuminated in the faint morning light. The larger wolf stepped towards Tom, locking its gaze on him. Meanwhile, the smaller one circled him with a graceful and predatory demeanor. Despite his training and bravado, Tom couldn't help but feel intimidated by these wild animals.

Tom's heart raced as he lifted his gun and aimed it at the oncoming wolves. But before he could pull the trigger, the smaller wolf, its eyes brimming with hunger, pounced forward. In a frenzy of fur and gnashing teeth, it knocked the gun from Tom's hand and lunged for the man's exposed throat.

As Tom Hughes took his last breath, he gazed into the piercing, glowing green eyes of the wolf before him. The animal began tearing off his shirt with its powerful jaws, exposing his chest. With a ferocious hunger, it ripped out his beating heart, devouring it with an enthusiastic vigor.

After the wolves savored their satisfying meal of the fresh heart, they proceeded to haul what was left of the deceased man into the thick cover of the woods. Once a symbol of power for the decorated marine, the gun was left behind, now rendered useless.

After the wolves finished their meal and melted into the forest's shadows, a plump orange tabby cat emerged from its hiding spot.

The feline cautiously approached the abandoned gun, using its nimble paws to expertly maneuver through the trigger guard. The cat then dragged the weapon toward the side of the road, carefully concealing it under a pile of dead leaves.

Just moments later, a tow truck drove past the exact location where the man had lost his life. It was headed to retrieve the mangled remains of a Sun-Moons car. If Tom had decided to walk in the opposite direction, he might have been picked up by the tow truck instead of becoming a meal for the wolves.

Meanwhile, at Crox's house, he couldn't shake the unsettled sensation that lingered from his intense dream. The visions of the wolf and the woman who transformed out of the green light continued to haunt his mind. Jax watched him closely, sensing the leftover apprehension that clung to Crox.

"The woods are drenched in blood," the black cat whispered, delving into Crox's mind.

"What do you mean, Jax? Whose blood?" Crox asked, his voice shaking with apprehension.

Jax's tail flicked back and forth in frustration, a sign that he was irritated by Crox's confusion.

"Dreams are not always mere figments of the imagination. The Shadow is gaining power, reaching beyond your nightmares." Jax stated,

"The Shadow is vanquished; we sealed the portal and banished it to its realm. Stop with this nonsense!" Crox yelled, seething with frustration.

"If you refuse to take action, more blood will be spilled, and you will bear the guilt," Jax retorted, then hacked up a hairball.

Ignoring the cat, Crox stormed out of the house and released a primal scream of frustration.

CHAPTER NINE

THIEVES

After a long and restless night plagued by bizarre dreams, Crox needed a distraction to ease his troubled mind. He wanted to escape his thoughts, and physical activity might do the trick. So, he decided to walk outside along Ramouth Church Road instead of his usual route through the dense forest behind his house.

Jax, the self-proclaimed protector, trailed closely behind him without making a sound as they walked along the lengthy driveway towards the road. The remnants of the strange dream still haunted Crox's mind as he walked.

The road twisted and turned, disappearing into the dense forest ahead. Crox's steps seemed to echo in the heavy silence, making him more uneasy with each passing moment. He couldn't shake off the feeling of being watched by unseen eyes from within the shadows of the trees.

Jax kept pace beside him, occasionally glancing nervously into the forest's depths. The air was thick and oppressive, as if the forest were closing in on them. Crox tried to calm himself by focusing on his breathing, pushing away the haunting memories from his dream.

A faint howl echoed through the trees as they continued down the road. Crox felt his heart skip a beat, and he looked at Jax, who had an expression of fear. The cat remained calm, gazing into the woods as if interpreting a language only he could understand.

Crox suddenly realized that the protection spell only extended to his house and yard, exposing him to danger while walking on the road. He quickened his pace and hurried toward home. Along the way, something in the ditch on the left side of the road caught Crox's eye. Following a set of fresh skid marks on the pavement, he noticed a large orange fur ball with a tiny head peering up from the ditch. This unexpected encounter startled both Crox and Jax. The chubby cat stood its ground, staring intently at Crox. Slowly, Crox approached the orange cat, but it swiftly darted into the nearby trees. In response, Jax released a high-pitched hiss towards the other feline.

"That's not nice, Jax, bad kitty," Crox stated sternly

"Screw you," came the spicey telepathic reply from the black cat.

Crox drew closer to where the orange cat had vanished and spotted a glint of metal hidden amongst the foliage. Intrigued, he bent down and pushed aside the leaves to investigate. His hand grasped onto something icy and metallic - it was a gun.

Meanwhile, Jax continued to pace nervously, eyeing the newly discovered weapon warily.

"This is not good," the black cat communicated telepathically, his pupils narrowing.

Crox straightened up, holding the gun tightly in his hand.

"Jax, do you have any information about this gun?"

"All I know is you picked up a gun, and now your fingerprints are all over it, stupid; I hope it wasn't used in a crime," the cat answered.

"Shit in the bucket!" Crox cursed out loud as he trudged back toward his house, placing the weapon in his waistband.

Once Crox returned to the safety of his home, he immediately grabbed his phone and called Relda. He urgently told her about the gun he had found on the side of the road.

An hour later, after finishing her workout at the gym, Relda arrived at Crox's house dressed in casual clothes instead of her sheriff's uniform, which she left in the backseat of her police cruiser.

She carefully examined the gun, noting its details and the exact spot where Crox had discovered it. She returned to the place where Crox had found the weapon and surveyed the surrounding area while Crox recounted how he had found the firearm.

While driving to Crox's house, Relda had spotted a brand new Cybertruck parked on the side of the road a couple of miles from where they now stood. After leaving Crox's house with the gun, she pulled up behind the abandoned vehicle and ran a check on its license plate. Surprisingly, it didn't come back as stolen, which Relda had expected.

The electric truck belonged to a man named Tom Hughes, who had no warrants, but the traffic accident from the night before of him striking a woman along this road was on file at the Sheriff's office and being investigated. Relda quickly walked around the truck and into the nearby woods, searching for any sign of Tom Hughes.

Relda confirmed that the vehicle's owner was not in the vicinity before calling her dispatch to send a tow truck for the abandoned truck. She assumed it had broken down after the accident and its owner had found alternate transportation.

After taking note of the vehicle's information and license plate number, she drove to the Sheriff's office to run ballistics on the weapon Crox had discovered. The two incidents might be connected. Upon returning to the Sheriff's department, Relda surrendered the gun to the evidence locker officer and directed Staff Sergeant Dean Pett to inform her immediately of any new information on its ownership or involvement in any crimes.

Relda's phone rang two days later, and she immediately recognized the number as Staff Sergeant Pett's. "Sheriff Michaelson, we've identified the owner of the gun you turned in," he said in a businesslike tone. "It belonged to a local man named Tom Hughes. We also have his car impounded after it was involved in an accident on Ramouth Church Road where a woman was critically injured.

Unfortunately, we haven't been able to locate Mr. Hughes. Officer Burrows is handling the investigation and will update you once we have more information. Currently, the gun does not appear to be connected to any of our ongoing cases." While Relda spoke with Officer Pett, her former lover Vonda was en route to visit Sun-Moon at the occult shop in downtown Fredericksburg.

Meanwhile- across town.

Sun-Moon was facing financial struggles and had asked Vonda to become a partner at Galinda's The Good Witch: Books, Curiosities, and Notions. However, Vonda had no intention of investing in the store or helping Sun-Moon. Instead, she saw an opportunity to obtain the incriminating materials and photos of influential figures in Fredericksburg that Sun-Moon possessed.

Vonda arrived at the occult shop thirty minutes after its scheduled opening time, only to find it closed. She pulled out her phone and tried calling both Sun-Moon's cell number and the shop's business line but received no response. Frustrated, she then redialed Sun-Moon's cell phone and was surprised when someone else answered.

The person on the phone introduced themselves as an orderly from Mary Washington Hospital. They informed that Sun-Moon had been brought in by ambulance and was currently being treated, but they couldn't provide any more information until they received consent from the next of kin.

Vonda stood outside her shop, processing the news she had just received. Sun-Moon was in the hospital, and it seemed like she would be there for a while. The shop would likely be empty since Sun-Moon was a one-person operation.

Vonda contemplated her options and decided that sneaking around the back of the shop and breaking in was her best bet since Sun-Moon was too cheap to put in a security system. She formulated a plan to grab what she wanted and make a swift getaway. With no one else on Caroline Street and no security cameras in sight, Vonda confidently approached the rear of the shop. She positioned herself out of view from any potential witnesses and shattered a window to create an entry point.

Carefully avoiding the broken glass, she climbed through the window and into the empty store. Her first target was the cash register at the front counter, which she found empty. Next, she searched through books on the shelves and in an armoire behind the counter but found nothing interesting.

Growing increasingly frustrated, she slammed her hands down on the counter and forcefully pushed the cash register to the ground. Vonda was not after money but something far more precious.

A blue folder lay on the counter under the spot where the cash register used to be. Inside were names, pictures, and details of influential figures in the region. This was Sun-Moon's list of people she was blackmailing – exactly what Vonda was looking for. She slyly tucked it into her pants and exited the store as inconspicuously as she had entered. In the distance, the sound of approaching sirens grew louder. Her heart raced as she hurried down the street, relieved to encounter no one who might have seen her. She turned onto Caroline Street and continued for several blocks until a police car whizzed by.

Vonda was sure no one saw her, but she took a few detours on side streets on her way home just to be safe.

Crox anxiously awaited Relda's call about the found gun. He paced back and forth in his living room while Jax observed with a smug look, flicking his tail leisurely.

Crox's eyes narrowed as he glared at the feline. "Why is this all happening to me? I am beginning to regret ever stepping foot on this property."

Just as he finished speaking, the phone rang, and Relda's number was displayed on the ID screen. Crox eagerly answered the call.

Jax couldn't help but communicate telepathically, "You always seem to find yourself in some type of trouble."

Relda filled Crox with what she had found out about the gun he had found. It belonged to a man named Tom Hughes, who had an accident near Crox's place and may have dropped the gun accidentally while walking in the dark. Relda also mentioned that they were trying to locate Tom.

Crox thanked her for the update but couldn't shake off the fear of all these accidents happening near his home. After hanging up, he still felt a sense of dread in the pit of his stomach. As he looked out the window, Crox saw the same big orange cat he had encountered on the road earlier. Like Jax's, Its bright green eyes seemed to hold more than just feline intelligence.

With a confident stride, the orange cat made its way toward the front of the house. It skillfully used its paw to nudge open the mail slot and deposited a small velvet bag before disappearing into the forest.

The noise of the mail slot closing startled Crox, jolting him out of his seat. He walked over to the entrance of his home, curious about the unexpected delivery that had been pushed through the mail slot. He carefully picked up the velvet bag, running his fingers over its smooth surface and noticing it lacked any labels or markings.

Jax alerted Crox telepathically, "Watch out; you never know what could be inside."

Crox nodded in confirmation and untied the strings on the velvet pouch. He discovered a small amulet with intricate patterns inscribed on it. There was also a bundle of dried herbs that smelled unpleasant. He stepped onto the porch and surveyed the area, but there was no sign of who had delivered the bag through his mail slot.

Crox spoke up, voicing his worries. "It appears our protective barrier spell has stopped working. We need to convince Vonda to summon the Circle of the Eternal Shadow."

Jax's voice was stern as he countered, "We cannot trust her. It could be too dangerous to invite her back here. The protection spell is working correctly.

Crox ignored the cat and grabbed his cell phone to call Vonda. When she answered, she seemed surprised by the call.

"Hey, what's up? Anything wrong?" Vonda asked suspiciously.

Crox confided in Vonda, "Someone keeps leaving things at my house, and I have a feeling they want to cause me harm."

Vonda replied, "I'm not sure who it could be. The protection spell should be working as intended. I'll reach out to the Circle and ask them to return and reinforce it. I'll also check with others to see if anyone knows who's been coming onto your property. I doubt it's the Shadow.

Crox expressed his gratitude,

"Thank you. I find it hard to believe that the Shadow has managed to break free from its realm, but there is definitely something going on. And those wolves are still lurking in the forest."

"Don't worry, I'll look out for you. Your safety is my priority. I must leave now, but I'll reach out to others to strengthen the protective spell around you," Vonda reassured.

Unbeknownst to Crox, Vonda couldn't help but smile with satisfaction as she hung up the phone. Her intentions to manipulate certain people in town with Sun-Moon's blackmail material were going perfectly according to her plans. She also had a way to use Crox's vulnerability to her advantage.

After their conversation, Crox retreated to his bedroom and collapsed onto his bed, exhausted from the stress and tension of the day. He closed his eyes, hoping for some relief and a moment of peace. Jax, always alert, curled up at the end of the bed and kept a watchful eye.

As Crox and Jax succumbed to sleep, a lone tubby orange cat peered in at them from outside the window. Its green eyes watched Crox intently.

The feline had been leaving little offerings through the mail slot, hoping to warn Crox of the dangers within the forest. The last of these gifts was a small bag made of soft velvet. It was the hex bag created by Sun-Moon to act as a way to infiltrate Crox's dreams, which allowed the wolf Amara to enter his dream state and communicate with him. Although they were unable to enter Crox's home and do him harm physically, they could still haunt him in his dreams.

Enemies lurked in plain sight and were much closer than Crox could imagine. The protection spell surrounding his property may not be enough to keep him safe from the danger that could enter his mind.

CHAPTER TEN

SLICKS STORY

Lola was privy to confidential information from her colleagues at the FBI regarding the gun found near Crox's residence. Subsequent inquiries showed that the legal owner of the weapon had been designated as a missing person, adding to the growing list of unexplained disappearances in the vicinity.

While Lola grappled with the notion that her former neighbor could be linked to the recent string of disappearances, her training and instincts led her to believe that Crox could potentially be a cunning serial killer blending into the community seamlessly. Despite not being officially involved in the FBI's investigation, Lola took it upon herself to uncover the truth.

Due to her prior friendship with Crox, she was confident in her ability to offer unique insights and make connections that others might overlook.

Driven to unravel the mystery, Lola returned to Stafford and immediately launched a search for any potential leads. Her investigation ultimately brought her to Mary Washington Hospital, where she interviewed nurses and doctors about Sun-Moon's accident and injuries.

Lola meticulously reviewed Sun-Moon's medical records, noting every little detail that could provide insight into the incident and Crox's potential involvement in the hit-and-run that caused Sun-Moon's disappearance. Before leaving the hospital, Lola discreetly made copies of the medical records and stashed them in her bag. She reminded herself to return once Sun-Moon was conscious and directly ask her about what happened.

On her drive back home, Lola's mind raced with theories and possibilities. She felt like she was getting closer to uncovering the truth, but there was still a crucial piece missing: why and how Crox played a role in these mysterious disappearances.

Lola needed to have another conversation with Crox, but she couldn't let on that she still suspected him of committing a crime. She was determined to continue her investigation of her old neighbor. She could be potentially stopping a serial killer. Driving down Patriot Highway towards Ramouth Church Road, Lola's attention was caught by Vonda's baby blue Jaguar as it passed by going in the opposite direction. There was something about Vonda that didn't sit right with Lola. She seemed overly happy, almost as if she were under the influence of drugs.

Lola turned onto Ramouth Church Road and Parked her car discreetly on the side of the road just past Crox's driveway. Lola made her way toward Crox's property, walking through the woods so he would not see her coming up the drive. The quietness and lack of wildlife in the forest made her uneasy. It was an odd sensation, as if something wasn't quite right.

Reaching the edge of the backyard, Lola caught a glimpse of warm light shining through the windows of Crox's house. Suddenly, an orange blur raced past her.

Lola whipped around to see what had darted in front of her, but before she could see what it was, a massive paw from out of the darkness swiped at her, causing he to tumble to the ground. Lola felt sharp claws rip through her clothes and puncture her skin. In a panic, she reached for a small flashlight in her pocket, but the animal's weight on her back pinned her down, rendering her defenseless except for the ability to turn her head back and forth. Her gun had fallen from its holster during the attack, but she didn't have time to look for it or use the flashlight as a weapon.

From the corner of her eye, Lola saw what had raced past her out of the darkness. It was an orange cat now attempting to hide behind a fallen tree as it cautiously watched what was happening to her. Turning to the right, she saw a large black and white wolf emerging from the dense foliage. She now assumed another wolf had attacked her and was holding her down.

The attacking animal sank its teeth into the back of Lola's neck, causing blood to gush out onto the forest floor. The terrified woman's screams pierced through the quiet forest as the wild animal greedily lapped up her lifeblood, its sharp claws digging deeper into her back, breaking her spine; the sound of bones cracking rang painfully in Lola's ears.

The wolf Lola had been watching approached her, and to Lola's shock, she heard it speak:

"Be quiet. No one can hear your cries for help. You will be our next meal, and we will relish the taste of your heart. It would have been better if you had just stayed out of these woods. Curiosity kills more than just cats."

Lola's mind was unable to comprehend the bizarre situation unfolding before her. The pain, coupled with the fact that a talking animal was involved, caused her brain to shut down. Another piercing scream escaped her lips as the wolf on her back jumped off, allowing her to collapse onto her back. In this position, her throat was now exposed and defenseless.

The wolf's jaws clamped down on her neck, abruptly cutting off her screams. The other wolf joined in, eagerly ripping away at her clothes until her skin was exposed. In a brutal move, Amara tore off Lola's right breast and continued to devour her flesh, tearing through her ribs and feasting on her still-pumping heart.

Crox was unaware of his former neighbor's screams of pain, though Jax, with his keen cat hearing, was unable to ignore the horrifying sounds of death. Only one phrase came to his mind."Pl ay stupid games, win stupid prizes, you nosey bitch." Jax could tell from the location and intensity of the screams that it happened near the boundary of the protective spell. The black cat made the decision not to tell Crox about the newest victim since his old neighbor's body would never be found.

Crox was dozing off on the couch, oblivious to his familiar feline slipping through the cat door and onto the back deck. The orange tabby made its way through the backyard and towards the treeline that marked the start of the woods. Jax's sharp senses were on high alert for any sounds or movements besides the usual creatures that roamed the forest.

Jax noticed the same orange tabby, one of the guardians of the forest, sitting a few feet away, its gaze fixed on him. Slowly, Jax approached the other feline, speaking cautiously, "Hey there, nugget head. Did you see what happened? What attacked that woman?"

The orange tabby looked annoyed at Jax before responding with a nonchalant shrug. "Don't be daft. You know full well what is in these woods. The Shadow released Amara and Mortimer, two souls transformed into wolves, to end the Circle of the Eternal Shadow. This means they need to kill Crox."

Jax's eyes widened, "Amara and Mortimer? Are they the wolves? But they were killed years ago. How did the Shadow release their souls into our realm?"

The orange cat explained, "The Shadow still holds great power and has many allies in this realm. So, its magic is still able to reach our world. It was not entirely banished from our realm.

One way the Shadow uses its powers to reach Crox is by using a witch to create hex bags, like the one I put through the mail slot. Additionally, the wolves have been ordered to hunt down anyone who enters the forest, gaining strength with every victim until they break through the protection barrier."

With a cautious expression, Jax turned to look at the chubby feline and asked, "You're more than just a guardian cat of the forest. There's something special about you. Did you also happen to leave behind the severed finger and hex charm?

Not only do I guard this forest, but I am also a protector of my dear Crox. The darkness stole my life, and now my spirit is trapped in the body of this feline, just like yours. But before that, I was known as Sean Palmer, Crox's partner. Unlike the other lost souls in these woods, I still hold onto all my human memories." The orange cat replied with a sense of sadness and longing.

Jax's voice was filled with anger as he hissed at the orange cat, "Why are you bothering Crox? Get your orange ass out of here and leave him alone. You used to work with his mother, who tried to sacrifice him to the Shadow. When it didn't work, the Shadow took your soul."

The orange cat replied, "I did work with Pittapat and was a Circle of the Eternal Shadow member. But I never intended for any harm to come to Crox; I loved him and tried to keep him safe. When I attempted to destroy the Shadow, it ended up killing me and trapping my soul. After Crox banished the Shadow back to its dark realm last year, my soul was released into this form. I suppose I came back as an orange cat because I used to have red hair. I have taken a new name. You can call me Slick."

Jax replied, sneering, "How clever of you, Slick. That's the perfect name for a thief to take. Stealing from the dead and leaving it at Crox's doorstep could incriminate him for murder. Maybe you should return to the forest and become dinner for the wolves."

Slick's eyes narrowed as he glared at Jax. "You have no right to pass judgment on me. You were a member of the Circle and your mother's most trusted ally and enforcer.

You knew her intentions all along and had the chance to stop her, but you chose not to because you were too attached to her, a momma's boy." Slick took a deep breath and continued, "I am doing everything possible to protect Crox. The wolves pose a real threat, and the Shadow's influence still lingers. I need your assistance in finding a way to neutralize them and keep Crox out of harm's way."

Jax hissed again and extended his claws, "You want redemption? Why should you be trusted? I won't let you near Crox; I should kill you myself."

Slick's voice echoed through the dense forest. "Stop! You need me," he pleaded. "I know this forest like the back of my paw and have been able to evade the wolves thus far. They haven't bothered any of the other creatures living in the forest. Together, we can thwart their plan to kill Crox before it's too late. The protection spell won't last forever."

Reluctantly, Jax sheathed his sharp claws but remained on guard. "Fine," he growled, "we'll join forces to stop Amara and Mortimer. But make one wrong move, and you're finished."

"Don't mention me to Crox. I don't want to cause him any more pain. But convince him to bring back the Circle of the Eternal Shadow members. I'll watch the wolves and update you if I learn more about their plans."

Slick continued, "To stop the wolves and end the Shadow, Crox must resurrect the original witch who created the creature. Only Victoria has the power to end this nightmare for good."

Jax's expression turned shocked, "But how can Crox bring back someone who died over a hundred years ago?"

Using his mother's grimoire, *Death is the Beginning*, he can bring the witch back to the land of the living. He needs to find the right spell for it. Even in death, Victoria Parham holds great power," Slick responded.

"I'll see what I can do," Jax said. "Keep an eye on things in the forest and try to gather all of the guardian cats. They're afraid of the wolves, but we might need their help.

"The felines that roamed the forest were once humans who were killed and had their souls imprisoned by the Shadow. With the assistance of members from the Circle of the Eternal Shadow, Crox managed to banish the Shadow back to its realm, freeing all of the trapped souls. They were then reborn as the cats who now inhabit the forest." Slick advised.

Jax replied with a hint of sarcasm, "Oh yes, I'm well aware, thank you very much. Look at me; I was there when Crox defeated the Shadow."

"What I'm trying to say is that only you and I (and possibly any other witches from our past lives) have been able to retain our human memories. The other souls have now transformed into cats; they may possess some supernatural abilities, but I doubt they will greatly help against the Shadow."

"Your understanding is not completely accurate; just gather all the cats in the forest and leave the rest to me. I need to return to my human now. Follow my instructions." Jax ordered

Feeling content with his demands, confident that the orange cat would comply, Jax returned to the house.

Crox remained blissfully unaware on the couch as Jax considered whether to divulge the new information. He doubted trusting Slick, but the orange cat's insights could be valuable. But Jax wasn't sure if he should inform his human that the love of his life, whom he assumed was long dead, was behind the mysterious gifts.

While Slick could communicate with Jax, he wasn't sure if the feline could do the same with Crox.

The black cat watched his human brother sleep soundly, deciding to leave him be for the time being. He knew that eventually, the truth would come out about Sean becoming Slick, and Crox would be devastated. But Jax hoped this wouldn't derail their primary goal: defeating the Shadow and its minions once and for all.

CHAPTER ELEVEN

GOODBYE SUN-MOON

Winter came early to the mid-Atlantic region, catching everyone by surprise. Crox sat on his back deck, his hands wrapped around a warm cup of coffee infused with a dash of Baileys, trying to ward off the cold that seeped into his bones on this frosty morning. Beside him, Jax sat stoically, keeping watch. The overnight snowstorm had taken away the vibrancy of the forest, leaving it barren and lifeless. The snow-covered branches only emphasized the vulnerability of the trees.

Crox spotted a set of tiny pawprints in the distance, leaving a trail on the snowy ground as they made their way toward his back deck. The paw marks revealed that a small animal had recently made its way to his house.

"I guess we had a visitor last night." Crox looked down at Jax and stated. The black cat looked up to him but kept his tongue. However, Jax thought the orange freak had better keep his distance if he knew what was good for him.

The biting cold air began to make Crox's nipples hard, prompting him to retreat into the warmth of the house. Jax stayed outside, his eyes fixed intently on the forest, ever alert. Crox settled onto the couch when his cell phone buzzed with a text message from Relda, asking him to call her whenever he had a free moment.

Crox felt a twinge of anxiety as he dialed Relda's number. Lately, she had never called with good news, and as the phone rang, he couldn't shake the feeling that this would not be a friendly call.

"I need you to come to the Sheriff's office immediately. There are a few things we need to discuss," Relda said, forgoing any pleasantries. Her tone conveyed a sense of urgency and concern.

Crox immediately agreed without hesitation to head down to the Sheriff's office. As he prepared to leave, Jax, who had just returned to the house, trailed him closely, sensing the shift in Crox's demeanor. The cat's intuition was uncanny. Although bringing a cat to the Sheriff's office would not typically be allowed, Crox believed Relda wouldn't mind if Jax came along as his emotional support animal. With Jax by his side, Crox felt better prepared to face whatever awaited him at the Sheriff's office.

Crox entered the Sheriff's office and was ushered into Relda's dimly lit office by an officer he did not know, with Jax quietly following behind. The shadows in the room added to the sense of secrecy and urgency.

Crox sat down in a chair, his nerves on edge as he awaited Relda. Jax jumped onto his lap, providing silent support. A few moments later, Relda came through the door and wasted no time getting to the point.

"We ran ballistics on the gun you found," she said gravely. "It belongs to Tom Hughes, a part-time security officer and retired Marine. But there's a twist—he's gone missing. I also found out that Sun-Moon was run over by Tom Hughes." Relda stated.

Relda continued, "There's a police report on the incident; he went missing after the accident. Sun-Moon is currently in the ICU at Mary Washington Hospital. It appears that after Tom hit her and reported the incident to our officers, he continued east on Ramouth Church Road towards Patriot Highway, where he pulled over. The truck Tom Hughes was driving was operable. I don't understand why Mr. Hughes stopped and got out with his weapon. I am afraid that, just like Mary Byrnes, we might not find him. I need to know if Sun-Moon visited you before she got run over." Relda asked.

The news about Sun-Moon's accident took aback Crox, and he needed a moment to gather his thoughts before responding. "What does this have to do with me?" he asked, surprised. "No, I haven't seen Sun-Moon. Our relationship has been strained since last year when she lied to me about her involvement with Vonda and the Circle of the Eternal Shadow. That betrayal created a rift between us that has yet to be healed." Crox struggled to make sense of the situation. "I can't offer much more information since I'm just as in the dark as you are," he admitted, frustration clear in his voice.

Relda leaned back in her chair, studying Crox's expression. "It's a strange coincidence that these events are all happening near your home—the gun, Sun-Moon's accident, and the disappearances of Mary Byrnes and Tom Hughes, not to mention the animal attack on your friend Willy. His body also has not been found. We need to determine if there's any connection between them and if there's a potential threat to you."

Crox sighed. "I don't know what's going on. It feels like I'm caught up in something beyond my control." Sitting quietly at Crox's side, Jax listened to the conversation, annoyed that his human was not telling Relda the whole truth.

"Tell her about your dreams. We will need her help when it comes time to stop the wolves and ensure the Shadow doesn't return to our realm," Jax said to Crox.

Attempting to hear Relda and Jax simultaneously, Crox barely heard Relda say, "I'll keep investigating, and we'll try to find Tom Hughes. In the meantime, don't go out of town. Let me know immediately if anything seems off or if you notice anyone acting suspicious around you."

As Crox walked out of the sheriff's office, he told the cat, "When we are in public, please refrain from speaking to me; it's distracting." Jax let out a loud meow, followed by a sharp hiss. His tail flicked back and forth to convey his displeasure at the request.

Crox decided to visit Sun-Moon in the hospital. He was suspicious as to why she would be near his home. Sun-Moon lived above her store in downtown Fredericksburg; why would she be on the back country road that led to his property? He did not think she knew anyone else on Ramouth Church Road. Also, what caused her car to go into a ditch in the first place?

Crox called the hospital to find out what room Sun-Moon was in and was advised she was still in the Intensive Care Unit and could not have visitors at this time; however, he could leave his contact information, and someone would call him when the patient was allowed to have visitors.

As Crox was being barred from visiting the battered patient, Sun-Moon was receiving an unexpected visitor. Disguised in a nurse's uniform, Hazel East stealthily made her way to the Intensive Care Unit, careful not to attract attention as she slipped into the hospital room.

Sun-Moon lay in the bed, surrounded by a tangle of tubes and wires; the battered woman was oblivious to Hazel's presence. Hazel closed the blinds on the door's small window, blocking anyone from seeing inside.

Hazel stood by the bed, her gaze fixed on the monitors beeping rhythmically, the ventilator softly whirring, and the IV pump clicking as it delivered measured medications. The symphony of mechanical sounds was almost hypnotic.

After briefly reconsidering her plan, Hazel decided to do what she had come here to do.

Hazel began to unplug the life-sustaining machines one by one, methodically silencing the alarms that would have otherwise alerted the nurse's station. This wasn't her first time resolving a conflict in such a manner, and she navigated the hospital's layout with practiced ease.

A twisted satisfaction gleamed in Hazel's eyes as she watched Sun-Moon's struggle unfold. As the patient began to choke on her own saliva, a cruel smirk played on Hazel's lips. Sun-Moon's eyes fluttered open and locked onto Hazel. She tried to scream, but her voice faltered, weakened by her injuries. With oxygen no longer supplied through the face mask, her breaths grew shallow and erratic.

Sun-Moon's skin lost its natural hue, turning a sickly blue as she struggled to breathe. Each movement caused her broken bones to radiate in pain, adding to her misery. Hazel grabbed the pillow beneath Sun-Moon's head and pressed it down forcefully over her face, depriving her of all oxygen.

"Let me end your suffering, you blackmailing bitch," Hazel spat with venomous hatred; as the life force left Sun-Moon's body. "This is the last time you profit over someone else's business." With each passing moment, Sun-Moon's struggles grew weaker until they finally ceased altogether, her body limp beneath Hazel's merciless grip.

Once Hazel was confident Sun-Moon was dead, she swiftly restored all of the life support machines to their previous settings and replaced the pillow behind Sun-Moon's head. In a matter of seconds, she exited the hospital room, leaving no trace of her presence.

Unnoticed by the hospital staff on the second floor, Hazel calmly boarded the elevator and descended to the lobby. Over ten minutes would elapse before Sun-Moon's demise was discovered. Later, while Sun-Moon's body was being transported to the morgue, Hazel was parking her car behind Galinda the Good Witch: Books, Curiosities, and Notions.

Despite being over seventy years old, Hazel still possessed the energy and vitality of someone half her age, a testament to the dark spells she had cast on herself long ago. With a swift kick, she forced open the back door of the occult shop, the hinges protesting loudly but was no match by the force of the kick, causing the door to fly open. Stepping inside the dimly lit shop, Hazel felt the lingering aura of its deceased owner.

Hazel went to the back room, where she saw the scattered decks of Sun-Moon's fraudulent tarot cards and other tools used to manipulate vulnerable minds. She couldn't help but wonder if Sun-Moon had the power of clairvoyance. And if she did, did she see her own death coming?

Hazel meticulously combed through the cluttered room, desperate to find the coveted blue envelope that held scandalous photographs of her and Harry Byrnes. He was married to Mary Byrnes, who had disappeared and was presumed dead.

Hazel's frustration grew as she searched in vain for the blackmail photos until she finally emerged into the main area of the store. Her eyes immediately landed on the overturned cash register and rummaged counter drawers, indicating that someone had already searched through. It was clear that Hazel had been beaten to the blackmail material.

Fueled by anger, Hazel stormed through the store, holding her lighter like a weapon as she ignited everything flammable in her path. The flames spread quickly, and soon, the entire occult shop was engulfed with the vibrant colors of orange, red, and yellow.

Hazel sped away, leaving behind a scene of chaos and destruction. Without smoke alarms or sprinkler systems, the fire raged unchecked and swiftly consumed the occult store.

When the fire department was finally alerted, it was too late to salvage anything from the condemned building. Sun-Moon's negligence in installing proper fire safety measures had proven costly, resulting in the building's total loss.

Hazel returned to her establishment, Simply You Salon, just a few miles away on Amaret Street, just in time for her next client.

While Hazel was busy with murder and arson, Vonda sat in her hot tub at home, engrossed in studying the contents of the blackmail list she had obtained from Sun-Moon's shop. The documents held a trove of incriminating information, including numerous compromising photographs featuring successful individuals in the community she was familiar with.

Vonda's gaze swept across the names listed on the blackmail dossier. The stolen information wielded influence over numerous individuals, some of whom held prominent positions within the town's social and political spheres. She began plotting a way to take advantage of this information and felt a sense of vindictive satisfaction, relishing her potential power. Her motivations were driven not by greed for money but by a desire for retribution against those who had slighted her.

As Vonda continued to sift through the documents, a particular photograph seized her attention. The image depicted an older woman with striking jet-black hair with streaks of purple hues, locked in an intimate embrace with an elderly gentleman sporting snow-white locks. Instantly recognizing the woman as a regular patron of Galinda, the Good Witch occult store, Vonda's attention was drawn to the man she was kissing—Harry Byrnes.

Harry Byrnes, a professor of religious studies at the University of Mary Washington, was known for his bland personality. Despite his unassuming nature, he held a prestigious position at the university and was married to the missing Mary Byrnes.

Vonda had encountered him during her enrollment in some night classes at the university and had been interviewed by him for his book on the occult. Considering his seemingly boring personality, she couldn't help but be taken aback by the revelation of his affair. It was a reminder that dark secrets lurk behind unassuming facades.

Vonda tucked away this morsel of information in the recesses of her mind, knowing it could be valuable. She longed to confide in her former lover, Sheriff Relda Michaelson, but she grappled with the dilemma of how to share it without revealing how she had acquired the knowledge.

The envelope contained a treasure trove of information: detailed accounts and incriminating photographs documenting the extramarital affairs and financial misconduct of local City Council members and prominent figures in the business community. Vonda intended to hold onto these files, keeping them close at hand for future use if necessary. However, her primary focus lay elsewhere—she was determined to uncover Sun-Moon's dirt on Freddy Montage.

Freddy, a second-generation Hispanic-American, owned a local used auto dealership in Fredericksburg, a business venture in which Vonda had invested. Their partnership soured when Freddy began siphoning money from the business and cheating her out of her rightful earnings. Despite her efforts to trace the missing funds, Freddy skillfully covered his tracks, leaving Vonda at a loss. After reluctantly extricating herself from the partnership, Vonda harbored a deep-seated resentment towards her former business partner, vowing to settle the score once and for all.

Sun-Moon's dossier of blackmail material was startlingly comprehensive. It revealed that Freddy had ventured into the dangerous world of heroin trafficking, both as a dealer and a user, while also maintaining membership in a notorious New York gang, raking in millions of dollars selling drugs. Sun-Moon had been extorting hefty sums of money from Freddy to safeguard these illicit secrets every month.

Vonda boiled with rage as she absorbed this revelation. "That conniving woman," she seethed inwardly. "She was profiting from my misfortune and had the audacity to solicit me as a partner in her bookstore, all while feigning poverty. For her sake, she better meet her maker before I get hands on her because I'm going to make her suffer, slowly.." Unbeknownst to Vonda, her vindictive wish had already been granted.

CHAPTER TWELVE

THE SHADOWS MINIONS

Slick, the orange cat, cautiously navigated through the snow. His paws left impressions that were quickly erased by the gentle breeze plowing the fresh snow. He was pursuing the giant paw prints of two wolves, each step a reminder of the danger he faced. Slick knew that if the wolves caught wind of him, he would become an easy target and end up being a snack. He kept a safe distance, relying on his keen sense of smell to track them while staying downwind to avoid detection. He was confident that his scent would not reach them.

The two wolves reached a clearing, and beneath the shade of a towering snow-covered tree stood a ring of stones. At the center of the circle, scorched into the earth, was a pentagram.

The larger of the two wolves stepped confidently into the circle. The smaller one sat patiently just beyond the circle of rocks. Slick, intrigued yet cautious, slowly approached, hidden behind the trees. His keen ears alert, and his body low to the ground.

As he drew closer, Slick could hear the wolf's deep voice. It seemed impossible for this wolf to possess such an ability; however, it was chanting a spell. The words of the enchantment resonated in the dark clearing. Slick's fur stood on end as the wolf summoned the evil entity.

"Shadow, hear my call. I summon you to me, invoking the powers of earth, wind, fire, water, and dark spirits. Speak now, Shadow of night, keeper of souls. Amara pleads for you to come to the realm of the living."

The temperature dropped even further on this already frigid night, and the air seemed to constrict in the clearing. From his hiding place, Slick watched with keen interest as a grey shadowy figure began to take shape in the center of the pentagram next to the wolf. The figure appeared to absorb all light around it, gradually taking on a solid dark form.

Once the transformation was complete, Amara addressed the Shadow respectfully. "I implore you to assist me in my mission. Release Mortimer and myself from Crox's protection spell over these woods, placed by him and his misguided friends. Give us the power to move freely and eliminate the one promised to you."

The fully formed Shadow spoke coldly, its voice echoing through the forest. "Amara, your progress has been lacking. You should have done my bidding by now. Summoning me to this realm unnecessarily weakens me. Why have you called me here? Where is Sun-Moon? She should be able to break whatever spell that binds you to this forest."

Amara bowed her head in submission as she looked at the looming figure of the Shadow. "Master," she spoke softly, "I beg your forgiveness for my failure. Sun-Moon has met with tragedy as I can no longer sense her presence. Without her, both Mortimer and I are rendered powerless in our quest. We need your power to break the spell that binds us to these woods."

The Shadow's figure shook with rage as it spoke to them, "The protection spell on the forest prevents me from reaching out. You must find a way to break it, or I will have no choice but to summon you back to me. And if it comes to that, your punishment will be brutal," the Shadow threatened, its voice dripping with malice.

Amara's ears flattened against her head in submission, and she averted her gaze and trembled slightly at the thought of failure and the consequences it would bring. The Shadow's eyes bore into her like two red, dark holes. "Yes, Master. We will find a way," the wolf replied, trying to hide her fear.

"Do not underestimate my warning. Time is running out for you." The Shadow replied.

"I will need Mortimer's help. He has no human memories and cannot speak; he will not fully obey me as his wolf form is dominant." Amara requested.

The Shadow's presence seemed to darken further, its form flickering threateningly as it replied. "Mortimer was not a true witch in his human form, so he could not retain his memories when I allowed his soul to return with yours," hissed the Shadow. "Be grateful I allowed him to be released from its torment and to be by your side. If his presence burdens you, I can easily bring him back with me and feed off his pain. Do not call on me again until you have completed your mission. Time is running short; I suggest you hurry and bring me Crox's body so I may claim his soul," the Shadow said with dripping malice.

Amara shuddered at the Shadow's words, "Yes, Master, I understand," she said quickly. "I am grateful for your mercy in allowing Mortimer to be with me. I will find a way to utilize his strength despite his limitations."

The Shadow's form dissipated into thin air, leaving the clearing in an eerie silence. Amara stood motionless momentarily and then turned to Mortimer, who stood by her side. His eyes reflected the primal instincts of his wolf form, no longer having a human soul. She had to find a way to harness his raw animal power and break the protection spell that bound them to these woods.

Slick remained motionless and out of sight, waiting for the two wolves to leave before sprinting off to find Jax. Crox needed to be alerted immediately; the consequences were greater now than ever before, and the fate of life and death rested on Crox to bring back the Circle of the Eternal Shadow.

Slick returned to Crox's house, relying on his feline instincts to navigate through the snowy woods with precision and speed, which took a toll on his tubby legs. The bitter cold seeped into his thick fur. Finally, he arrived at the house and slipped inside through the cat door, grateful for the warmth of the interior.

"Why do you think you can just come into my house?" Jax demanded sharply. "You are not welcome here. You are nothing but a feral animal from the woods." He glared at Slick with suspicion and annoyance. Slick took a moment to catch his breath, ignoring Jax's harsh words.

Slick shared the chilling details he had witnessed in the forest clearing. With urgency in his voice, the orange cat recounted the summoning of the Shadow and explained how Amara and Mortimer were using Sun-Moon to break the protection spell over the forest. "Lord only knows how long that old witch has been working with the Shadow," Slick stated after his tale. The orange cat then went to the water boal and helped himself to a drink.

Jax's tail twitched with agitation as he listened intently to the news. "So, the wolves and Sun-Moon are working together to break the protection spell and release the Shadow," he said, his voice dripping with disgust. "I always suspected that women couldn't be trusted." He paused momentarily before adding, "But Sun-Moon is in the hospital, so she can't cause any problems. I'll warn Crox about this betrayal." Turning to Slick, he added, "And now it's time for you to get your fat ass out of my house."

Slick's fur stood on end, and he gave a low hiss in warning toward the black cat. His body tensed, ready for a potential fight. But realizing this was not the moment to engage in battle, he quickly turned and left.

The chilly air of the forest welcomed Slick back, and he trotted away into the darkness, his paws sinking softly into the snow with each step.

Crox sat in his home office, fully immersed in paperwork. He had received a batch of real estate sales contracts from his office manager, Armand, and was poring over them with intense concentration. Unaware of the orange cat's visit, Jax entered the room silently and noted Crox's unwavering focus. After a brief moment of observation, Jax decided to interrupt him.

Jax telepathically stated, "There's a problem. Sun-Moon is collaborating with the wolves in the forest and they were sent here by the Shadow. Amara, one of the wolves, has the ability to summon the Shadow. She must have been a powerful witch when she was human. The other wolf was just a regular human whose soul was taken by the Shadow and lacks any supernatural powers."

"Whoa, slow down, little one," Crox interrupted, his brow furrowed in worry. "What are you saying? How could Sun-Moon be working with the Shadow or any of his minions?"

Jax proceeded to share all the details he had gathered, making sure not to reveal his source. Crox's expression grew darker as Jax spoke, and his concern turned into fear. Jax had no intention of telling Crox about Slick, perhaps one day, but not now.

Crox whispered to himself in disbelief, "Sun-Moon? Involved with the Shadow? Using her power to summon wolves and break through the protection spell?" He had always known Sun-Moon could not be fully trusted, but this was a betrayal beyond his wildest dreams. Everyone near him seemed to be a traitor.

Crox dialed the hospital, determined to get Sun-Moon's room number. If they refused visitors again, he would have to devise a plan to slip in undetected and confront her about her involvement with the Shadow. He needed answers desperately and wouldn't rest until he had them.

The receptionist at the hospital's information desk didn't provide Sun-Moon's room number but instead announced her death.

The receptionist asked if Crox knew anything about her family, but he had no information to offer; he knew nothing of her family. Shocked, Crox ended the call and stared at his phone. With Sun-Moon dead, he knew he may never unravel the truth of her connection to the Shadow.

Crox paced anxiously in his office, uncertain about what to do next. Reflecting on his connections to the supernatural, he considered Vonda and Armand, both former Circle of the Eternal Shadow members during his mother's reign as high priestess. Both had ultimately betrayed him.

Despite their disloyalty, Crox knew they held a unique position of power within the cult group. As the sole blood descendant of Pittapat, his mother, he, however, possessed the inherent right to lead the occult group. The grimoire spell book authored by his mother could only be wielded through a blood descendant, ensuring that no one else could truly claim leadership. In light of this, Crox recognized his obligation to reassert his authority within the Circle and bring back the coven.

Crox hailed from a lineage of witches, yet his magical abilities were restricted. While he possessed the gift of communicating with Jax and performing elemental spells from the grimoire, his powers were limited. To access more advanced forms of witchcraft, Crox relied on the collective strength of other witches.

"What do you think we should do, Jax? You always seem to have a thought," Crox inquired of the black cat, seeking his counsel.

Jax took a moment to consider Crox's question before responding telepathically, "We need allies. Sun-Moon's betrayal indicates that reuniting the coven is crucial to defeating the Shadow once and for all. Merely trapping it in its realm isn't sufficient protection for you any longer."

"We should contact Vonda and Armand," Jax continued. "They can gather the members of the circle. You need their support, and you must lead them as their high priest. But proceed cautiously; we can't be certain where their loyalties lie."

Crox let out a heavy sigh, acknowledging the truth in Jax's words. "I'm reluctant to work with those who've betrayed me, but you're correct," Crox conceded. "Facing the Shadow alone is futile. I can't evade my destiny, and I can no longer shirk my responsibilities.

Crox grabbed the grimoire, "*Death is the Beginning*," and delved into the spell book; he stumbled upon a section detailing the ritual to reunite the Circle of the Eternal Shadow. It was as if his mother had foreseen the group's eventual dissolution. The spell involved summoning the spirits of each former member and binding them to the leader—in this instance, him. It was a complex ritual requiring meticulous preparation, specific ingredients, and, above all, his blood.

The most accessible items to acquire for the ritual were the herbs and plants. Fortunately, a local plant nursery in Fredericksburg, known as the 'Enchanted Garden,' specialized in unique botanicals. Crox could obtain the Wolfbane, Belladonna, and Hemlock required for the binding ritual.

In addition to the botanical ingredients, the spell necessitated a black mirror. This mirror served as a conduit to summon the original cult leader, Victoria Parham, from death's grasp. Victoria Parham was the first witch of Stafford County, and her presence was crucial for the ritual's success.

Crox thought he could acquire the special mirror he needed at Galinda's the Good Witch: Books, Curiosities, and Notions. However, with Sun-Moon dead and no family to take over the shop, there would be no legitimate means to obtain it. He would have to resort to breaking in and stealing the mirror.

The most challenging aspect of the spell lay in acquiring personal items from each individual he intended to bind to himself—items like hair, nail clippings, or jewelry. Moreover, Crox recognized that his connection to the supernatural was not particularly powerful. He must find a method to enhance his witchcraft abilities to compensate for this limitation.

Crox compiled a list of individuals he suspected had once been part of the Circle of the Eternal Shadow. He intended to contact Vonda for the names and contact information of those he couldn't recall. He simultaneously noted down the required items for the spell. Suddenly, a series of loud howls echoed from the forest, sending a shiver down Crox's spine and filling him with an unshakeable dread.

In response to the unsettling sound, Jax burst into the room, his fur bristling and his entire demeanor conveying a sense of alarm. "The wolves are enraged, and they're more dangerous than ever," Jax conveyed urgently, even through telepathy. "I advise against going outside, and I pray no one else ventures into those woods," he added, his voice tinged with panic.

Crox nodded in agreement with Jax's advice and resolved to remain indoors for the evening. He hoped that no unexpected visitors would show up. He couldn't bear another disappearance or murder. Crox carefully returned his mother's spell book to the safe. He then walked through the house, ensuring all the doors and windows were locked.

CHAPTER THIRTEEN

NIGHT-TIME MEETING

Vonda sat in her favorite poolside spot at Honey Suckle Hill, letting the sparkling water cool her feet. But even as she tried to relax, the eerie howls of the wolves kept creeping into her thoughts. With her phone in hand, she spoke to Freddy, their voices competing with the distant chirping of cicadas. It was a call to schedule a meeting to try and fix their damaged business partnership, but Vonda knew it would also serve as an opportunity for revenge.

Choosing a secluded location on Ramouth Church Road, Vonda hoped for privacy where they could discuss matters without interruption. Beneath her friendly tone, Vonda had a hidden agenda - she wasn't interested in finding a solution but instead sought to make Freddy pay her what she was owed.

Vonda couldn't help but notice the full moon shining brightly in the night sky as she drove to their designated meeting spot. The stars twinkled like diamonds, captivating her attention. The sight reminded her of the Beatles' song "Lucy in the Sky with Diamonds," she felt a sudden urge for a joint and a shot of tequila to calm her hatred towards Freddy.

The plan was simple: intimidate her ex-partner, Freddy Montage. She would meet him alone on Ramouth Church Road, armed with the incriminating evidence she had obtained from Sun-Moon's store. Her goal was to become the new blackmailer, seeking revenge for the betrayal she had suffered and reclaiming the money lost in their failed used car dealership venture.

Vonda approached the designated meeting spot, her eyes scanning the road illuminated by the moon's glow. The trees cast sinister shadows that seemed to dance in the eerie atmosphere. She parked her car further down the road and walked back to the meeting spot, knowing that keeping her car hidden would give her an element of surprise.

Carefully approaching the abandoned house on Crox's property, Vonda avoided setting foot in the surrounding forest. She knew the protection spell was in place, shielding the property from the potential threats lurking in the woods. As long as she stayed within the boundaries of the spell's barrier, she would be safe from the evil forces trapped inside.

Freddy had no idea that Vonda knew the supernatural world, as he remained oblivious to such things. To him, she was just another target to exploit and discard at his whim. But tonight would teach him a lesson. Freddy would soon realize that Vonda was not to be underestimated and would come to fear her in ways he never thought possible.

When Freddy arrived, his anxiety was evident in his fidgeting movements, and he scanned his surroundings with caution before exiting his car. Unaware of Vonda's true intentions, he didn't see her as a threat. However, he knew better than to give her the upper hand. Therefore, he was on high alert just to be safe.

Little did Freddy know, a baby-blue Jag was parked a quarter mile up the road. He assumed he had arrived first since no other cars were in sight. Suddenly, a female voice across the street called out, "Freddy, did you really think you could betray me and get away with it?" Vonda's words dripped with contempt.

Freddy was taken aback, his words stumbling out in a startled jumble. "Vonda, what in the fuck? You nearly scared me out of my skin!" His heart raced, and adrenaline surged through his body at the sudden sound of Vonda's voice.

Vonda emerged from the shadows from across the road and stepped onto the moonlit road, purposely positioning herself in Freddy's line of sight. "I know about the heroin and how you betrayed me by selling your poison. Now, I'm here to collect my share," she announced.

"What in the world are you talking about, you crazy bitch? I have no time for your madness," Freddy retorted, trying to maintain control with a show of bravado.

Vonda's laughter was cold and menacing, piercing the silence of the night. "You know, I have something you desperately need to keep hidden, or it could ruin your pathetic excuse for a life." With a dramatic gesture, she produced a large envelope.

Freddy's eyes widened in suspicion, though he maintained a calm façade. "And what exactly do you think you have on me? Your accusations are meaningless without evidence. What proof do you believe you possess?"

Vonda stepped closer, her gaze predatory and intense. "I took this from Sun-Moon's shop before her unfortunate death. Now, you have two options: either you pay me my rightful share of the used car business along with a percentage of the drug sales,-

or I ensure this envelope finds its way into the hands of the authorities. Bubba's waiting, and there is no lube in prison."

Freddy's faux bravado wavered, evident in his quick glances at the sealed envelope. The consequences of what Vonda held and its potential impact hit him like a ton of bricks, causing sweat to form on his forehead. Sun-Moon had been aware of Freddy's illicit drug dealings for some time now and had been blackmailing him for months. The evidence contained within the envelope could be enough to send him to prison for decades.

The fear in Freddy's eyes did not go unnoticed by Vonda, who relished the power she now held over him. Her voice remained threatening as she spoke, a subtle warning. "You know what happens to drug dealers when they get caught. A simple call to my ex-girlfriend, Sheriff Relda Michaelson, could ruin your life and leave you butt hurt and I don't mean metaphorically. But I'm giving you a chance to make things right. Pay me what you owe, and we can put this whole thing behind us."

Freddy hesitated, realizing that Vonda had the upper hand in this confrontation. He was well aware of the potential consequences if his illegal activities were exposed, and he didn't want to become a Bubba's bitch in prison. "Alright, you win," he finally conceded, knowing he had no other option. "Just tell me what you want, and I'll get it for you.

"Vonda's smug expression showed her satisfaction with her victory. "Smart move. I'll send you the details of where and when to deliver the money; we can discuss the amount later. But don't forget, this isn't just about money; it's about respect. You should have thought twice before crossing me."

Despite outwardly agreeing to Vonda's terms, Freddy's mind was already racing with plans to eliminate her and retrieve the evidence of his involvement in the heroin trade. He suspected she had copies hidden elsewhere, making it difficult for him to ensure her permanent silence here. To make matters worse, he had no idea where the other incriminating documents could be.

Vonda noticed Freddy seemed lost in thought and began to walk backward toward the woods' entrance, oblivious to his surroundings. Unbeknownst to him, he had crossed the protective boundary around the forest. Vonda sensed the danger and drew closer. She hesitated at the edge of the forest, her instincts warning her of the potential dangers lurking within its shadows.

The haunting howls of wolves suddenly shattered the night. "Freddy, stop! Don't go any deeper into the woods!" Vonda's urgent voice cut through the darkness.

Freddy halted instantly, his eyes wide with shock. Glancing around, he realized he had strayed into the thick forest, where tall trees loomed ominously in the moonlight.

"What was that?" Freddy asked, his voice trembling with unease. However, he did not make a move toward Vonda, who was just outside the protective barrier.

Vonda hesitated momentarily, considering whether to reveal too much to Freddy. She knew of the evil within the forest but struggled with how much to share. Before she could devise a reason to discourage him from going further into the woods, a chilling scream from the forest echoed through the night.

She saw Freddy being thrown to the ground, writhing in agony and clutching his stomach as blood poured out. His screams reverberated through the trees.

"Get out of there! Come to me!" Vonda shouted, keeping a safe distance from the forest. She was not about to risk her safety to save this fool. Suddenly, Freddy's eyes widened in sheer terror. He yelled out, "Something's attacking me... a wild dog or something. Help me." He stammered, his voice trembling between cries of agony and horror. The words tumbled out in a frantic rush, punctuated by the raw fear that colored his every word.

A large black-and-white wolf emerged from the shadows, its powerful body moving with an unsettling fluidity. Vonda felt her blood run cold as she recognized Freddy's peril—it was one of the wolves unleashed by the Shadow.

The wolf towered over Freddy, then pressed one of its heavy front paws against his face, suffocating him while its sharp claws dug into his eyes. Freddy's screams grew louder, his body thrashing in agony as his eyeballs were brutally pulled from their sockets.

Vonda's voice rang out in fury, shouting for the wolf to leave Freddy alone. She fumbled in her pocket for her .22 pistol, but it slipped from her grasp and fell to the ground with a loud clang. Frozen in fear, she could do nothing but watch as the horrifying scene unfolded in front of her. The wolf ignored Vonda's desperate pleas, focusing solely on Freddy. With one final scream, Freddy went limp and motionless, his life ending before her eyes.

Ignoring Vonda's presence, the wolf savagely tore into Freddy's chest, blood and flesh flying everywhere. Vonda recoiled in horror at the gruesome sight, like something out of a satanic ritual. Finally, the wolf pulled out Freddy's still-beating heart and devoured it hungrily.

The wolf towered over Freddy's lifeless form, his once-piercing screams now silenced. It stared at Vonda with sinister eyes, savoring the last bits of Freddy's heart. Then, it opened its mouth and spoke to her in a strangely human voice that Vonda recognized all too well. Fear and confusion gripped her as she struggled to process the fact that this creature could speak. But deep down, she also felt relief, knowing she was standing just out of its reach.

"Amara?" Vonda gasped, her voice trembling in disbelief. Memories flooded her mind, taking her back to when she was a Circle of the Eternal Shadow member, sitting next to Pittapat, Crox's mother, and the revered high priestess of their coven. She remembered how Pittapat had sought more power and control over dark magick by summoning the spirit of a long-deceased witch, Amara.

Even then, Vonda had felt the evil energy radiating from Amara's spirit essence. The wolf nodded slightly, its eyes glowing with a wicked light. "Yes, it is I. But I am not the same Amara you once called upon in your coven's rituals. I am now bound to the Shadow.

"Why have you come here?" Vonda asked, her voice shaking with uncertainty.

Amara's smile stretched wider, revealing her sharp incisors. "My desires are numerous, but my greatest one is to regain my human form and be reunited with my lover, Mortimer. However, for now, let's just say I'm here to collect what is owed to my master."

"How did the Shadow manage to release your soul into the realm of the living?" Vonda questioned.

"Foolish woman," the wolf sneered, its mocking tone laced with wickedness. "When Pittapat begged for my help in conquering her enemies, I only agreed with the Shadow's permission. It is more powerful than you will ever know."

Vonda couldn't resist asking, "But how could that have been possible?" Her fear was momentarily forgotten as curiosity took over.

Amara's patience was wearing thin as she spat in annoyance. "These questions are tiresome," she snapped, her eyes flashing with irritation. "I am here to claim Crox's soul for the Shadow. But do not worry, dear Vonda. I will call on you when you can serve me if you refuse. I will make you suffer when I kill you.

Amara's warning was apparent as she turned away from Vonda. "Continue with your petty vendettas, but do not dare cross me. My wrath is not something you want to face." With one final menacing glare towards Vonda, Amara disappeared into the dark forest, taking Freddy's mutilated body with her.

Vonda stood in shock. "I won't let you harm Crox," she yelled, her voice trembling.

Amara's laughter echoed in the forest's darkness, sending a chill down Vonda's spine.

"FUUUUCCCK!" Vonda screamed.

As she returned to her vehicle, Vonda's mind was in turmoil. Frustration boiled inside her as she realized Freddy's death had eliminated any hope of recovering her losses from their failed business venture. A cold fear then took root. The Shadow was coming back.

CHAPTER FOURTEEN

STRANGE VISITOR

As Vonda sped down Ramouth Church Road, putting the horrific scene of her ex-partner's death behind her, Jax was dealing with an unexpected visitor: Slick, the orange cat. Annoyed by Slick's use of the kitchen cat entrance to enter his home, Jax's frustration only grew upon learning what Slick had come to tell him.

Slick's voice was filled with frustration as he asked, "Do you know Amara has claimed another victim? What are you going to do about these wolves and stop the killing?"

When Amara's name was mentioned, Jax was suddenly filled with fear. He was all too aware of who she was.

In his previous life as a human, he had sought guidance from her spirit and was fully aware of the darkness she possessed within.

"Thanks for informing me. Now leave," Jax commanded, his tone laced with anger and hostility.

Slick pressed his face against the kitchen island, marking it before finally leaving, squeezing through the cat door to return to the forest. Jax entered the bedroom to wake Crox and share the news of the wolf's attack. After failing to rouse him with a paw or nudge, Jax sat on Crox's face and faked hacking as if he were about to throw up. This jolted Crox awake immediately.

"What the hell, dude?" Crox asked sleepily

"There's no time to waste," Jax urgently relayed, his feline eyes filled with concern. "The wolves have struck again; Vonda led someone into the forest, and they're now dead."

"Wait, what?" Crox asked with confusion.

Jax quickly explained everything he knew about Amara and his past work with her when she was a spirit. Now, the Shadow has sent her to the land of the living to kill him. The cat also stressed the immense danger the Shadow still posed, even while trapped in its other realm.

Crox's frustration manifested in the tone of his voice as he spoke. "We have to put an end to Amara and the Shadow once and for all," he declared, rising from the bed. "I can't stand by and watch them continue to harm innocent people, and I refuse to let that demon regain power in our world." He strode to the kitchen, now fully awake. Why had Vonda been meeting someone in the woods near his property? She knew the dangers lurking in the forest well and had helped him build a protective barrier against those ferocious wolves. What was her motive?

Crox thought to himself that he needed to inform Relda about the possible attack. Although he doubted a body would ever be found, it was still his duty to bring it to her attention.

After a satisfying breakfast, Crox texted Relda, asking her to stop by when she had some free time. In response, Relda called and informed him that she had been occupied with the investigation into Mary Byrnes' disappearance and Willy Williamson's animal attack.

However, no bodies had yet to be found. Willy's husband, Will, wasn't much help when he arrived at the hospital; he had gone catatonic from the shock of what he witnessed. His statement didn't make much since. The information she had came from Lola, who had seen the animal attack.

Crox inquired, "What was Lola doing with Will and Willy? I didn't know she knew them, and why were they on my property so late at night?"

Relda responded, "I didn't take her statement, and I'm not privy to their relationship. Based on the initial investigation information I was given, I assume they were out-capturing images of nature."

Crox muttered, "It would have been considerate if someone had simply asked permission to be on my land before trespassing." Then he thought, "Fuck around and find out."

Relda agreed to visit him later that evening and update him on her investigations while they enjoyed drinks and cigars.

Crox ended the call and decided to contact Lola. He was curious about why she was on his property at night and eager to hear her side of the story about Willy. Unfortunately, when he called her, it went straight to voicemail.

Crox approached Jax with a mischievous grin. "Wanna go shopping?" he asked, jerking his head towards the door. "Might as well stock up on supplies for the house. There is not much else I can do around here. Jax's sleek black fur stood on end as he responded telepathically, "I think I'll stay here and keep watch." Crox rolled his eyes. "Suit yourself, but don't come crying to me when you get lonely."

Crox went into the bathroom and, as he likes to say, shit, showered, and shaved. He slipped on one of his favorite Hawaiian shirts and shorts. At this stage in his life, he could dress comfortably and not worry about impressing others.

Just before leaving, he grabbed a list of necessary ingredients for a spell he wanted to cast from his mother's grimoire. It was a binding spell that would bind the members of his mother's coven to him. Crox had decided to reunite the Circle of the Eternal Shadow with him as its leader.

He was headed toward downtown Fredericksburg. Crox's first stop was the quaint plant nursery on Amelia Street. After her husband's passing, Joyce Lloyd used the life insurance money to fulfill her lifelong dream of owning a nursery. Leaving behind her job as a Realtor at Crox Home Sales, she opened The Enchanted Gardens. Now, tending to plants and herbs was not just a hobby but her full-time occupation. In the final stages of her life, Joyce took pleasure in crafting healing elixirs from the bountiful garden and offering them to those needing physical, emotional, or spiritual care.

Upon entering the Enchanted Gardens, Crox was enveloped in a delightful mixture of lavender and rosemary scents. Joyce, a tall and graceful woman with long silver and blonde hair, welcomed him with open arms. Her wise violet eyes shimmered as she spoke.

"Crox, my dear, what brings you to my humble little shop? Are you getting up to no good?" Joyce asked.

Crox returned her warm smile and closed the distance between them. "I need some supplies; I know your shop is the best place to get them," Crox said, handing her the list of items he was looking for.

Joyce's eyes lit up with excitement as she went over the list. "Dealing with the supernatural, I see? Well, you've found yourself in good company. What can I assist you with?"

Taken back, Crox asked, "What do you mean? I am just planning on adding some new plants around the house."

"Sure," Joyce said with a smirk.

Feeling uncomfortable with the conversation, Crox took the list back and said, "I can get them myself so that you can wait on other customers."

"Mm-hmm, okay," The shop's owner said snarkily.

Joyce stepped back and started buzzing around the store, welcoming customers and aiding them with their purchases. Crox went through the rows of shelves, carefully scanning for the necessary ingredients to complete the binding spell.

Crox avoided looking at Joyce, not wanting to engage in any more idle chatter or respond to her prying questions. He glanced at the self-checkout area as he put the final item into his basket. Seeing Joyce still occupied with other patrons, he quickly scanned and paid for his items, leaving the store while the nosy owner was still engaged with other shoppers.

He couldn't help but wonder if Joyce had also been a Circle of the Eternal Shadow member since seeing him shop for plants and herbs used in magick did not surprise her. After leaving Enchanted Gardens, Crox headed to his next destination.

Determined to retrieve the black mirror he had seen at Sun-Moon's store last year, Crox drove towards Galinda's The Good Witch: Books, Curiosities, and Notions. His mind whirred with thoughts of a break-in and stealing the mirror. However, upon arriving at the store, his heart sank as he saw the charred remains of what was once the storefront. The stench of smoke still rose from the burned-out building.

Crox's hands trembled as he realized the black mirror was most likely destroyed in the fire. He stood on the sidewalk, staring at the ashes of his aspirations, struggling to devise a new plan to gain the power to lead the Circle of the Eternal Shadow. Without the black mirror, how could he call on his mother's spirit to help him bind the coven to him?

Sitting in his truck, Crox stared at the shattered windows of an occult store, feeling lost and unsure of what to do next. His mind raced with possibilities as he wondered, "What should I do now?"

Suddenly, a female voice came from the backseat, making Crox jump and causing his heart to hammer against his chest. The bodiless voice caught Crox off guard.

As he tried to regain his bearings, he saw a form starting to appear out of thin air in the rearview mirror. Once the form was fully materialized, Crox recognized the visitor.

It was Janice Hildress, a former member of the coven and a formidable witch in her own right. "How did you manage to get into my truck?" Crox's voice shook with anger and fear as he demanded an explanation.

"I'm not truly here, my my. Did your mother teach you nothing? I am astral-projecting to you. My body is at home, but my spirit is here with you," Janice explained calmly.

Crox took a deep breath and maintained his composure. "Why have you sought me out?" he inquired.

"I am here to assist you. My tarot cards have revealed the path you are on and the challenging task that lies ahead," Janice answered matter-of-factly. Crox couldn't help but shudder at her words, realizing she had access to knowledge about his destiny that he could only dream of possessing.

"Your tarot cards have predicted my present and future?" Crox exclaimed, his disbelief gradually dissipating as he grew accustomed to conversing with an astral-projected witch.

Janice's ghostly figure glimmered in the low light seeping through the tinted truck windows. Her soft laughter reverberated within the confined space.

"Crox, my dear, the future is not set in stone. The cards only show potential paths, not certainties. But fear not, for I am here to guide, advise, and help you find alternatives to relying on the treacherous black mirror."

"Okay, what options do I have?" Crox pleaded, his voice tinged with desperation. I need to gather the members of the Circle of the Eternal Shadow and establish myself as their leader. Have your tarot cards come up with a way to do this?"

A loud siren exploded inside Crox's mind, causing blinding pain. Crox grabbed his head and heard the witch in the back seat say, "Don't mock me, you little faggot."

Janice leaned in closer, her translucent eyes penetrating Crox's very soul. "There are other ways to communicate with the spirit world. The mirror is a powerful tool, but not the only one. You can do a black séance, a dark ritual that might allow you to communicate with spirits and demons and bind them to your will. In time, I will come to you again and walk you through it; for now, I must return to my body or risk being lost to the spirit realm," Janice stated as her form began to dissipate into a shimmering mist, leaving behind a faint scent of lavender and sandalwood.

Sitting alone in his truck, Crox gazed at the back seat where Janice's form had been, lost in deep contemplation of the witch's proposal. The thought of conducting a black séance terrified and captivated him, but he couldn't deny the thrill of facing the Shadow and its wolf death squad.

Crox arrived home to find Relda inside, sitting in Jax's beloved Paul Bunyan rocking chair. She greeted him with a sly smile and wore her weathered police uniform. "I see you found my spare key?"

Crox let out a deep sigh as he entered the living room and went over to the bar. he poured two glasses of bourbon, handing one to Relda who took it and then lit a cigar, taking a long drag before speaking. "So what's going on now?"

Crox nodded, his brow creased with concern. "I have a suspicion that Vonda deliberately lured someone into the woods, and that person met their demise at the hands of the wild animals I reported to animal control. Hasn't anyone in your office found anything? Hell, the whole Sheriff's Department has combed my property multiple times, yet people are still going missing or being killed. Shit, my old neighbor thinks I'm a killer."

"So, if I understand correctly," Relda said, blowing smoke from her cigar. "Why do you believe Vonda led someone into the woods? The Sheriff's Department has thoroughly searched those woods and found nothing but an abandoned Jeep on your property. As far as I know, the Jeep is still there. There is reason for you to be under suspicion. I don't think you have done anything but are holding out on me. You know more than you're telling me."

Crox ignored the comment and motioned towards the door. "Let's go look at the area where the Jeep was left. perhaps your officers missed something." Crox suggested.

The two walked down the road toward the driveway where the vehicle had been left, Jax following at their heels. Relda stopped and turned to Jax, "No animals allowed," she declared firmly.

Jax didn't cower or avoid eye contact; he stared back at her, hissing defiantly.

Crox let out a deep, rumbling chuckle and reached out to gently pat Jax on the head. "Be good, my little one. We wouldn't want to ruffle Sheriff Relda's feathers, would we?"

Jax let out a small snort and walked back toward the house as Relda and Crox continued their walk to where Freddy Montage had met his death.

CHAPTER FIFTEEN

DARK WITCH

Relda and Crox strolled along the empty road in silence, both lost in their own thoughts. Crox strained his ears as they walked for any signs of wildlife coming from the nearby forest. He had brought his .38 Smith & Wesson, just in case, but didn't mention it to Relda.

When they finally reached the driveway of the abandoned house on Crox's property, they saw the black Jeep Wrangler still parked there. Jax had been telling the truth. Relda quickly dialed the Sheriff's office on her cell phone, requested dispatch to run the license plate number, and called her back.

Crox moved around the Jeep, attempting to open the doors, but they were securely locked.

The Stafford Sheriff's dispatcher called Relda back and informed them that the Jeep belonged to Freddy Montage and had not been reported as stolen. Crox's eyes narrowed suspiciously. "Freddy Montage? Isn't he Vonda's former business partner at Starship Auto, the used car dealership?"

Relda's face turned to stone as she expressed her anger. "Why was Vonda involved in business with someone like Freddy? He's a known drug dealer. She's above that." Crox raised his shoulders in a gesture of confusion. "I only met him once at a party at Vonda's house. I had no idea he was dealing drugs."

Relda noticed a wallet in the locked vehicle's center console through the driver's side window and thought the Jeep's owner may still be nearby. She called out for Freddy, but there was no response. As she was about to venture into the woods, Crox grabbed her arm and stopped her.

Crox's voice was filled with concern as he warned, "If I were you, I wouldn't go into those woods. There have been too many people now who have gone missing; I would feel better if we had more backup.

"Don't be ridiculous; we're both armed," Relda said. I know you have a gun on you; I want to take a quick look around. I won't go far." As she approached the edge of the thick wall of trees, Relda's flashlight created eerie shadows in front of her.

The ground was damp and uneven; twisted roots and fallen branches hid the path ahead. Suddenly, her light landed on an area that appeared to have recently been trampled upon.

Curious, Relda crouched down to inspect the disturbed soil and broken branches when she heard a rustling noise not far from her. Her heart raced as she cautiously reached for her gun, prepared to defend herself against any potential threat.

Instead of a vicious, lurking predator, a plump orange tabby cat jumped out from the shadows. Its green eyes were fixated on Relda, almost as if it were analyzing her. "Stupid cat, go away!" Relda shouted in irritation as she fell on her butt.

Crox's heart raced at the sound of Relda's raised voice, and he wasted no time charging through the thick trees to ensure she was okay. When he caught up to her, Relda aimed her gun at the cat, but it seemed undaunted by her weapon.

"What's going on?" Crox panted, trying to catch his breath.

Relda lowered her gun with a shaky hand. "Just a damn cat," she muttered, still recovering from the adrenaline rush.

The cat looked back and forth between Relda and Crox before darting off into the trees, its tail flicking back and forth in amusement.

As they started walking back to the driveway, a loud howl pierced through the trees, causing Relda to jump and grab Crox's arm.

"We need to get out of here," she exclaimed, her voice trembling with fear; this caused Crox to worry; if Relda, with all her police training, was scared, they better get out of there quickly.

As soon as they were safely back at Crox's house with the doors securely locked, Relda immediately contacted animal control to search the forest again for any signs of wolves or coyotes. However, Crox was confident they weren't dealing with ordinary animals; something more menacing lurked in the forest's shadows. Jax watched them from his favorite chair, switching his tail impatiently, waiting for Relda to leave so Crox could fill in on what caused them to run into the house with their tails between their legs.

After another bourbon to calm her nerves, Relda took out her weapon and serviced the front yard, making sure nothing was outside, and then bid Crox goodnight and got in her car, and sped out onto Ramouth Church Road like her ass was on fire. Crox watched her leave, wishing he had asked her to stay, as she wasn't in the best frame of mind to be driving.

Crox re-entered the house and was greeted by Jax, who spoke to him telepathically. "What did you discover?" Jax's voice sounded concerned. Crox let out a deep sigh before answering, "Not too much. Relda and I stumbled upon an abandoned Jeep registered to one of Vonda's past colleagues in the woods.

There were signs of a possible struggle in the woods, but no sign of a body or blood."

"I told you not to go in those woods," Jax scolded firmly.

Crox shrugged off the comment and asked if anything had happened while he was gone. Jax gave him a smug look before strolling to the kitchen and yowling loudly for his dinner. While Jax dined on kibble mixed with tuna, Crox retreated to his office. He pulled *Death is the Beginning* from his safe and searched for the specific spell. He needed to bind members of his mother's disbanded coven to his will. But there was one problem: he needed a black mirror to complete the spell and had no idea how to acquire one.

Crox then began thinking of his visitor, Janice Hildress, who had arrived in his truck earlier through astral projection. He knew little about her except that she was a powerful witch who could project herself astrally. She had mentioned conducting a black séance to complete the binding spell, but Crox was unsure how to proceed without her guidance. Crox continued to ponder his situation, his fingers tracing over the worn pages of the grimoire. He searched for references or instructions to guide him in performing the dark ritual of binding another's will to his own. But the pages remained frustratingly silent, withholding their secrets from him.

A feeling of urgency nagged at the back of his mind. He knew he had to locate Janice Hildress and understand the complexities of the black séance before it was too late. Jax entered the room and jumped onto the desk, breaking Crox out of his intense musings. The cat gazed intently at the grimoire, its emerald eyes mirroring the words on the page.

"Do you know how to do a black séance?" Crox asked the cat. Jax let out a low meow, his expression serious.

"That is very dark magick; only a select few who dabble in the forbidden arts know of such things," the cat replied.

Crox's heart sank at the news. He knew he would have to tread carefully if he wanted to proceed with the binding spell.

"What do you know of this Janice Hildress?"

Jax's eyes narrowed as he stared at Crox, weighing his following words carefully. "Janice Hildress was a high-ranking member of the Circle of the Eternal Shadow and an advisor to our mother, the high priestess. She is a practitioner of the dark arts; she uses human sacrifices in many of her spells," Jax communicated telepathically.

Thoughts raced through Crox's mind as he processed the idea of having someone like Janice on his side. He had always been cautious of his mother's coven, and this new information only heightened his wariness. However, he knew he would need their aid in defeating the Shadow. He frantically searched for Janice's contact information online, but it seemed she had disappeared from the digital world. Frustration gnawed at Crox as he scrolled through countless search results with no success. If Janice were a coven member, perhaps Vonda would know how to reach her. He called Vonda, hoping she could provide him with Janice's phone number or other contact information.

Vonda's response was curt and distant, her voice dripping with thinly veiled annoyance.

"I'll contact Janice," she stated flatly, "and if she wants to talk to you, she can reach out herself.

"Crox asked again for her contact information, but Vonda flatly refused. Crox felt a surge of anger and frustration well up in his chest.

"Does that woman really think she holds all the cards?" he yelled in frustration after she hung up on him.

"At the moment, she does," Jax chimed in telepathically, his tone dripping with sarcasm.

Feeling irritated with the cat and betrayed by Vonda's actions of not giving him Janice's address or phone number, Crox decided he needed a break. He left Jax to his own devices and stormed out of the house. He climbed into his truck to go for a long drive and clear his head before dealing with more drama. The engine rumbled to life as he peeled out of the driveway, the sound of the Hemi V8 drowning out all other thoughts and worries for the time being.

Crox felt a familiar dizziness wash over him as he drove along the winding country road. It was like being on a weed-induced high and experiencing an out-of-body sensation. He quickly pulled his truck to the side of the road, turned off the engine, and gripped the steering wheel tightly, causing his knuckles to turn white.

Hoping to rid himself of the disorienting feeling, Crox closed his eyes tightly. But when he opened them again, he found himself in a poorly lit room filled with rows upon rows of old books, glistening crystals, and various decks of tarot cards. The air was thick with incense.

Crox blinked multiple times, trying to center himself, when he heard a deep, alluring voice say, "Welcome to my lair." The woman's voice echoed through the dimly lit room, and Crox turned to see Janice Hildress. She stood in the center of the room, looking both sultry and regal, draped in a dark purple velvet dress with a long slit up to the thigh.

"Well, well, Crox," she purred, "it seems you were able to answer my call and use astral projection to come to me."

Crox's heart raced as he tried to understand how he had arrived here. His voice sounded strange, unlike his usual deep southern drawl. "How am I here?" he asked, his fear showing through his tone.

Janice flashed a wicked grin as she answered. "I needed to see if you were powerful enough to astral project through the spirit world," she explained. "It seems you are a stronger witch than what your mother led me to believe you were."

Confusion clouded Crox's mind as he tried to make sense of her words. "I don't understand," he said, unsure and afraid of what was happening.

"Don't worry about that now," Janice interrupted Crox, her eyes blazing with excitement. "I want to discuss the black séance."

Crox, who was nothing but a translucent form, tried to pay attention to Jancise as she spoke about the black séance. However, he found himself more fascinated being in this astral form outside his body.

While she rambled on about human and spirit sacrifices, Crox tried to protest that he didn't understand, but all of a sudden, Janice stabbed him with a silver knife. Instead of blood, a thick, black smoke seeped out of the wound. He couldn't believe what just happened as he gazed at the wound and then back at Janice in shock. He couldn't believe she had just stabbed him without warning. He began to feel weak and lightheaded but realized there was no pain.

Janice's words echoed in his mind, "As long as you get back to your body quickly, you will be Okay; fail to do so, and you will die."

Time was of the essence. He closed his eyes, channeling all his concentration to return to his physical form. In a matter of moments, he opened his eyes and found himself back in the driver's seat of his truck.

Weakness crept into Crox's muscles, but he fought to stay conscious. Taking deep breaths, he had harnessed the magick within him to transport himself to Janice and back to his body. Despite the stab wound in his side, he felt no pain, but the experience left him trembling. Once he felt stable enough to drive, he turned the truck around and returned home.

Jax was lounging on the front porch, "That didn't take long," Jax commented. Crox scowled at the cat and muttered, "Shut up."

Jax let out a snicker and replied, "Touche'."

Crox curled up on the couch, wrapping a heavy afghan around him, and turned on Netflix to help shut off his mind and block the emotions of fear and trepidation he felt.

Meanwhile, Janice Childress was parking her white Mustang Cobra under the train bridge on Sophia Street in downtown Fredericksburg, next to a bar called Brock's, searching for an unwilling victim.

She would need blood from an unwilling living person to complete the black séance ritual she was going to do herself; Janice had attained one unwilling sacrifice when she stabbed Crox while he was in the spirit realm by astral projection.

Like a predator preparing for the kill, Janice prepared herself by unbuttoning her blouse, a silver knife used to stab Crox strapped to her thigh.

The night was quiet, but she could hear the distant sounds of music and laughter from the nearby bar. She waited patiently under the bridge for an unsuspecting sacrifice to stumble into her trap.

Finally, a young, handsome man who looked like a college student from Mary Washington University emerged from the bar, clearly intoxicated and looking for a good time. Little did he know that instead of getting lucky, he would be getting murdered.

The young man noticed the attractive older woman standing alone, wearing a tight dress that hugged her curves. He sauntered over to her, thinking he might be able to score some head before heading home for the night. As he got closer and prepared to deliver his most winning pickup line, Janice suddenly attacked, plunging the silver blade into his left eye and then swiftly cutting his throat.

His screams of shock and pain were muffled, his vocal cords severed. The scent of blood and alcohol mingled in the air alongside the odor of urine. Janice had successfully captured her live offering.

Janice left the lifeless body on the street beneath the towering train bridge. She drove away back to her home, looking like a woman without a care in the world.

Janice couldn't help but hum a little tune her mother used to sing to her when she was just a young girl, free from any guilt associated with killing an innocent stranger. "Jump and dance, laugh and sing; what joy these days will bring with happy children shining in the light of day,"

Once back home, she gathered the necessary materials for the black séance that awaited her. Her long fingers traced over an ancient spell she had stolen from Pittapat many years ago. Her lips moved silently over the page as she recited the words that would empower her to control the Circle of the Eternal Shadow members.

Chapter Sixteen

SPIRIT REALM

Vonda found herself striding through the bustling streets of downtown Fredericksburg, her mind set on one destination: Simply You Salon. The small, historical city was alive with the sounds of chatter from shoppers strolling the streets, the scents of coffee and freshly baked bagels wafting from a nearby restaurant. As she walked, Vonda couldn't help but feel a pang of sadness at the thought of Freddy's untimely demise and the loss of his debt that came with it. Instead of dwelling on her misfortune, she had hatched a plan to make up for it by collecting money from Hazel East, one of Sun-Moons blackmail victims.

Vonda made her way to the salon, plotting her next move to recoup her lost financial potential. The morning sun beat down on her skin, warming her as she weaved through groups of shoppers and panhandlers begging for money. She knew that no matter what obstacles stood in her way, she would not rest until she had made her money back - one way or another.

The door to Simply You Salon swung open with a gentle chime, announcing Vonda's arrival. She paused to take in the sleek and modern black-and-white decor that adorned every surface of the salon before making her way toward Hazel East's workstation. Hazel, currently attending to an older woman with a sour puss expression, looked up and warmly greeted Vonda with a smile. The scent of lavender and eucalyptus wafted through the air, calming Vonda's nerves as she prepared for her confrontation with Hazel.

Hazel's impeccably styled jet-black bouffant hair stood out starkly against her porcelain skin, accentuated even further by her perfectly applied bright red lipstick. Every strand seemed to be in place, not a single hair out of line. Despite her deceptively harmless appearance, Vonda couldn't ignore the churning feeling in her gut that she had felt ever since she had decided to take over Sun-Moon's blackmail. The rumors and blackmail information surrounding Hazel only added to her unease. Still, Vonda pushed those thoughts aside as she reminded herself of her true purpose for being there - to recoup what she had lost when Freddy was killed. Vonda couldn't help but wonder how far Hazel would go to protect her secrets.

"Hello, darling!" Hazel exclaimed in an excessively sweet voice. "What brings you in today?" However, her narrowed eyes gave away her suspicion of Vonda.

I just need a trim, Vonda responded.

Hazel pointed to a chair for Vonda to sit in and wait. She advised she would be along after checking out her current customer. Vonda sat in the chair, her fingers tapping nervously on the armrests as she waited for Hazel to finish. After the old sour-puss woman left, Hazel went to work setting up her workstation.

Despite Vonda's impatience, Hazel took her time setting up her tools; it seemed to Vonda that the hairstylist was being purposely slow. Finally, Hazel called Vonda over and began trimming dead ends from her hair.

Hazel rattled on as she began trimming Vonda's split ends. She spoke of her booming business and alluded to making certain powerful and married women look their best at one of Fredericksburg's finest salons. Hearing Hazel's rambling words, Vonda's head ached.

Vonda had enough of the chatter and sharply interrupted, her tone laced with accusation. "I hear you have a certain penchant for making sure powerful and married men get happy endings as well."

The pupils of Hazel's eyes dilated in response, giving her a feral, untamed look that made Vonda's skin crawl. The old woman's lips curled into a sly and devious smile as she coolly replied, "I'm not quite sure what you're insinuating, dear."

Vonda looked up to Hazel, her voice dripping with venom. "Don't try to play innocent with me, Hazel. I have the evidence, and if you don't want your dirty secret affairs exposed, you'll pay up. I am sure it would do wonders for your business."

A flash of anger and fear flickered through Hazel's eyes, but she quickly regained control and replied, her tone icy and calculated, "You've got nothing on me, sweety. And even if you did, let's just say I don't respond kindly to threats."

With perfectly painted red nails, Vonda opened her designer handbag, and with a sly smirk, she slid out a small envelope. She placed it on the table between them, and Hazel couldn't help but feel a sense of unease about what was inside.

"Take a look, honey. It's just a taste of what I have," Vonda said in a sickly sweet tone as she pushed the envelope toward Hazel. "Names, dates, and some rather compromising photos. I'm sure the folks in this small town would love to see them."

Hazel tensed up, but she had no fear in her eyes, only hatred.

"You know, sugar, the last person who tried to shake me down ended up dead," Hazel said coolly, trying to maintain control of the situation.

Vonda's eyes narrowed, and her faux sweetness disappeared. "I don't think you're in any position to threaten me, you old slut," she spat viciously.

Hazel's anger boiled over at the insult. She balled her hands into fists and gritted her teeth. "Get the hell out of my salon!" she demanded through clenched teeth.

With one final icy glare at each other, Vonda calmly rose from her chair and stated, "Bless your heart." She gracefully tucked the envelope back into her handbag and strolled toward the door, giving Hazel one last wicked smile before leaving the salon without paying for the haircut.

Hazel watched Vonda sashay through the parking lot to her baby blue jaguar. Her black painted nails dug into her client book, and in a low, menacing voice stated, "That bitch is going to see what karma is all about."

Hazel locked the storefront door and flipped the "closed" sign before entering the back room and opening a small closet door. She pushed aside hanging hair-cutting capes to reveal a small space with a table used as an altar. Hazel lit a black candle that was placed in the center of the table. She then put a glass bowl filled with Vonda's hair trimmings and sliced her palm with a sharp knife, allowing her blood to mix with the hair and water. She chanted a spell, the words calling upon dark forces to do her bidding, "By the light of this dark flame, I call upon night to bring pain. May hurt freely flow to this blond one." Hazel repeated the chant three times, blew out the candles, and flushed the bowl's contents down the toilet.

Back in Stafford, Crox was flipping through the worn pages of the old grimoire. He was searching for answers, desperate to understand the intricacies of conducting a black séance. Jax was lounging on the couch, watching his human get increasingly frustrated. Jax spoke up telepathically, "Having trouble, are we?" the cat's voice echoed in Crox's mind.

Crox looked up from the book and stated sharply, "I need to figure this out. Janice said a black séance is the key to binding the Circle of Eternal Shadow members to me as their leader."

Jax tilted his head, studying Crox with an intense gaze. "You're treading in dangerous waters." The cat warned. "Be careful. Every action has consequences."

Crox sighed, running a hand through his hair. "I know, but I can't sit back and let the Shadow return to our realm. I have to do whatever it takes to stop it before any more bloodshed happens."

The leather-bound grimoire, its pages yellowed with age and crackling under Crox's touch, seemed to come alive. The pages began to flip on their own, landing on a page filled with symbols representing the dead and a spell to call forth the power of the spirits to bind another's will.

"Jax, I found it," Crox declared triumphantly.

"What is it?" Jax asked, leaning in closer to see the text.

"The binding spell," Crox replied with a sly grin. "It will not only bring the Circle of the Eternal Shadow members to me and be at my command. It will bind them to me."

Jax's expression turned grave. "But at what cost? Dark magick always comes with a price."

Crox's smile widened as he reached to pet the sleek black cat. He took a deep breath, steeling himself for the task ahead. The spell he was about to cast was powerful and dangerous. To bring the scattered members of the coven back to Stafford County and bind them, Crox would need to call upon the dead through a black séance.

The one he needed to call on was the witch Victoria, the first high priestess of the coven known for her mastery of dark magick. He needed to bring forth her spirit back to the living world.

Victoria had lived over a century ago in Kentucky with her husband, Shane, and their four children. But when she used her magick to kill her brother-in-law during an argument, the towns-people turned on her and forced her family to flee from their home. The clan eventually landed in Stafford, Virginia.

Victoria and her husband started a cult called the Circle of the Eternal Shadow on the land now owned by Crox. Only a few members of the occult group were part of the inner coven of witches; the majority were just misled, mindless followers.

The witch Victoria also called forth the Shadow to our realm and used its powers to avenge her when she was shaded or to help extend her powers over the cult.

Crox knew that calling forth Victoria Parham through a black séance would be risky. She had been a formidable person in life, and even in the land of spirits, she could possibly be dangerous. Crox hoped she would still have control of the coven, even in death, and would be willing to give him the power he needed to become their leader.

He had almost what was needed to call on Victoria from the land of the dead but would need one thing that he had a feeling Janice Hildress possessed: the silver knife, which was required to kill an innocent living victim as well as someone in the spirit world.

Crox remembered when he was called to Janice through astral projection, which pulled his soul from his body. She had also stabbed him with a silver knife just as he was about to return to his body, so in a way, he was a spirit, and she had made a victim of him.

Who would be the living victim? The thought of someone else dying on his behalf made his skin crawl.

Since he could not call Janice and didn't know where she lived, the only way to find her was to astral project to her, but he wasn't sure he could on his own.

A page in the spell book mentioned astral projection and out-lined how one could perform it. Crox flipped through the pages until he found the page he was looking for. It described a ritual involving meditation, visualization, and the recitation of a specific chant. The spell dark spell also called for sacrifices using a specific weapon. Crox closed his office door so as not to be interrupted by Jax. He began to meditate, bringing Janice Hildress's face to the forefront of his mind.

With Janice's face etched in his mind, Crox recited the spell, "By the stars above and the earth under my feet, I call upon my ancestors to move my spirit through time and space, where I will freely roam. I journey through the spirit realm with a focused mind and a strong will. So let it be."

As Crox continued to recite the spell the second time, he felt a strange sensation enveloping him, as if his spirit was being lifted from his body. He continued to focus on Janice Hildress, visualizing her and the surroundings of the room she had brought him to, willing himself to be there.

Suddenly, he felt himself being pulled through a whirlpool of multiple colored lights, and in what seemed like an instant, he found himself standing in Janice's living room. She looked up from the book she was reading and smiled. She was not startled at all to see him standing there.

"Very well done. You amaze me," Janice said, her voice sounding like a parent speaking to their child who had just learned to use the potty.

Crox took a moment to compose himself, adjusting to the feeling of being in the spiritual realm. Smoke poured from his stomach where Janice had stabbed him. He placed his hands over the wound as if stopping the blood flow.

"You will not be able to stay in the spirit realm for long. Your wound is a fatal one, so if you stay here too long, you will die," Janice said with a smug look on her face.

"So can I safely say I was the sacrificial victim of the spirit plane, as part of the black séance? Crox asked.

"My, don't you learn quick. I have the knife that you will need to call on the dead to do your bidding." Janice said with a smile

"Who was the living victim?" Crox asked.

"That is none of your concern; just know you have what you need. I will bring it to you when the time is right. Now go unless you never want to be in your body again," Janice said flatly, "I am so happy you are coming into your power. Your mother would be proud of you."

Hearing the reference to his mother caused the skin on his arm to prickle. "I don't care what my mother would think; she was pure evil, and because of her, I am dealing with a power I may not be able to stop."

Crox focused on returning to his body, feeling the pull of the spiritual realm tugging at him. With a final glance at Janice, he recited the incantation backward, willing himself to return to his body.

After reciting the spell one time, Croc felt the familiar sudden jolt, and his consciousness snapped back into his body. He gasped for breath, feeling the sensation of being back in the realm of the living. The wound in his stomach started to ache, but he knew as long as he did not go back into the spirit world, not succumb to the stabbing.

CHAPTER SEVENTEEN

BACK FROM DEATH

Crox lay motionless on the floor of his office, slowly emerging from his trance after projecting himself through the spirit realm. Jax observed him closely from the corner of the room, waiting for Crox to stabilize himself.

"You never cease to amaze me, Crox. Your ability to achieve astral projection without outside assistance shows your incredible growth in your powers," Jax communicated telepathically, genuinely impressed by his human brother's newfound skill.

Crox's voice was hoarse as he asked, "How did you enter the room? I had the door locked."

"Don't worry, my dear brother. I have my ways," came the cat's smooth reply before it quipped, "Now, where exactly did your spirit wander off to?"

" I went to see Janice Hildress. I think she was in the inner sanctum of the Circle of the Eternal Shadow," Crox explained, still trying to catch his breath and make sense of what had just happened.

"Be careful with that one. Janice was an advisor to our mother when she was at her worst. Janice also seemed always to have her own agenda, and I never trusted her.

"I need to call on the spirit of the witch Victoria to complete the binding spell successfully. Without her, I fear I won't be able to accomplish it. Thankfully, this other witch has what I need to call upon Victoria's aid.

Jax looked up at Crox, swishing his tail back and forth, almost looking puzzled, then responded,

"Do you know the type of magick Janice Hildress is into? Many innocent people have died at her hands for her to work in the dark arts. If she can do the black Seance, that means she has killed an innocent person."

"What is done is done; she has the last item I need to call forth the Witch Victoria. If she has blood on her hands, well, that is on her, not me." Crox said, though his face showed the guilt he felt.

Jax turned and walked out of the room without saying another word.

Slick was outside, looking through the window and listening to the exchange. He became concerned when he found out Crox had been able to astral project. This meant he was coming into his full power, greatly worrying the orange cat. Crox was never meant to use his magick, both for his sake and for those around him.

When Crox was young, his mother bound his powers; she worried that the Shadow would tempt the young man to do its bidding. Crox's power was not as advanced as that of his brother Jaxson, which meant that he would be useless in keeping the Shadow contained and could easily become seduced by the entity.

Binding Crox's powers and making him believe he had no supernatural gifts worked until Pittapat died, and her binding spell over Crox started weakening. This was the start of Pittapat's slide into the dark arts, which allowed her to be seduced by the Shadow herself and then suffered death at its hand when she failed to do its binding and bring it Crox to kill and trap his soul.

Across town, Janice Hildress sat at her altar, preparing for her dark ritual in the seclusion of her home. She had first prepared a protection spell to prevent Crox or anyone else from coming in through astral projection or any other supernatural means. She had decided to do her own black séance, calling on the one Crox sought, Victoria Parham.

Janice had her reasons for bringing the original leader of the Coven back from the dead. She realized Crox did not have what it took to lead the great coven Circle of the Eternal Shadow. She would need to be the one to take charge and bring back the occult group under her leadership.

Janice sat on the floor before the small table she used as her altar. On top of an old photograph of Victoria Parham, the first leader of the Circle of the Eternal Shadow, she placed two black candles. Next to the candles, she placed the knife with the silver blade she had used to stab Crox while he was in the spirit plane and the one she used to kill the stranger down by the dock.

Janice spoke her spell aloud, "By the light of the moon, at this midnight hour, I call upon thee, my mistress Victoria Parham, first leader and guide, beloved spirit and true high priestess of the Circle of the Eternal Shadow; I am your humble servant who freely gives of my will to you. Accept this blood sacrifice of both the living and the spirit; take a living form; move among us in the land of the living."

The light around Janice seemed to dim as she continued to chant the spell. The temperature dropped, causing goosebumps to form all over her body from the chill. The sky outside opened as the rain poured down and lightning cut through the night sky.

Janice's eyes rolled back until there was nothing but the whites, which glowed with an unnatural intensity. A mighty wind swept through the room, extinguishing the candles placed on the altar and knocking off knick-knacks that adored the side tables. The only source of light to see came from the occasional flicker of lightning that electrified the night sky.

The black séance had begun to take effect. The room seemed to vibrate like a train was passing the house. The howling sound of the wind outside the window became so loud Janice had to cover her ears as she channeled the power to bridge the gap between the living and the dead.

The storm outside raged on, with thunder and lightning crashes finally fading away. However, the rain continued to pelt down furiously, creating an ominous background noise that mirrored the sound of Janice's racing heart. As she clutched onto the knife with its gleaming silver blade, she sensed someone entering the room. The temperature seemed to decrease even more, and the air grew dense and stifling, making it difficult for her to breathe.

A deep purple glow emerged in the center of the room, gradually taking shape and transforming into a tall shadow resembling a tree. The light then shifted from a flat surface to a three-dimensional figure, revealing the silhouette of a woman draped in a long black gown. Her skin was pale, and her hair flowed down her back in vibrant shades of red. Once the transformation was complete, Janice was mesmerized by the woman's eyes, sparkling with emerald hues. It took her breath away to see her high priestess, Victoria Parham, standing before her in the flesh.

Janice bowed respectfully as Victoria's spirit fully materialized into human form. "My Mistress Victoria, I summoned you from the realm beyond. I offer you the sacrifices of the living and the dead. I need your guidance. Janice said respectfully.

Victoria's eyes swept over the room and then locked onto Janice. "Janice Hildress, you have called upon me; speak your intentions, my servant."

Janice hesitated momentarily, responding, "I seek to bind the Circle of the Eternal Shadow members to me. A man named Crox is attempting to thwart the Shadow's plan to come back to this realm. I don't think he is powerful enough to do so. I need your guidance and power to complete the binding spell of the Coven and help me become a leader to confine the Shadow if it returns."

"You silly fool, you will never lead my coven," Victoria said flatly.

Janice's eyes widened in shock and fear. "But, my priestess, I have faithfully served the coven, and performing the black séance to bring you back shows I have the power to lead the coven and control the Shadow."

Victoria laughed a cold and haunting sound that echoed through the room. "I am no longer in the realm of the dead, you silly whore. I care not of your petty ambitions. My loyalty lies with the Circle of the Eternal Shadow, not with power-hungry witches like yourself. I will once again control the coven. You should not have summoned me from my grave. You shall not see another day."

Victoria then raised her arms like those of a Greek goddess. She looked at Janice and began to cast her spell: "I call on the powers of the goddess Loviatar, ruler of pain and suffering. From your darkness, I ask, heed my call; I am your worthy servant, Victoria; put this unworthy soul before me to death and have her be seen no more."

Without warning, an invisible force seized Janice, lifting her off the ground. Her body began to bend backward, breaking her spine. She screamed in painful agony. The shadows in the room came alive, engulfing her body. Blood poured from her eyes as her body continued to contort in unnatural ways.

Victoria stood by, a wicked smile playing on her lips as she watched the witch who had brought her back to life suffer in agony. The sound of Janice's bones snapping brought her immense pleasure. "Please, spare me!" Janice pleaded, but Victoria ignored her cries and exited the room. As Janice's head twisted violently, her neck breaking, Victoria calmly made her way into the darkness of the night.

Victoria was adorned in a long, flowing black evening gown, which trailed gracefully behind her. Her slender feet were bare, allowing the cool grass to tickle her toes as she walked. Her raven-red hair cascaded in loose curls down her back, glinting in the moonlight. But her piercing emerald green eyes sowed the darkness within her. Janice had unleashed a powerful evil, far greater than the Shadow, onto the world. Victoria Parham's presence in the living world was like a dark stain spreading through the night. Each step she took seemed to command the very elements, and the thunder and lightning started again, this time more intensely, as she made her way to the forest of Ramouth Church Road.

Unaware of the new arrival from the spirit realm, Crox sat in his office, consumed with guilt over the thought of an innocent person being killed for his sake. His connection with Janice during their astral projection had given him valuable information about the black séance and the binding spell. However, he was still missing a crucial piece: the silver-bladed knife used to sacrifice an innocent.

Crox considered how he would obtain the knife but realized he didn't have Janice's contact information. Although he could visit her through astral projection, it was a risky move after she had stabbed him in that form before—the idea of dying while out of his body was too unsettling to try it again. He would have to find out where Janice lived through Relda, who may be able to find her address or phone number through her police resources.

Since Relda was the Sheriff of Stafford County, she had access to DMV records and could easily obtain Janice's home address. Crox needed to figure out how to get Relda to give him that information.

As Crox pondered his options, Jax sauntered into the room. "We have a problem. I sense a new life energy has been summoned to this realm. Something dark has been unleashed into the land of the living."

Crox furrowed his brow. "What do you mean? What kind of energy?"

The words echoed in my mind, "A new soul has been released from the realm of the dead. Something evil."

A shiver ran down Crox's spine, sending a chill through his body. He could feel a cold, dark presence stirring in the pit of his stomach, which left him uneasy and on edge. The cat's words rang true, a foreboding feeling settling over him as he realized that something had indeed crossed over from the land of the dead and now lurked beyond the confines of the forest. It was an ominous realization that made his skin crawl and his heart race with fear. But there was no denying it - the danger had spread beyond the boundaries he had once thought safe.

"Any idea who or what this could be?" Crox asked.

Jax's green eyes reflected a combination of worry and doubt as he shook his head. "I couldn't make out who it was, but the energy is strong and evil. It's unlike anything I've ever sensed before."

"Okay." Crox said, "We will deal with it when the time comes. Let's complete this binding spell. It is the only thing I can think of to do now."

Crox stared out the window; a tear rolled down his left cheek. He thought to himself, "All I ever wanted was to live a normal life, but no matter how I try, this shit always finds its way back to me. I hope I am strong enough to stop this madness."

Taking a deep breath and wiping away the moisture on his face, Crox got his bearings together. There was no time for self-pity. He had to put on his big boy pants and handle his business.

Jax approached Crox and placed a paw on his foot. Telepathically, the cat said, "You are not alone, my brother. This is family business, and I am here to help you deal with anything that comes at us."

Crox looked down at the cat and smiled. He was not alone. This was a family affair; perhaps if he called on his mother's soul, the family would strengthen, and he would find the strength needed to win this war against evil. Or die trying. Better his death than that of more innocent people.

CHAPTER EIGHTEEN

DREAM VISITOR

Crox was jolted awake by a sharp pain between his shoulder blades. It felt like someone had stabbed him in the night, leaving him groggy and disoriented. As he rubbed at the sore spot on his neck, he had been sleeping on the lumpy couch all night, tossing and turning from an unusual nightmare.

This dream felt different from any other; it seemed personal and important as if trying to send him a message. Crox's dreams were sometimes more than just random thoughts or images; they sometimes told of the past, present, and future. They were also a way for him to connect with those in the spirit realm.

Crox found himself in a dream, standing among tall grass and vibrant wildflowers in a lush green meadow. In the center, an impressive oak tree stretched its branches towards the swirling clouds above. A thick fog rolled in, shrouding everything in a hazy mist. Despite the slight chill in the air, Crox couldn't help but be captivated by his surroundings.

The sky was a beautiful mix of shifting colors - purple and green mingled with orange and gold, from the rays of the morning sun casting through the clouds, creating an eerie misty atmosphere. As Crox gazed at this dreamlike scene, he felt both calm and trepidation at the same time. What did this dream symbolize? And why did it feel so vividly real?

A figure materialized out of the swirling haze, gliding gracefully towards him. It was a woman in a vibrant purple muumuu that billowed around her like a cape, its oversized and flowy design enveloping her small frame. As she drew closer, Crox couldn't believe his eyes—it was his long-dead mother, Pittapat. She had tied her hair back in a ponytail, and her sunken cheeks made her look worn and tired. But he recognized her thin lips and somber expression. It was indeed his mother.

She spoke to him in a raspy voice: "My son, I have come from beyond the grave to ask for your forgiveness. I know what I did to you - binding your magick and then offering your soul to the Shadow - was wrong. But it wasn't out of malice, but out of fear."

She explained how their bloodline held power over the Shadow, but with that power came vulnerability to its allure. Pittapat shared that long ago before she became a high priestess, their family had kept the creature confined to the forest where Crox now resided. However, in trying to control it, she had become consumed by its darkness.

"The Shadow threatened to consume us all, including Jaxson and his daughter Starleena," she confessed sorrowfully. "I thought I had no choice but to contain it within the forest, even if it meant sacrificing you."

"What are you talking about? Your desire to control the Circle of the Eternal Shadow led you to do these things." Crox yelled angrily.

Pittapat continued her story, "By obeying the commands of the Shadow, I ensured that it remained trapped within the forest. The one who summoned the Shadow into our realm- my great-grand-mother was the daughter of Victoria Parham. Our bloodline is connected to the one who brought this evil entity into our world, giving me the power to control and use it for my own purposes. When I was initiated into the Coven, Victoria appeared in my dreams and revealed our connection. She had also sacrificed another witch from our bloodline in the past, and the Shadow demanded that I fulfill that promise. After I took over as leader of the coven following Charlotte's sudden departure, I no longer needed assistance from the other coven members to control the Shadow. I discovered that I could do it alone."

Crox's voice dripped with bitter sarcasm as they confronted his mother, "So you were lying the entire time you were in charge, and I was just a pawn, a lamb to be slaughtered?"

Pittapat warned in a barely audible whisper. "Watch your mouth, son; even in this dream state, I can still cause you harm."

Pittapat's face twisted in an evil smile, making the hairs on the back of Crox's neck stand on end. Crox knew his mother's warning was not to be taken lightly.

Pittapat's tone suddenly grew gentler. "I strayed from the path of righteousness and turned to darkness for strength to defend my people. The Shadow's seductive promises twisted my actions, and I became a mere pawn in its dark schemes. I even was going to sacrifice you, my son, thinking it would give me more power to contain it and keep it locked away in the forest forever. But now, in death, I see that the creature was slowly consuming my soul, making me do these evil things.

Crox listened intently, his mind racing with questions but unable to articulate them. To his surprise, Pittapat seemed to read his thoughts and began addressing some of his unspoken concerns.

"I know you want to unite the coven under your leadership and prevent the Shadow from escaping its prison realm," she warned. "But be careful, my son. Janice Hildress has unleashed a force into the living world that is far beyond your understanding. The Shadow is cunning, its power reaching beyond the forest's boundaries. You must deal with this new threat first."

"What did Janice release? Jax and I both sensed something," Crox asked.

As the mist surrounded Pittapat, her voice echoed through the air. "When the time comes, you'll know what needs to be done," she whispered. "Trust in yourself and the strength passed down through our bloodline; you will discover a way to defeat the darkness within the forest." With a final nod, she disappeared into thin air, leaving behind only a faint trace of lavender. The mist lingered, enveloping everything in a pale green fog as if trying to hold onto her essence. But Pittapat was gone, leaving behind a mysterious message and an uncertain future.

Sitting on the couch, Crox rubbed his sore lower back and tried to calm his mind after the bizarre dream. The thought of being related to Victoria, the first witch, was unsettling. His mother's half-hearted apology only added to his frustration with her justifications for her actions.

As he got up and headed towards the kitchen, Jax followed closely behind. "I can tell your night wasn't restful. Why don't you get a haircut and then head downtown? You could grab lunch and check out some of the art galleries on Caroline Street."

Crox agreed it was time to tame his unruly locks, which were starting to make him resemble Albert Einstein without the genius. He also wanted to catch up with Relda and take her to lunch. After feeding Jax boiled chicken and kibble and enjoying a bowl of Captain Crunch himself, Crox texted Relda to invite her to join him for lunch.

She happily agreed, mentioning that contacting him was on her to-do list. Relda told him to meet her downtown Fredericksburg, and they could stroll through the shops.

After taking a long, hot shower, Crox felt the tension in his back muscles loosen, and the frustration from his unsettling dream slowly dissipated. He was finally starting to feel like himself again.

Jax observed as Crox's car pulled out of the driveway. The cat then darted through the cat door and ran to the far end of the backyard. Jax made sure only to go as far as the property's edge, avoiding entering the woods where danger lurked.

The black cat began yowling loudly, summoning his forest spy, Slick. He knew this would put Slick in harm's way, as the wolves would likely hear his call and come running.

If the orange cat couldn't evade Amara and her partner Mortimer, he would likely be their next meal. He had to rely on his cunning and stealth as he made his way to Jax.

A howl reverberated through the thick forest, sending shivers down Jax's spine. The wolves were distant, but their howls still stirred fear in his heart. He hoped that Slick was nearby and would reach him soon. His prayers were answered when he spotted the round shape of the orange cat emerging from the trees a few moments later.

Jax made a gesture with his tail, indicating Slick to follow him. The two cats headed back to the house. Once inside the comfort of the kitchen, they settled down. However, Jax couldn't shake off the feeling of danger lurking just outside. His feline intuition was on high alert, and Slick seemed to sense it, too. They exchanged a knowing look as they both felt the presence of the wolves watching them from the shadows of the forest.

Meanwhile, Crox and Relda took advantage of the beautiful weather in downtown Fredericksburg, unaware of Jax's meeting with Slick and the growing tension at home. They wandered down charming streets and explored an art gallery called Canal Quarters before pausing for lunch at a quaint local cafe named Amy's.

Relda sensed something was bothering Crox and asked, "Is everything okay? You seem lost in thought. What's going on now? Please don't tell me someone else has gone missing."

Crox forced a smile and shared his latest vision about his mother. Relda was no stranger to his dreams; she knew he used them to speak to spirits. Seeing him use his dreams successfully over the years helped her solve cases of missing persons. She listened without judgment.

Unlike Crox, Relda kept her clairvoyant talents hidden. They had helped her solve numerous crimes and eventually climb the ranks to become one of the first female deputy Sheriffs in Stafford County and later the first black, lesbian supervising Sheriff. Her promotion was a significant milestone for the traditionally conservative county and may have only happened because of her unique powers, which she had not even told Crox about.

Crox's mind suddenly jolted with a thought: he needed a haircut. "I should really get my hair trimmed," he told Relda as they strolled through the bustling downtown shops. "Care to join me? And after, we can grab some coffee and maybe check out that new art gallery, Artfull Dimensions."

"Sounds like a plan, but where do you have in mind?" Relda questioned.

"Let's go see that witch hairstylist Hazel East, who supposedly cursed Mary Byrnes," Crox replied.

"I don't think that's a good idea. You know she's still under investigation for Mary's disappearance and the fire at Galinda's occult bookstore. Do you want to trust her with sharp scissors near your throat?" Relda exclaimed.

Crox let out a deep chuckle. "I thrive on living dangerously," he said with a sly smile.

Meanwhile, Vonda sat parked outside Simply You Salon. Her mind was consumed by thoughts of her recent encounter with Hazel. She knew that blackmailing the old witch would bring about a lot of trouble, but she couldn't resist the rush of power and control it gave her to hold such incriminating information over the old woman's head.

As a survivor of the town's seedy underworld, Vonds relied on her charm and cleverness to navigate dangerous situations and emerge victorious.

Vonda couldn't shake the feeling that her actions this time may have set off a chain reaction beyond her control. Sitting in her car parked outside Simply You Salon, she saw Crox and Relda enter the hair salon.

The soft chime of the bell above the door announced the visitors as Hazeconversedng with a customer; she looked up and saw Crox come in. The sudden shift in her expression conveyed all too clearly: I am going to kill you.

Relda noticed the tension in the air, but she remained composed. The once cheerful and carefree salon now felt ominous, as if a dark energy had entered the room. While Hazel's attitude was contemptuous, Crox appeared unfazed as he boldly strode towards her.

"How are you doing, sweetie? I need a quick trim. Can you fit me in?"

"Are you fucking kidding me with this shit? Why are the two of you here? I won't allow a couple of queers to harass me." Hazel hissed, her lips so tight that her dark red lipstick smeared her lower jaw.

"No, ma'am, I just want a cut; I am not looking for any trouble," Crox said smugly.

"Look, you little asshole, I have the right to refuse service to anyone, and I am refusing service, so get the fuck out of my shop!" Hazel screamed.

"Listen, there is no need for that," Relda said with authority.

"Chill, Sheriff, I got this," Crox said, motioning Relda to stand down.

"Look, I know the last time we were here was on an official matter, but I only came here today to get a haircut," Crox stated.

"Please leave," Hazel said, though with much less venom.

From her car parked outside the salon, Vonda watched Relda and Crox exit, wondering if they had come because of her and the blackmail information she held against Hazel. She became furious at the thought of that deceitful witch calling the police on her without considering it was her ex-lover who she had reached out to in an attempt to cause chaos for Vonda.

Vonda's hands curled into fists as she felt a surge of rage wash over her. How could Hazel betray her trust and expose their private affairs to Relda? Her initial plan of using the blackmail for financial gain was replaced with a burning desire for revenge. With narrowed eyes, Vonda vowed to make Hazel pay for trying to ruin any chance of reconciliation between herself and Relda.

Stepping out of her powder blue Jaguar, Vonda's red high-heeled boots clicked menacingly against the pavement. She confidently held a sleek Smith and Wesson .38 pistol in her right hand as she approached Simply You Salon's entrance.

CHAPTER NINETEEN

HELLO MY QUEEN

The door to the salon slammed hard against the wall as Vonda burst in, causing the small window at its center to shatter into pieces. Hazel spun around in shock to see Vonda, her eyes wild, holding a gun pointed directly at her.

"You thought you could betray me and go to the police instead of paying what you owe?" Vonda hissed with hatred. "I won't let my life be ruined because of your old ass."

An eerie silence filled the salon as Vonda advanced towards Hazel, her hand shaking as she held onto the gun tightly.

As Crox and Relda made their way to their car, they heard the sound of shattering glass and quickly headed back to the salon.

When they arrived, they saw Vonda pointing a gun at Hazel, who was standing motionless.

"Vonda, what the hell is going on?" Crox shouted. The shiny silver gun caught the sunlight and momentarily blinded him. Relda instinctively reached for her weapon, her hand hovering over the grip as she tried to defuse the situation. "Vonda, put down the gun and tell me what's going on."

Hazel's eyes were fixed on the weapon pointed at her chest by Vonda. She spoke, fear evident in her voice, "Please, let's talk about this."

Relda attempted to reason with Vonda, pleading, "We can find a way to resolve whatever issue you have, Hazel, without causing harm. Please, put down the gun."

Vonda heard a voice in her mind, but it wasn't hers. It spoke to her in a familiar and unsettling way: "Why are you doing this, Vonda? This woman is not your enemy. You should never have tried to extort her; she belongs to me, and I will not allow you to harm her."

Her body stiffened as the voice continued to speak. Vonda couldn't identify whose voice it was, but it was communicating with her through telepathy. Vonda's muscles began to tense as she fought to rid herself of this voice in her head, but it was useless. The unseen presence also seemed to have taken control over Vonda's body.

Despite her best efforts, Vonda's hand remained locked onto the gun; she attempted to drop it but found she no longer controlled her hand. Panic set in as she desperately struggled to regain control of her own body.

"I said put down the gun!" Relda's voice boomed in the distance of her mind. Vonda turned her head, trying to respond, but her mouth refused to cooperate. The woman she still loved stood before her, but Vonda could only watch helplessly as she no longer had control over her body and could not speak.

Vonda's focus remained on her captive as she tightened her finger around the trigger of her gun. The force of her grip would surely leave a mark on her palm.

Suddenly, a gust of wind rushed through the salon, extinguishing all the lights and plunging the room into darkness. The temperature instantly dropped as the howling wind entered through the shattered front door. At that exact moment, Vonda's right arm moved on its own, slowly raising under her chin. With a distinct click, she cooked the hammer and pulled the trigger. The loud bang of the gunshot reverberated throughout the salon, filling every corner of the room.

Crox's heart thumped erratically in his chest as he tumbled to the ground, shielding himself from the potential ricochet of the bullet. The room fell into a tense silence, the wind gone and light now filtering in through the broken door. Crox cautiously opened his eyes and removed his hands from his ears, relieved to find that he was still alive.

The aftermath of Vonda's suicide was a gruesome sight, spread out before him like a horrifying painting. Her lifeless body lay on the floor, her head split open with blood and brain matter pooling around her. It looked like something out of a low-budget horror film, but there was no fake blood or special effects here - it was all too real.

Hazel stood still, her expression unmoving except for the smirk that had spread across her lips.

Relda rushed to Vonda's side, frantically checking for any signs of life. "Someone call an ambulance!" she yelled to Crox, who fumbled with his phone to dial 911.

While Crox spoke rapidly with the emergency operator, Relda cradled Vonda's head, desperately trying to stem the flow of blood and tissue spilling onto the polished floor. In their state of shock and panic, neither of them noticed as Hazel calmly stepped over Vonda's body and walked out into the parking lot, leaving behind a trail of chaos and death.

Hazel went down Ramouth Church Road in her large gold Lincoln Town Car, still reeling from the horrific scene she had just witnessed.

While being held at gunpoint by Vonda, a mysterious voice had spoken to her telepathically, requesting a meeting. A powerful witch had caused Vonda's demise and now summoned her.

As she turned off of Patriot Highway onto Ramouth Church Road, Hazel couldn't shake the cold shiver that ran through her body. Despite the warmth of her car's heater, her mind was consumed with thoughts about these woods, where she had sent Mary Byrnes to her death. It was a decision that weighed heavily on her conscience even now; she had not meant for Mary to be killed.

Her instructions were clear: park at the abandoned driveway and await further directions. But Hazel couldn't shake off the growing sense of danger as she drove closer. Was this a trap? After some hesitation, she pulled over to the side of the road. Before entering the woods, Hazel would perform a spell to ease her fears. She retrieved a small pocket knife from her glovebox and sliced her palm, using the blood to draw a pentagram on her forehead.

She recited the protection spell, "Earth, fire, wind, water, and spirit. I summon thee to protect me from all harm. Neither the living nor the dead shall break my body, mind, or soul. May my spirit lend me their strength and provide me with protection." Once Hazel finished her chant, she exited the large luxury vehicle and headed toward the exact location where Freddy met his end.

Hazel lingered in the driveway, unsure if she had indeed heard a voice in her mind. She was about to leave when the voice spoke again, this time from deep within her psyche. "Hazel East, I thank you for answering my call. You have been selected as one of my subjects, and you will serve me. Follow the path through the woods; my wolves will lead the way. Do not fear them. Your attempt at a protection spell is useless against me. As long as you obey my commands, no harm shall befall you."

Hazel's legs shook with fear, but she knew she had no other choice but to obey. She took cautious steps towards the edge of the trees, her eyes darting around in search of any signs of danger. As she entered the forest, darkness enveloped her, and the only sounds were the rustling of leaves and distant owl calls.

Despite her fear, Hazel continued on with the help of her cell phone's flashlight app to guide her way. After what felt like an eternity of navigating through the dense woods, two massive wolves emerged from the shadows. The larger one stared directly at Hazel, its gaze eerily human-like. After a few moments, the black and white wolf turned and began walking, followed closely by the smaller one. Hazel cautiously followed suit, making sure to keep a safe distance in case she needed to make a quick escape back to her car.

The wolves led Hazel to a small open space, where she saw a figure concealed by the darkness of the forest. The person's features were obscured from her view.

"Do not fear, my child. Bow before your queen," commanded a deep yet feminine voice that reverberated through the trees.

The woman emerged from the shadows and stood in the clearing, revealing herself to Hazel, who was taken aback as she recognized the stranger - none other than the legendary first witch of Stafford County, Victoria Parham. Over a hundred years after her death, she had returned from beyond the grave. Hazel respectfully kneeled before her. Victoria smiled at her and bid her to rise.

"What do you need of me, my queen?" Hazel asked respectfully.

Victoria's lips curled into a smile as she answered. "Crox wants to revive my coven, the Circle of the Eternal Shadow, and use it to banish the Shadow back to its realm for good, but I can not allow this.

Hazel stuttered, "But why me? I am an old woman who barely has any magick left. What can I do?"

"I've also been keeping an eye on you from the spirit realm," Victoria continued. "I know the extent of your abilities. You will play a crucial role in my new reign over my coven." Crox will either pledge his loyalty to me or meet his demise. You are more powerful than you realize, my servant. Your soul will be granted eternal life if you do as I say." Victoria instructed. The wolves watched the two women with disinterest, tough wanting to tear them both apart.

Enthralled by the idea of immortality and the power it would grant her, Hazel eagerly nodded in agreement to Victoria's proposal, knowing deep down that she had no other choice. Victoria handed her a small vial filled with a dark liquid and instructed, "Get Crox to drink this. It is a potion that will slowly work its way through his body, weakening him. Bring him back to this exact spot where I will be waiting."

Meanwhile, while Hazel was deep in conversation with Victoria amidst the dense trees of the forest, Crox and Relda sat in the dreary waiting room at Mary Washington Hospital. The fluorescent lights hummed above them, casting a cold, clinical glow on their faces as they grieved over the sudden loss of Vonda. Her absence felt like a gaping hole in their hearts that could never be filled.

Crox held Relda tightly, trying to soothe her shaking body as she sobbed uncontrollably. He knew there were no words that could ease the pain of losing someone you loved so deeply. As they sat there, lost in their thoughts and sorrow, Relda suddenly stood up and began to remove her blood-stained shirt.

She couldn't bear to wear it any longer, the physical reminder of the tragedy that had claimed Vonda's life. A nurse standing nearby noticed her distress and handed her a clean nurse's smock to change into. Relda gratefully accepted it and quickly put it on, feeling a sense of relief as the fabric covered her torn and stained clothing.

Looking at Crox through tear-filled eyes, she asked him softly, "Do you know what we'll say to the detectives from Fredericksburg about what happened at the salon? I don't even know what I saw, and I am a trained police officer ." Her voice trembled as she began to cry again.

"We'll tell them exactly what happened, love. We'll get through this together." He answered. Crox's heart clenched as he realized they would have to relive the horrific events once again when questioned by authorities.

Crox knew it would not be an easy task, but together, they would find the strength to face it. He was unsure what happened himself. One moment, Vonda was about to shoot Hazel, and the next, she was turning the gun on herself.

As they finally emerged from the sterile, fluorescent-lit hospital, Crox and Relda were momentarily blinded by the intensity of the midmorning sun. They had been inside for over 12 hours, trapped in a never-ending cycle of worry and grief. The sudden flood of warmth on their skin felt good, but a chill came over Crox as he began to feel things would never be the same again. Soon, they would have to face the harsh reality of attending a funeral for Vonda.

CHAPTER TWENTY

GRIEF & PROTECTION

The air inside the Fredericksburg Police Station was heavy and tense as Crox and Relda were ushered into an interrogation room.

The walls were stark white, with a lone clock ticking loudly in the corner. Sitting across from them was Detective Josie Lamas, a young woman with a no-nonsense expression and piercing brown eyes that seemed to see through their rehearsed story.

"Alright," she said in a calm, professional tone. "Let's start from the beginning. What happened at Simply You Salon?"

Crox and Relda exchanged a nervous glance before Crox took a deep breath and recounted the previous day's events. His voice shook as he described their innocent visit to the salon for a haircut. His hands trembled as he spoke of Vonda's tragic suicide.

"We had gone to the salon for a haircut and were walking to our car when we heard a loud bang; it was the glass shattering in the front door. We went back to see what had happened, and that is when we saw Vonda holding a gun.

We tried to talk her down, but she seemed out of control as if she were on something. Before we could do anything, she shot herself," Crox explained.

"That's strange. There was no trace of drugs or alcohol in her system." Detective Josie Lamos remarked, her voice laced with suspicion. She then turned to Relda and asked, "Is there anything you want to add, Sheriff?"

Relda shook her head. "It's all true. Everything Crox said happened exactly as he described it. We were caught off guard and didn't have time to react."

Detective Lamos observed them intently before speaking again. "Based on the evidence, this appears to be a clear case of suicide, although we may need to ask you some further questions later. But for now, you are free to leave; by the way, you said you went to the salon to get a haircut, but it doesn't look like you got one; why is that?."

"Hazel said she didn't want to serve me because I'm gay," Crox stated, hoping his voice didn't betray his lie.

"I see- a hairstylist who doesn't serve the gay community. Interesting," Officer Lamos said, looking at Crox in a way that indicated she clearly didn't believe him.

As they stood up to leave, Detective Lamos stepped in front of them, blocking their exit. "Just one more thing: Do you know why Hazel East left before emergency services arrived? I want to get her statement."

"I have no idea," Relda replied quickly. "Our focus was on Vonda and stopping the bleeding."

Josie Lamos handed Relda a business card, her voice still laced with doubt. "Thank you. If anything else comes to mind, please give me a call."

The drive back to Crox's house was silent as they retreated into their thoughts. When they reached the front porch, Jax was waiting for them with a concerned look in his eyes; he could sense the sorrow and turmoil surrounding them.

"What happened?" Jax asked Crox telepathically as they walked inside.

Crox let out a heavy sigh and ran a hand through his hair. "It's a long story. Let me grab a drink first, and then I'll fill you in."

Emotionally drained, Relda paid no attention to Crox talking to the cat. She went into a spare bedroom and closed the door. Crox knew she needed some time alone but was glad she had stayed instead of driving home. He wanted to be there for her.

Pouring himself a generous amount of whiskey, Crox relived the events at the salon with Jax. He recounted everything, from Vonda's unexpected arrival to her tragic death and how it seemed something had control over Vonda's body.

She was there to shoot Hazel, not herself. Jax listened intently, his tail flicking back and forth as he absorbed every detail. Jax remained quiet until Crox was done with the story.

"I'm sorry you had to see that; it must have been horrific," Jax said sympathetically, his emerald eyes reflecting in the low light. "I believe a powerful witch may have taken control of Vonda's body; it couldn't have been Hazel, as her power is not strong enough. But she might know who was really pulling the trigger."

Crox nodded and took a large sip of the whiskey, hoping it would calm his frayed nerves. He walked over to the spare bedroom and opened the door, revealing Relda curled up in a fetal position, her face streaked with tears.

As he gazed at her sleeping form, Crox couldn't help but feel a deep sadness for Vonda's passing and the pain it was causing Relda. Despite the issues he had with Vonda, he would miss her. He also knew that Relda would need time to process her grief, and he promised himself to support her in any way she needed.

In the dense forest outside Crox's house, Slick crouched behind a large oak tree, peering through the leaves at the witch Victoria.

The resurrected witch was deep in thought. Her fingers twisted around the handle of a tree branch as she murmured incantations to herself. Slick could see the vindictiveness on her face as she spoke the spells to regain control of her coven. Slick couldn't just sit by and watch. He knew he had to warn Jax before it was too late.

Slowly, the fat cat crept away from the tree, careful not to make a sound as he made his way out of the forest and to the house. His heart pounded with fear as he wondered what Victoria would do if she caught him listening in on her. Reaching the cat door and proceeding into the house, much to Jax's irritation, Slick urgently relayed all that he had heard from Victoria's conversation with the old witch Hazel and the spells she was attempting to cast to regain her power as high priestess. Jax knew they had to act fast before Victoria regained control over the Shadow and the wolves.

Crox sat in the living room, lost in thought as he waited for Relda to wake up. He was oblivious to Slick and Jax's conversation in the kitchen. Suddenly, Crox's senses were overwhelmed by the powerful sensation of someone approaching his home – one he had never felt before. He quickly ran to the front window but saw nothing. He then went out onto the back deck and surveyed the backyard and surrounding woods, searching for any signs of the unknown presence. All he could hear was the distant hoot of an owl, but he saw no one.

Jax climbed onto the deck, his eyes fixed on his human brother. The cat spoke up, "I sensed it too; there's something other than the Shadow's wolves lurking in that forest. If you also feel its presence, your abilities are growing stronger. I fear that this entity may be too powerful for our protection spell for it to defend us against what is out there. Perhaps you should wake Relda and leave from this place."

Crox remained rooted to the spot on the deck, gazing out into the dark night, looking for whatever evil preyed on him from deep in the woods. His fear was beginning to turn to anger.

He responded without turning to look at the black cat: "My home is my castle. I refuse to be driven out by the Shadows, the Wolves, or anything else. Whatever comes for me, I'll be ready. I will not run in fear."

Staring up at the glittering stars above, Crox's mind and body were consumed with exhaustion from the weight of the stress. After a few minutes, he scooped up Jax and carried this tiny body to bed. He then collapsed onto the mattress and quickly drifted into sleep, where there were no ominous warnings or haunting dreams, just a blissful and all-encompassing unconsciousness that offered temporary relief from the day's chaos.

In the dead of night, as the humans and feline slumbered peacefully, Victoria released the first subject of her new reign from her grasp. With a cruel smile, she watched Hazel stumble out of the forest, her fear palpable with each heavy step toward her car. Hazel had a mission to complete, and failure was not an option, for if she failed, only death would be a merciful escape compared to the torture that awaited her. Amara and Mortimer, the two wolves under Victoria's control, escorted the old witch back to her car.

As they walked through the darkened woods, Victoria sat in the center of a clearing where an old altar stood, remnants of a pentagram still etched into the earth from long ago. The stones formed a ring around her, their jagged edges glinting in the moonlight as she called upon the elements to open the door to other dimensions - a doorway that would bring forth unimaginable horrors.

Crox woke up feeling energized and surprisingly content the following day despite the urgency of finding Hazel East before the Fredericksburg police did. He needed to uncover the truth about Vonda's death; it was clear that something supernatural had occurred, and Hazel, being a witch, may hold the key.

Relda was still in a deep slumber in the spare bedroom. He woke her with a gentle shake, noticing the bloodshot eyes from her previous night's tears. The lingering weight of sorrow hung heavy in the air, but there was no time to dwell on it just yet.

Crox prepared breakfast for them, including scrambled eggs, toast, and strong coffee, while Jax indulged in some wet cat food mixed with tuna.

"I have to go home, shower, and brush my teeth. I feel completely gross." Relda sighed, dreading the task ahead of her. "And I must call Macy, Vonda's sister, and tell her the news. I'm not looking forward to that conversation."

"We also need to find Hazel before she speaks with the authorities," Crox reminded her urgently.

Relda nodded, sipping her coffee and rubbing her tired eyes. "You're right. We need to find out why Vonda went to that salon with a gun. It was obvious she intended to shoot Hazel, but why? Once I deal with Macy, Vonda's sister, I let her know what happened and help her plan the funeral. After I'm done, I'll request some days off from work, and then we can meet up later today to check on Hazel at the salon or her home."

Crox agreed, and they finished their breakfast before parting ways. Relda headed back home while Crox planned to search through his mother's old grimoire. He could feel his magick abilities growing stronger, but he still didn't know what or how to control them. Perhaps the spellbook would hold some answers for him.

With Jax following closely at his heels, Crox entered the office and sat at the desk. He opened the old book with its worn pages, realizing he had failed to return it to the safe after his last reading session. In the future, he would need to be more cautious; he couldn't risk this powerful book falling into the wrong hands.

As he delved deeper into the mystical text, Crox stumbled upon a passage written in a flamboyant, extravagant style of calligraphy. The ornate writing was difficult to decipher, causing Crox to read each word slowly. The passage discussed a way to control another, known as telepathic possession. It explained how one could seize control of someone's mind and manipulate their thoughts and actions. It also warned of the potential dangers and disastrous consequences of such possession.

The more Crox read, the more he became convinced that Vonda had fallen prey to this telepathic possession. He ruled out Hazel as the culprit, as she seemed genuinely scared and confused during their encounter. Crox also didn't believe that the Shadow could have taken control of someone in this realm; it would have already done so if it could.

So, who or what could be responsible for this possession? Crox wondered. He continued flipping through the grimoire pages when he came across a protective spell that promised to keep him safe no matter where he went, providing him peace of mind even when away from home. His eyes widened as he read the instructions of the protection spell, which called for a blood sacrifice. Without hesitation, he picked up a letter opener from the desk and stuck it in his left index finger, making it bleed.

Crox then took the blood and drew a pentagram on his forehead. Crox then began to recite the words of the protection spell, "By the power of earth, fire, wind, water, and spirit, I call upon the elements to protect me from harm and death. Neither the living nor the dead shall break my body, mind, or soul. May my spirit guides walk with me on this path, and their strength be mine."

As he finished saying the final words, he felt a surge of energy coursing through his veins, a magick shield forming around him to ward off any danger that may come his way.

He knew that this spell might come at a price, but at this moment, nothing mattered more than protecting himself from the darkness that sought to harm him. Crox's confidence swelled as he donned this added layer of protection, ready to face whatever lay within the forest. So sure of his invincibility, he dared to test the spell by venturing deep into the dark and foreboding woods beyond his backyard.

CHAPTER TWENTY-ONE

NIGHT-TIME STROLL

Crox stepped out into the cool night air; a breeze brushed against his skin and sent chills down his bare arms. He took a deep breath, savoring the crisp scent of leaves and earth filling his senses. In this peaceful moment, he felt he was on the brink of a breakthrough in understanding his powers as a witch.

Crox leisurely walked around his backyard, admiring the half-moon in the sky that would soon become full. A red ring of shadow surrounded the moon, creating an eerie yet beautiful sight. Jax had been left inside the house at Crox's request. This time, he wanted to be alone and feel the comforting embrace of his protection spell without any interruptions.

Crox also intended to survey the edges of his property and test his spell's strength without worrying about Jax's well-being.

Stepping over the property's protective boundary and into the dark, foreboding woods, Crox immediately felt a powerful presence hanging in the air. He had experienced this sensation before but couldn't quite remember where. Trusting his intuition, he navigated through the dense trees and underbrush, guided by the bright moon's light.

After what seemed like an eternity of walking, he stumbled upon the clearing where the circle of rocks with the pentagram burned into the ground. As he entered the heart of the forest, he saw flickering candles casting an alluring yellow glow.

Crox's heart raced uneasily as he approached what appeared to be a makeshift altar. A thought echoed in his mind: "Curiosity killed the cat."

As he cautiously approached the circle, Crox caught a flash of movement out of the corner of his eye. He turned too quickly to get a better look, only to lose his footing, twisting his ankle and causing him to tumble backward onto the rough ground. The sharp rocks and twigs scraped against his skin as he landed with a thud, the pain shooting through his body like an electric shock.

From the shadows emerged the creature that had run past him. Suddenly, it pounced on Crox's stomach, knocking the wind out of him. Crox rolled onto his side, trying to dislodge the animal while gasping for air. When he finally regained his breath, he checked to make sure he hadn't soiled himself before looking at the tubby orange cat that had landed on him.

The feline sat patiently as Crox composed himself. After checking his ankle and ensuring he could still walk.

Crox stood up and brushed off the dirt from his backside. He chuckled at himself for being tripped up by a cat and was grateful that he wouldn't have to change his underwear.

"Alright, you got me," Crox chuckled. He reached down and gently scratched behind the cat's ears, eliciting a contented purr from the feline.

"You must be the guardian of this place, huh?" With its thick orange fur and piercing green eyes, the cat seemed to radiate an aura of protectiveness as it gazed back at him. Its tail twitched in response, almost seeming to nod in agreement.

The orange tabby purred contentedly, nuzzling its head against Crox's palm. A strange sense of familiarity struck him; petting this cat felt like something he had done before, even though he couldn't recall ever seeing this fat orange cat. A slight breeze rustled through the trees, snapping him out of his daze.

Crox regretted not bringing a weapon with him into the forest. He knew the protection spell might not even be effective against whatever or whoever was emitting the powerful energy he sensed or the wolves that could be hiding in these woods. But he was relieved to have met this friendly cat instead of encountering wild predators.

Crox bent down and picked up the orange cat while stroking its soft fur. As he did so, he gazed intently at the flames dancing on the candles arranged in a circle on the ground. The flickering light cast elusive shadows around the clearing. He felt the presence of someone watching him, but he did not feel a sense of danger. He turned his head, looking all around, only to be met with the forest's darkness.

"So this is where you like to hang out, huh? Do you know who lit these candles?" Crox spoke to the cat, attempting to cut through the eerie quiet. The feline responded with a soft meow before leaping out of his grasp and gracefully strolling into the center of the ring of rocks. It gazed up at the crimson half-moon high above. "Do you consider this your sacred space, my fluffy friend?" Crox chuckled as he watched the cat cock its head in his direction, almost as if it understood him.

Suddenly, the distant sound of howling pierced through the trees, causing Crox to freeze in fear and causing his testicles to retract into his scrotum. It was far away, yet too close for comfort. At that moment, Crox decided against continuing to test his protection spell. He hurried back towards his home with the cat held firmly in his arms to prevent it from escaping.

As Crox neared his house, he spotted a figure standing on the front porch, bathed in the faint light of the porch lamp. It was Relda, her arms tightly crossed and her expression a mix of worry and anger.

"Crox, where have you been? I've been beside myself with worry," Relda exclaimed as he drew closer.

"I took a stroll through the woods and met this little guy," Crox answered sheepishly, raising the plump orange feline for Relda to see.

"Hmm, he's quite chubby," Relda remarked with a touch of teasing in her voice. Why were you wandering around in those woods at night? Have you lost your ever-loving mind? Do I need to remind you of the dangers lurking out there?"

Crox chuckled nervously, rubbing the back of his head in embarrassment. "I know, I know. It was foolish of me. But I needed some time outside for some fresh air and wanted to see if the protection spell from my mother's grimoire I cast worked."

Relda's expression turned angry as she scolded Crox, "Do you honestly believe some silly magick spell can protect you from wild animals? I thought you were smarter than that, dumbass."

Crox winced at her harsh words, knowing she was right. He had been reckless. He took a deep breath to steady himself before responding. You're right," Crox said earnestly, meeting Relda's gaze. "I shouldn't have gone out alone, especially at night. I let my curiosity get the best of me, and I promise it won't happen again."

Relda's anger slowly faded away as she locked eyes with Crox. She could see the sincerity in his eyes and felt her heart soften. Without hesitation, she reached out her arm and placed a gentle hand on his forearm, a small gesture of forgiveness and understanding.

Losing Vonda had left her emotions raw, and she couldn't bear the thought of losing another friend. "Just please promise me you'll be more careful in the future," she said softly, trying to hold back tears. I don't want to lose you, too."

Crox nodded, a lump forming in his throat at her words. He knew he needed to be more mindful of his actions for his safety and those who cared about him.

Crox promised Relda he would be more careful. They entered the house with Crox's arms still cradling the orange cat, who purred contently. Finding this unique feline in the woods made Crox feel things would turn out alright. He couldn't explain why he felt a connection to the cat, but it was almost as strong as his love for Jax.

From the forest's darkness, Victoria had watched as Crox stumbled back in surprise when an orange cat leaped out of the underbrush. She was confident Crox had no idea the cat was once a human, its soul now trapped within this feline form. In this forest, all the cats were once living men and women who had fallen victim to the Shadow and had their souls trapped by the entity.

When the Shadow was banished back to its realm, these souls were released from its grasp and transformed into cats. Though she didn't know why, Victoria didn't care unless they interfered with her plans; if they did, she would eliminate them without hesitation.

Victoria sensed Crox was growing stronger but couldn't pinpoint what was causing this transformation. All she knew was that she needed to tread carefully around him. She needed him alive for now, especially since he possessed some of her bloodline powers.

The first witch of Stafford County considered revealing herself to Crox but decided to hold off for now. She needed more time to plan her next move carefully and wanted complete control over the situation before making herself known. For the time being, she would remain hidden, silently observing Crox and his friends.

Watching from the shadows would allow her to gather valuable information about his strengths and weaknesses. Her ultimate goal is to regain her full power and have him serve by her side. Victoria followed Crox as he returned to his house, where the Sheriff was waiting.

Victoria could feel a slight magical force within this woman as well. After Crox and Relda disappeared into the house, Victoria telepathically summoned Amara and Mortimer to join her in the forest clearing as she retreated into the shadows.

Once inside, Crox poured Relda a glass of chardonnay, and they began to make arrangements for Vonda's funeral. Vonda's sister, Macy, wanted no part in it due to their longtime feud with Vonda, which was still fueled by her resentment and jealousy toward her older sibling.

While the two humans discussed their deceased friend's memorial plans, Slick wandered around the house in search of the litter box. After finishing all the food in Jax's bowl, Slick explored further until he came across Jax in Crox's office.

Jax's voice rumbled with a low growl as he bared his teeth at the orange cat. "What are you doing here?" he snarled.

Slick's voice rose angrily as he spoke, his eyes throwing daggers toward the black cat.

"Crox dragged me here. What of it?"

Jax let out a hiss and lunged at Slick, his sharp teeth bared in a vicious snarl. The two cats tore through the house, claws slashing and fur flying as they hissed and spat at each other, their eyes blazing with feral rage.

Relda let out a chuckle as she observed Jax's obvious displeasure with the new addition to the household. After a moment of tearing into each other, they seemed to realize they were being watched, and the two cats quickly composed themselves. Their fur was sticking up in all directions as they innocently gazed up at Relda, pretending nothing had happened.

"Don't try to fool me with those innocent looks," Relda laughed, shaking her head.

Crox calmly observed the cats' playful antics while taking small sips of his wine. Despite the mayhem they were creating, he couldn't help but be amused and smile. He felt a sense of joy and contentment wash over him, grateful for this moment of simple pleasure.

Crox walked Relda to her car, leaving the two cats to continue their battle for dominance. As they made their way outside, Crox asked about Hazel East. "I have a friend in the Fredericksburg police department who told me that Vonda's death is being treated as a suicide.

They sent an officer to get a statement from Hazel, but she is not considered a suspect. The police will probably contact her several times before closing the case." Relda advised.

"Do you want to do a stakeout? Hazel eventually has to show up at her house or salon. I can take the house if you prefer to take the salon," Crox suggested.

"I just want to bury Vonda and let it be. I can't get involved in following someone without probable cause; besides, it's outside my jurisdiction; I could lose my job," Relda replied.

"I understand. I'm here for you if you need anything. I love you," Crox said as he hugged Relda.

He watched as Relda drove away and then walked back inside the house. He could hear the cats causing damage, and he let out a sigh as he entered, finding Slick sitting on top of Jax.

Jax's mind roared with telepathic fury as he screamed at Crox, "Get this fat ass off me!"

Crox chuckled as he scooped up the orange cat and took him to his bedroom, closing the door. When he returned to the living room, Jax was seated on the couch, waiting for him.

"Get rid of that wild animal," Jax ordered.

"I don't think so," Crox replied. He is not feral; in fact, he is quite friendly. There's something about him that I can't quite put my finger on. He's going to stay here with us. Now I just need to come up with a name for him."

Jax launched himself onto the back of the couch, his sharp claws unsheathed. He crept up behind Crox's head and pounced, slashing the back of his legs with unbridled fury until blood seeped from the wounds.

"Damn you!" Crox roared in pain as Jax leaped off and landed gracefully on the floor. Jax sauntered toward the kitchen with a defiant yowl, his tail flicking in satisfaction.

"Call him Slick," he declared, his voice laced with malice. "A name fitting for a slippery snake like him."

CHAPTER TWENTY-TWO

HUNT FOR HAZEL

After escaping getting shot and watching Vonda blow her brains out, Hazel went into hiding. She was determined to stay off the radar of the police. She found a cheap and unassuming motel called Paynes Motel on Princess Anne Street and paid in cash to avoid any records that could lead to her arrest if a warrant was out for her.

Hazel contemplated her next move while sitting on the shabby bed of her dimly lit room. She knew she had to be cautious and lay low until she could figure out how to fulfill Victoria's task.

Her plan was simple. Hazel would lure Crox away from that dyke cop and have him consume the potion Victoria had provided. It would render him unconscious so she could take him deep into the forest where Victoria and her two wolves would be waiting.

Hazel understood that the only way to get him into the clearing of the forest was through this method. She didn't believe he would go willingly. However, she faced another issue: even if he consumed the potion and fell unconscious, how would she manage to transport his heavy body through the woods? With Crox's weight being at least a hundred pounds more than her own and her lack of physical strength due to her age, it seemed impossible to drag him by herself.

While Hazel was strategizing how to kidnap Crox, he was searching public real estate records for any additional properties or businesses that Hazel may have owned and could be hiding out at. Unfortunately, the only information he found was her salon and home address on Bridgewater Street in Fredericksburg.

Crox glanced over at Jax, who was still sneek attacking Slick, stating firmly, "Listen up, Jax. I need to leave for a bit, and I expect you to behave while I'm gone. That means no picking on Slick. Understand?"

Already plotting his next vicious attack on the orange cat, Jax looked up with feigned innocence and answered, "Sure, I'll be a perfect angel. Slick won't have a thing to worry about."

"Don't give me that crap," Crox snapped, "Slick is part of this family now, whether you like it or not. And if I come back to find even a scratch on him, there will be serious consequences." Jax's eyes dilated with anger. The black cat was not happy being scolded.

"Touch'e," came Jax's snippy reply. After Crox left the house, Jax went to find a hiding space for his next attack on the orange Outlander.

Crox's first stop was Hazel's home, where he hoped to find some clues to help him track her down. He doubted she would return to the salon while the front door was being repaired.

Driving slowly by the small white bungalow on Bridgewater Street, Crox noticed that all the houses in the neighborhood looked like tiny one-story single-family homes built in the early 1950s. The house blended in with its surroundings and would quickly go unnoticed. Nobody was out on the street, making what he would do easier.

Crox parked his truck a block away from Hazel's place to avoid attracting attention from the neighbors. He walked confidently up to her front door and knocked, but there was no response. After waiting a few seconds, he knocked again, this time louder.

Still, there was no sign of life inside; it seemed that Hazel was not home. Disappointed, Crox returned to his truck and reached for his cell phone to call his old friend, Kevin Merrick. Crox and Kevin had been friends since their teenage years, and Kevin had always been skilled at picking locks.

"Kev! It's Crox. Long time no see," Crox exclaimed as he answered the phone.

"Crox! How have you been, man? I haven't heard from you in a coon's age. What's new with you?" Kevin responded.

"It's been good, bro. I need you to help me out with something. I'll tell you more when you get here. Are you free right now?"

"Absolutely, I've got your back. Give me a few minutes to finish what I'm doing, and then I'll head to your place."

"Great. I'm currently on Bridgewater Street in Fredericksburg, behind the 2400 Diner. Can you come by here?" Crox asked.

"I know that area well. Do you have a specific address? I'll be there in about twenty minutes."

"There is no need for an exact address; just look for my truck parked nearby and try not to park too close," Crox instructed.

"So, what's going on?" Kevin asked before Crox hung up.

Before he could answer, Crox chuckled and ended the call.

Crox knew he could always count on Kevin, who was the type of friend that didn't require explanations. Kevin was a doer, not a questioner, which was precisely what Crox needed in this particular situation. Sure enough, within fifteen minutes.

Kevin arrived at their designated meeting spot, parking his blue Volkswagon Passat a couple of blocks away. With his tall stature and beard, Kevin had a mischievous glint in his eyes that made him stand out as a good ol' Southern boy. It was almost like he could read Crox's mind; without being asked, he brought along his lockpicking tools, knowing they were about to break into somewhere.

They approached the side of the house, aiming to enter through the rear. The tall fence shielded them from the prying eyes of curious neighbors. Kevin lifted Crox onto his shoulders, enabling him to climb over the fence and land safely in the backyard.

"You're getting heavy, man. I might get a hernia carrying you like this," Kevin laughed.

"Shut up, asshole," Crox responded.

Crox couldn't help but notice the backyard's condition —it was a mess, with overgrown weeds and grass. It was clear that no one had bothered to tend to the yard in quite some time. Crox led the way to the gate and opened it for Kevin to enter.

Together, they made their way towards the back door. Kevin pulled out his trusty lockpicking tools and effortlessly unlocked the cheap lock. Crox was amazed at how skilled Kevin was at gaining entry so quickly.

As they searched through every room in the neglected house, the layers of dust and worn furniture told a story of a sad life that lived within these walls. However, their extensive search yielded no clues or leads on Hazel's whereabouts. It seemed as though she hadn't been there for a while. Standing in the dusty living room, Crox couldn't shake the feeling that they were missing something important.

Kevin rubbed his hands against his jeans and thought aloud, "Maybe she's hiding somewhere else, or perhaps she left town. What could she have done? It appears from this house that she's just an old woman who doesn't know how to clean."

Crox replied vaguely to the question about why he was searching for Hazel: "She's been missing for a few days now, but it looks like she hasn't been in this house for quite some time."

Crox looked around the hoarded room and noticed a door hidden behind an armoire. With Keven's help, they moved the large piece of furniture, fully exposing the door. Upon opening it, they discovered a set of stairs leading down to a basement.

Making their way down the creaky stairs, the musty scent of the basement invaded their senses. The space was filled with countless soiled boxes, discarded pieces of furniture, and even more cobwebs. Crox and Kevin began rummaging through the clutter, searching for anything helpful in locating Hazel.

In one corner of the basement, tucked away behind some old chairs, Crox noticed a small barn door. It blended in so well with its surroundings that it would have been easily overlooked if one wasn't paying close attention. Curious, he opened the door to reveal a hidden room below the house.

The room was dimly lit, and Crox fumbled to find a light switch, using the flashlight on his cell phone. In the center of the room stood a wooden table covered in dusty tarot cards, a crystal ball, and various jars of herbs.

Crox's eyes widened as he realized this was Hazel's private altar room, where she practiced her witchcraft away from prying eyes. Standing behind him, Kevin whistled in amazement,

"Look at all this stuff. Do you think any of it is valuable?" Crox scowled at him and replied firmly, "We are not here to steal; I'm just looking for information."

Crox carefully inspected the room, hoping to find clues leading him to Hazel's whereabouts. His eyes landed on the tarot cards placed on the altar, and one card stood out to him—the Devil card.

"It seems Hazel was involved in some dark practices," Crox muttered under his breath. "But where could she have gone?"

Despite conducting a meticulous search of the secret altar room, nothing of great significance was found that would give clues to Hazel's whereabouts.

Despite Crox's assurance to Kevin that they were not there to steal anything, he couldn't resist slipping the Devil card into his pocket when Kevin wasn't paying attention.

Crox strolled towards the stairs leading them out of the damp and moldy basement. "Let's get out of here, Kev," he said. The men exited the same way they entered, Crox making no attempt to conceal their break-in. He wanted Hazel to be aware of it. As they left through the back door, Crox paused to scribble a note on Hazel's grocery list pad on the refrigerator: We need to talk. It was signed, you-know-who.

As Crox made his way out of Hazel's backyard, she sat parked a block away and watched him leave. The man he had been with went in a separate direction. Hazel's Ring doorbell had alerted her to their unauthorized presence in her home. She was relieved that they didn't appear to have stolen anything.

However, she knew it would be best not to go home yet; she didn't want to risk reencountering those trespassers or the police. Hazel was not aware they had deemed Vonda's death a suicide. Seething on how these invaders had violated her sanctuary, Hazel tapped her purse where Victoria's potion was safely stored. "Crox will pay," she thought bitterly.

Hazel decided to silently trail Crox from a safe distance, ensuring not to attract his attention. "If Victoria didn't want you alive, I would take you out right now," Hazel thought as she followed his Ram 4x4 truck toward Simply You Salon.

Crox drove to the salon, unsure if Hazel would even be there. To avoid attracting attention, he parked his truck a few blocks away and walked the rest of the way. The shattered glass had been replaced, but the hasty repair job on the door wouldn't keep out any intruders. Looking through the window, Crox could see that the salon was empty. He debated whether to wait for Hazel or give up on finding her for now.

Ultimately, Crox chose to head back home. It seemed like this stakeout had been a waste of time and effort. As Crox made his way home, Hazel trailed behind him at a safe distance in her gold Lincoln Town Car.

Unaware that Hazel was stalking him, Crox pulled into his driveway while she parked on the side of the road several hundred yards away.

Crox stomped into his house, a mixture of frustration and disappointment weighing heavily on his shoulders. His visit to Hazel's home and salon had been unfruitful, leaving him no closer to finding her. He went to the living room, where he saw Jax and Slick sitting beside each other, seemingly in harmony for once.

"Well, you two have adjusted to the new living arrangement. I'm pleased to see you getting along," Crox remarked as he plopped onto the couch.

Just as Crox started to unwind, a knock sounded at the door. He stood up and went to answer it, surprised to see Relda standing there with a bag of groceries in her arms.

"With everything happening, I thought we could use some food and a distraction," Relda suggested warmly.

Crox was grateful for the gesture and welcomed her inside. They spent the evening cooking together, reminiscing about Vonda, and enjoying each other's company. The presence of Relda and the cats brought a sense of normalcy, a much-needed reprieve from the constant reminder of death that seemed to surround him. They both began to feel a sense of healing as they laughed at memories of better times on Honey Suckle Hill. Meanwhile, Hazel made her way through the forest, calling out telepathically to Victoria while trying to avoid running into the wolves.

A wicked smile crossed Victoria's lips as she stood in the clearing, hearing Hazel's call. She could sense the old witch's fear; it was like a drug, filling her with pleasure. Victoria commanded Amara and Mortimer to lead Hazel through the forest to her. The wolves vanished into the darkness, their haunting howls reverberating into the night. Victoria laughed wickedly, her voice bouncing off the trees and causing the birds to flee through the air as she waited for her pets to bring her the slave.

CHAPTER TWENTY-THREE

COVEN REBORN

As Victoria waited for Hazel to join her in the dark clearing, she began to chant a spell, calling upon the Shadow to emerge to the living realm. "Daylight fades, giving way to everlasting darkness. Enter this realm where evil will reign. May the screams of the sacrificed be swallowed in your void. Hear my call, under-lord. Come forth."

The temperature plummeted, and a bright purple glow filled the clearing. The candles Victoria had placed around the stone circle flickered violently, and the ground trembled beneath her feet. A sudden burst of wind tore through the forest, wailing in all directions. With each passing moment, the moon's light grew brighter, casting long shadows that twisted and melded together into a monstrous shape. And then, in an instant, the purple light dissipated, revealing a swirling vortex of black smoke that solidified into the form of the Shadow.

Victoria couldn't tear her eyes away from the menacing figure before her. Its red eyes seemed to look straight into her soul. The creature hung suspended in the air, radiating pure evil. "My treacherous servant, Victoria," the Shadow's voice slithered like a poisonous snake. "Why have you returned to the land of the living? The grave is where you belong."

Victoria stood tall and unafraid, her eyes blazing with fury. She would no longer submit to the will of the Shadow. With a steady gaze into the faceless form, and declared, "You may have taken my mortal body, but my spirit cannot be extinguished. I have returned, ready to take over my coven and regain its power to control this realm."

"Bring me the promised one, and I will allow you to continue to live; fail me, and I will take your soul and feed on it for eternity." The Shadow's voice echoed.

"It shall be done, but first, I demand the return of my coven. I need your dark power to summon all those who once worshipped you to come and pledge their eternal allegiance to me as their high priestess once again."

The Shadow's cold laughter rang throughout the dark forest as Victoria knelt before it. "I will grant you the power to rebuild your coven," the Shadow hissed, its red eyes blazing brighter. "But remember, your loyalty belongs to me alone. I will make sure your soul rots in eternal agony if you cross me."

Victoria bowed even lower, her mind swirling with schemes for vengeance against those who had betrayed her. A wicked smile spread across her face as she began to recite the spell, utilizing the power of the Shadow to extend its reach across the globe and into the minds of her former coven members.

"My subjects, I shall enter your thoughts and control them," she hissed, her voice echoing through the minds of all members of the Circle of the Eternal Shadow. "No protection spells can block my will. Hear me, my loyal followers of darkness. The Circle is reborn under my command. Come to me, heed my call."

Victoria's voice rose in volume, and her agitation increased as if she was channeling the energy of the earth itself. A pulsing lime-green light enveloped her body, intensifying with each passing moment. Her eyes rolled back into her head, their whites glowing fiercely against the darkness. The air crackled with electricity, charged by the dark power of the Shadow.

Hazel cautiously navigated through the dense woods, making her way toward the clearing as Victoria's spell continued to spread its reach across the world. Suddenly, Amara jumped out from the shadows, startling Hazel and causing her to lose her balance. As she tried to regain her footing, Mortimer appeared behind her, his sharp teeth bared, ready to pounce. But before he could attack, Amara let out a blood-curdling howl, stopping Mortimer in his tracks.

Amara glowered at Hazel as it began to speak. The wolf's voice was husky yet feminine, almost seductive in its command. "Our Queen wishes to see you," she said, her eyes gleaming with a dark intensity. The wolf beckoned Hazel to follow her deeper into the darkness, her steps silent and swift on the forest floor. The air around them was heavy with the musky scent of wild animals.

Hazel's heart raced, both from fear and disbelief. She may have been a witch herself, but never before had she encountered a talking animal. It was too much for her elderly mind and body to handle, causing her to collapse from shock. Her body began to convulse, and a sharp pain went down her right arm.

"Get help, please. I think I am having a heart attack." Hazel pleaded as she rolled in agony on the ground, clutching her chest. Terror began to wash over her as she struggled for air, unable to breathe. Her body contorted from the pain and fear in unnatural positions.

Amara circled her with a predatory glint in its eyes. Mortimer's hesitation was brief before he launched himself at the helpless old witch, his powerful jaws clamping down on Hazel's neck with brutal force.

The smaller wolf's sharp fangs tore through the delicate flesh of Hazel's throat and pierced her jugular, causing a violent gush of blood to spray across the forest floor, creating a gory art masterpiece in crimson red.

As Mortimer devoured Hazel's heart, Amara coolly remarked that their queen should not be angered with them, for the witch was already doomed to die. With blood still dripping from their muzzles, the two wolves scampered back to report to Victoria about the unfortunate death of Hazel.

Tension hung heavy in the air at Crox's house. The dark energy penetrating from the forest made the cats pace and growl. Jax's fur stood on end. Crox felt a sharp stab of pain shoot through his skull, causing him to wince and clutch at his head. Suddenly, a vision crashed into his mind like a tidal wave.

He saw Hazel trapped and helpless in the woods, surrounded by the two wolves. The scene was so vivid and terrifying that Crox could almost feel her fear and desperation as if it were his own. His body trembled as he stumbled back, gasping for air, the vision fading but leaving behind a lingering sense of dread.

Relda rushed to his side; worry etched on her face. "What happened? Are you alright?" she demanded, gripping his shoulder with concern. But Crox could only stare ahead with wide eyes, feeling as ghostly pale as death itself. Crox's voice trembled as he spoke, his eyes still wide with shock. "I saw her... Hazel. She was in the woods, surrounded by the wolves. It felt so real, like a vision."

Relda's features tightened, her furrowed brow revealing her concern as she intently listened to Crox's words. "A vision? Surely, it must have been a figment of your imagination," she questioned, her tone laced with worry and doubt.

Crox shook his head. "No," he insisted, his voice laced with anguish and fear. "This was different. It felt too real. I know in the depths of my soul that Hazel is dead." He clenched his fists, nails digging into his palms as he spoke.

Relda paused momentarily and then stated, "We can't search tonight. It's too dark, which could be dangerous. I'll contact animal control again and report a sighting of a coyote in the area; they will not believe it's a wolf since they have been out looking for them before and haven't seen any traces of them. Coyotes are common around these parts. While they're out searching, perhaps they'll find evidence of Hazel's remains if she was out there and was killed." Her tone was grim.

Crox hesitated before saying, "Alright, it's probably safer if we stay indoors tonight." But some of him still wanted to go out, if only to test his personal protection spell again.

Relda looked at Crox with a smile, "Since I'll be staying the night and didn't bring an overnight bag, do you happen to have an extra set of pajamas and a spare toothbrush? "There should be a few extra toothbrushes in the bathroom down the hall. I can lend you a T-shirt and some gym shorts to wear for sleeping. We should get some rest now. We can call animal control in the morning," suggested Crox.

Amara and Mortimer entered the clearing, seeing both Victoria and the Shadow surrounded by a glowing lime-green mist. Victoria was reciting a spell to telepathically communicate with members of the Circle of the Eternal Shadow, no matter where they were in the world. The two animals sat down on the ground and patiently waited for their queen or master to speak.

"Listen and obey, my loyal subjects. I have returned to the realm of the living and will lead us to greatness once again. Join me in the clearing where the Shadow resides; we will harness its power together." Victoria called out telepathically as the Shadow watched in silence. Victoria's voice echoed through the minds of her coven's previous members, thanks to the Shadow's powerful magick. There was no escaping her reach now. With a threatening tone, she warned them that if they did not obey her commands, their lives would be filled with agony and misery.

Despite the fear and loyalty that still bound them, some members had mixed reactions to the resurrected witch's call.

Some of the past coven members felt compelled to obey and began making their way to Stafford County, pulled by Victoria's words. But others, having moved on from their dark past, resisted the call and tried to block the witch's intrusion from taking over their minds.

Witches, both males and females with varying levels of power, scattered around the world, felt the unsettling presence of Victoria's telepathic summons. She continued to chant, tapping into the Shadow's power to strengthen her call. The air in the clearing grew dense, and the lime-green light that surrounded her seemed to pulsate in response to the dark magick she was harnessing.

As the night dragged on, the reactions to Victoria's call continued to be mixed. Some who resided nearby made their way to the clearing, unable to resist the irresistible call; their faces were expressionless, with a look of surrender in their eyes. Others fought back, desperately trying to protect their minds from Victoria's control.

Among the group of individuals who refused to give in was a remarkable witch named Charlotte. Years ago, she had broken away from the dark ways of the coven and fought to maintain her independence. When the intrusive presence entered her mind, Charlotte immediately identified its source.

"I won't be a pawn in your quest for power again," Charlotte muttered as she began to cast defensive spells to protect her mind from Victoria's telepathic summoning. She also reached out to others who had defected from the coven, warning them to resist the pull of the original high priestess and use all their abilities to save themselves from falling back under her and the Shadow's control.

Victoria felt the defiantness radiating from Charlotte and a few others. With the Shadow's formidable power at her command, she unleashed a deafening ringing sound into their minds. The piercing tones caused excruciating pain and intense bleeding within their brains as if they were being squeezed and crushed from within. Blood began to trickle out of their ears.

It was as if their skulls were boiling under the immense pressure of Victoria's dark spell. As the horrifying consequences of rebellion unfolded, fear swept through those still uncertain about submitting to Victoria's call. Some, unable to withstand the unbearable mental strain, reluctantly surrendered to her dominion as their wills crumbled under her wrathful force.

Victoria reveled in Charlotte's suffering. How dare she try to disobey. The pain Victoria inflicted upon her was torturous and unrelenting until finally, Charlotte's will broke, surrendering to Victoria's commands. "Yes, my queen," she sobbed, her voice weak and defeated. I hear you," Charlotte begged for mercy, pleading for the torment to end.

A twisted grin spread across Victoria's face as she relished in her control. Her role as high priestess granted her immense power, and she took pleasure in dominating those who had once stood beside her. Victoria's hold on the Shadow grew stronger with every new mind brought under her sway.

"You have what you need; your followers will soon arrive, and you can summon me back to this realm permanently. But for now, my strength wanes, and I must return to the dark realm. Do not call upon me again until you possess the means to bring me back completely," demanded the Shadow.

Victoria bowed her head to show obedience, her long red hair falling in a curtain around her face. She watched the Shadow slowly dissipate, its form melting into nothingness. Victoria felt the surge of power coursing through her veins slowly wane, leaving her drained. She knew that with the circle members' loyalty—even if it were out of fear—she would be unstoppable, and her power would return once the coven was reunited.

The forest guardian cats had been watching from a distance, their eyes gleaming with curiosity and suspicion. Once the Shadow was gone, they scurried off, their padded paws barely making a sound on the forest floor. The wolves, however, remained close by, their powerful bodies flanking Victoria as she sat on a large rock in the clearing.

The green eyes of the wolves shone with fierce loyalty and allegiance to their queen, whom they would protect at all costs, as they waited for the arrival of the Circle of the Eternal Shadow members.

Mortimer's howl pierced the stillness of the forest, a primal call that echoed through the trees and seemed to shake the very ground beneath their feet. It was a rallying cry, summoning all creatures to come and heed their queen's will. From all corners of the forest, animals of the forest emerged - small rabbits with twitching noses, sleek foxes with alert ears, and even majestic deer with antlers held high. With bowed heads and trembling bodies, they paid homage to Victoria, the undisputed ruler of these woods.

CHAPTER TWENTY-FOUR
TESTING THE LIMITS

As the sun rose, sending its first rays across the sky, Crox felt his fears from the night melt away. In the light, he felt invincible. It was strange how darkness could paralyze him, yet daylight brought him a sense of power and courage. He knew he needed to act quickly before Relda awoke and tried to stop him. The urgency filled him, pushing him towards the unknown dangers of the forest.

Throughout the long night, he felt a strong pull from within the woods calling out to him.

And now, driven by an indescribable force, he had to discover what happened to Hazel. He knew she had been out in the forest last night. Crox wasn't entirely confident in the effectiveness of his protection spell, but he had it on him just in case.

Crox also brought along his trusty Smith & Wesson .38 special, prepared for any danger that might come his way. Despite his fear of what dangers may lie ahead in the heart of the woods, Crox felt an undeniable energy pushing him onward. He delved deeper into the trees, a sense of unease growing within him. The foliage thickened, blocking out most of the sunlight above. Crox's heart raced as he pushed through, guided only by an inner instinct that seemed to guide his every move.

Amara and Mortimer trailed closely behind, monitoring Crox's every move from a safe distance. Victoria had warned them not to engage with him. From the shelter of the thick trees, various cats of different sizes and colors also kept an eye on Crox as he wandered through the woods, instinctually staying hidden from the two vicious predators.

Crox couldn't shake the unsettling sensation of being observed, but he pressed on through the dense forest, feeling like an invisible hand was guiding his steps. Eventually, he emerged into a small clearing illuminated by soft sunlight filtering through the trees.

In the middle of the clearing lay a body, unmoving. Crox's heart sank as he approached. His vision from last night was confirmed as he recognized Hazel's lifeless form. Her insides were brutally torn out and strewn about her, a gruesome scene that made him nauseous.

Crox couldn't hold back the contents of his stomach any longer and began spewing vomit onto the ground next to the dead woman.

He knelt next to her, carefully examining the brutal wounds that covered her chest and throat. The wolves had unleashed their savage attack on her, leaving behind a ghastly sight that made Crox question how the existence of such cruelty could exist in this world.

As he analyzed the gruesome scene, he couldn't shake off the feeling of still being watched. He heard rustling in the nearby bushes and turned swiftly, but no one was there. It was almost as if the very spirit of the forest was observing his every move, waiting for him to make his next move.

Out of nowhere, a blinding red light engulfed the forest, forcing Crox to shield his eyes. A woman's voice echoed in his mind, saying, "Greetings, Crox. Thank you for responding to my call. I see you have stumbled upon what remains of my servant, Hazel." The voice continued, "It is unfortunate that she failed to complete her task, but you are here now, and my wolves have been well-fed." Crox frantically looked around, attempting to locate the source of the voice amidst the intense red glow. But it was futile; he could barely see a few inches before him.

"I am Victoria," the voice declared with authority. "I have returned from the grave to reclaim my throne as Queen and High Priestess over the Circle of the Eternal Shadow. You will serve me willingly or suffer a fate worse than death. Any futile attempts to defy me will be utterly useless. The power of the Shadow belongs to me, and it will consume you just as your mother promised long ago."

Crox's screams filled the empty clearing, a mixture of anger and fear echoing off the trees and reverberating through the air. The defiance in his voice was apparent as he declared, "I will never submit to you or the Shadow! I will defeat you both!"

Crox pulled out his gun, waving it haphazardly. He could not pinpoint Victoria's location as her voice came from within his mind. "Your defiance will lead to your demise today, along with those you hold close. Your friend, Relda, will suffer unimaginable torment at my hands; my wolves will slowly tear her apart in front of you. And as for those bothersome cats who have captured your heart, they will make a delicious feast for my pets," Victoria warned. "Your mother always said you were stubborn little shit. She told me all about you when she called upon me as her spirit guide while I rested in my grave. Any resistance to my commands is futile. The Shadow has claimed you and its power is absolute. "Victoria's voice resounded in Crox's mind.

Crox reminded himself that he had the protection spell and the forest guardians on his side and summoned his inner courage.

With confidence ringing in his voice, Crox declared, "You may wield the power of Shadow's dark magick, but my will and protection spell will shield me from any harm."

His words echoed like thunder through the clearing. Suddenly, a bright bolt of lime-green light burst forth from Crox's outstretched hands, pushing back against the suffocating red glow threatening to consume him.

Victoria's high-pitched cackling laugh reverberated through the dense forest as she taunted him with cruel words. "Your feeble attempts amuse me," she sneered. "But you cannot possibly hope to withstand the unstoppable force of the Shadow. You are merely a mortal, insignificant and powerless against the will of darkness."

Victoria's venomous words slithered like a snake into his mind. Crox felt a surge of uncertainty wash over him. Could he truly stand against this evil? He knew his magick was limited, and if his protection spell failed, he could become just another missing victim. The forest's darkness loomed around him, pressing in with an ominous weight. Suddenly, out of the shadows, a chorus of growls and vicious hisses erupted from the shadows, drowning out the sound of Victoria's wicked laughter and cruel taunts.

Emerging from the shadows, a horde of cats appeared, their emerald green eyes glowing fiercely. Crox heard a voice say in his mind. "We stand by your side, Crox," their voices echoed in unison inside his mind, a chorus of feline solidarity. We will not let the Shadow consume you. Escape now while you still have a chance. The wolves are nearby." Victoria's laughter faltered slightly at the sight of dozens of cats. "Do you truly believe these insignificant creatures can defy me?" she sneered, her voice oozing with frustration and rage.

Crox's heart raced in his chest, surrounded by a swarm of snarling, hissing cats. Panic and confusion overwhelmed him as he cried, "Who are you?" A chilling chorus of voices echoed in his mind, commanding him to run as fast as he could and not look back.

Crox scrambled to his feet and took one last look at Hazel's mangled body before obeying the voices and bolting away from the clearing. He ignored Victoria's menacing threats that seemed to taunt him as he sprinted toward his home. The cats followed closely beside him, some ahead of him, leading him through the dense forest to safety.

Crox felt that the journey through the woods was never-ending; every step made him fear that something would pounce on him at any moment. The forest sounds grew louder, ringing in his ears as if the trees were ready to attack. Despite his growing terror, he pushed forward, knowing that escaping Victoria and her wolves was his only chance at not being fed to the Shadow. He couldn't bear ending up like Hazel with her throat ripped out—the image fueled his urgency to run even faster. He had foolishly tested the limits of his magick against the Shadow's dark forces, but he knew deep down it was no match for the witch Victoria or the Shadow.

Crox finally broke through the trees and emerged into the open space of his backyard. He stumbled over a tree branch as he crossed the boundary of his property, but he managed to stay upright. Exhausted from the run and adrenaline-filled excitement, he collapsed onto the grass and rolled onto his back. The cats that had guided him out of the woods followed him into the clearing, their glowing eyes watching over him protectively.

After catching his breath, Crox sat up and took in his surroundings with relief. He was grateful to be back within the safety of his property. The mysterious felines who had led him out of danger now surrounded him, their presence comforting and intriguing. He knew there was more to these cats than meets the eye, but for now, he was just thankful to be alive. There came a noise from the direction of the house, and the cats of the forest hurried back to their hiding places in the forest.

Relda had burst out of the back door, running full speed through the yard, followed closely by Jax and Slick. Once by his side, she immediately bombarded Crox with questions, her words coming out in a frantic rush."What happened? Where were you? Are you okay? You promised to stay out of the forest-ASSHOLE!"

Crox struggled to find the right words to convey the horrors he had witnessed in the woods. "It's Hazel...She's dead. The wolves tore her apart," he said in a whisper.

Relda's face turned pale with shock. "I specifically told you to wait for animal control. Are you trying to get yourself killed, or are you just trying to make me angry?" Relda's tone rose to hysterical levels as she spoke.

"Girl, you need to take a chill pill," Crox replied with a hint of sarcasm.

Relda's anger dissipated as she took a deep breath and tried to calm herself down. "I'm sorry. It's just... the thought of you going out there alone, especially after what happened to Hazel..." Her voice trailed off, her concern visible in her eyes. "I'm going to call for backup. The Sheriff's office should be notified," she insisted.

Crox shook his head firmly, conveying a strong sense of disapproval. "No, let's not do that. Hazel's body won't be found.

We can't involve anyone else." He gently touched Relda's arm, giving her a pleading smile.

As they sat on the soft grass, the sun rose higher in the sky, casting a warm glow over the landscape. But despite the comforting light, a lingering feeling of unease persisted in the air. Relda sighed, understanding Crox's desperation. "Okay, I won't call for help just yet."

Jax and Slick flanked Crox in a protective stance. Their piercing green eyes scanned the surroundings, ever watchful. Despite their fierce demeanor, they tried to comfort Crox, nuzzling him gently with their soft fur and emitting low purrs of reassurance.

"How are we supposed to keep him safe if he continues to act recklessly? Surely, you can reason with him. He understands your language," Slick lashed out in frustration.

Jax sighed, defeated, as his tail swished back and forth, stating, "I understand your frustration, but you were in a relationship with Crox for years. You know how stubborn and fiercely independent he can be. The only one powerful enough to stop Victoria is Pittapat, my mother. I need to have Crox do the spell to resurrect her."

"But is that truly our only option? Your wicked mother deserves all the torment she's experiencing in death; she had me killed and tried to kill her own son unless you've forgotten," Slick growled.

Jax acknowledged the truth in the words of the orange cat. His mother, once a formidable witch, had succumbed to darkness and wreaked havoc on those around her. Yet even in death, she possessed the power to fight against the evil plaguing Crox. "To bring back Pittapat, Crox must perform the dark Séance.

The blood of her offspring and the spell from the spell book should be sufficient to restore her human form and break free from the clutches of the shadow," Jax advised Slick with conviction.

Slick's jaw clenched as he reluctantly nodded, a surge of anger rising in his chest. He knew deep down that Jax was right, but he refused to admit it out loud. "Fine," he growled through gritted fangs, "but if she even thinks about trying anything, I'll rip her throat out with my claws."

Jax rolled his eyes, barely containing his annoyance at Slick's bravado. "Oh, how terrifying," The black cat thought sarcastically. "Your flabby butt couldn't even kill a squirrel."

CHAPTER TWENTY-FIVE

JAX SILENCED

Relda supported Crox as they returned to the house, resisting the temptation to alert her colleagues at the sheriff's department. Once inside, Crox collapsed into a chair, visibly drained from seeing the sight of Hazel's mangled body in the forest. Her concern for his well-being overshadowed Relda's frustration with him.

"I have to get ready and head to the funeral home to arrange Vonda's funeral. Will you be okay?" she asked.

Crox nodded, motioning to his caretakers, Jax and Slick, nearby. "I'll be fine," he assured her. "You won't tell anyone about this, right?"

Relda looked at Crox briefly and answered, " I gave you my word, so don't worry. Go back to bed and get some rest. I will return this evening, and we can discuss an action plan." Crox nodded in appreciation, fatigue evident in his tired eyes.

After Relda left, he grabbed a throw blanket from the armoire in the front parlor and returned to the family room, where he collapsed onto the couch and drifted into a deep slumber within minutes. Jax and Slick crept over to him, cautiously climbing up next to him and gently rubbing their heads against him while emitting soothing purrs.

Once Crox was out of the forest and into his backyard, which was still under the protection spell and he could not be touched by Amara and Mortimer, the two wolves turned back and silently made their way through the forest toward the clearing where their queen, Victoria, awaited their return. As they approached, they saw their queen's eyes still glowing with remnants of the Shadow's power.

Victoria turned to face them, her gaze scanning them like a predator assessing prey. "You have done well," she hissed, her voice laced with malice. "But our work is far from over. The Circle of the Eternal Shadow must be reunited, and with their collective power, I shall rule this entire region once more."

Amara knelt on the ground, her head bowed in submission. "Our queen, what is your next command? Shall we continue to patrol the forest, or do you have a more specific task for us?"

Victoria's wicked smile spread across her face as she said, "Kill any cat you come across in these woods. From what I have seen, there are plenty to choose from. Let none remain alive."

"With pleasure," Amara growled, her eyes glowing with a fierce hunger as she let out a deafening howl that echoed through the forest. Mortimer snarled in response, ready to follow his mate without hesitation. The wolves ran off, disappearing into the trees as they prepared to carry out Victoria's merciless decree of slaughtering the forest cats.

Victoria sat at her altar in the center of the rock circle, on top of the pentagram. She began to recite her own protection spell. "By the dark of night, where shadows dwell, I cast a barrier. No harm shall pass, no curse shall bind; this shield I summon." The spell would protect her from hexes or curses from any of the witches of the coven.

Back inside the safety of his home, Crox lay uncomfortably on the couch with his furry comrades slumbering soundly beside him, no longer worrying about the dangers lurking just outside their door. Jax and Slick were sprawled out, while Crox was forced to curl up into a small ball to make room for them. The two cats seemed to take up every available inch of space on the large couch.

Sleep, however, did not bring peace to Crox; instead, he found himself trapped in a dream world he could not escape. He heard whispers echoing all around him in this dark and lonely landscape. "My son, there is no escape," a haunting voice murmured from the shadows. Crox strained his eyes to see the source of the voice, but there was only an endless void surrounding him. As he cautiously inched forward, the whispers grew louder and seemed to come from all directions.

Suddenly, a bright white light pierced through the darkness, revealing a ghostly figure standing before him. His mother, Pittapat, her eyes were hollow and empty of a soul. Crox couldn't help but feel sadness as he looked upon her face, which once was beautiful in life but now twisted and contorted in agony.

"Why do you resist, my son?" the ghostly figure spoke with an eerie resemblance to his mother's voice. Embrace the darkness within you; it is your destiny and the only way for you to survive." Crox was rendered speechless and unable to respond. You cannot escape what is meant to be. I have promised you to the Shadow; its hold on you is absolute."

Crox struggled to move away from the ghostly voice that sounded like his mother, but the voice's hold on him was strong. Her voice grew louder as she began to sing a haunting lullaby, "Hush, hush now, my son; it is time to let go- and embrace what shall be. Release all your worries and surrender my son. Close your eyes and still your mind, then you will find, my love, in the shadows." Crox could feel the dark void consuming him. The song echoed in his head, tempting him to give in to his mother's words. But deep within his soul, a glimmer of resistance remained.

"Wake up!" a powerful voice echoed within his mind. "This is not real; it's just an illusion trying to confuse you. Wake up!" the voice continued to scream, urging him to break free from the dream. Crox woke up with a jolt, his heart racing in his chest. He looked over at the sleeping cats, who were unaware of the dream struggle he had just faced. He was shivering from a cold sweat covering his body.

Unable to get back to sleep, Crox decided to use the time to research a few spells. He went to his home office and began poring over his mother's spellbook, determined to strengthen his protection spells for his waking and dream states. As he flipped through the pages, he couldn't shake the feeling that they were somehow changing before his eyes. Though he had read the book countless times, he couldn't find the markings he had made on certain pages. Surprisingly, he stumbled upon spells and incantations he had never seen before.

Now fully awake and alert, Jax and Slick strolled into the office and perched themselves on the window sill. Their eyes followed Crox's every move as he combed through the old pages of the grimoire, searching for the perfect spell, not sure what that spell would be, only hoping it would call to him. After what seemed like an eternity, his finger finally landed on a page, his eyes lighting up with excitement as he found what he had been seeking.

The "Mind Guard" was an enchantment crafted to ward off the effects of hallucination spells and safeguard the caster from any invading psychic influences, whether awake or asleep.

Crox shooed the two cats out of his study before closing and locking the door behind them. He stood behind his desk, placing both hands on a page containing the mind guard spell and reciting, "I call upon the forces of light and darkness. Surround me from above and below. Shield my mind from all harm that dares try to enter. Shield me in my waking and sleeping hours."

As the words left Crox's lips, a shimmering white light encircled him, creating an invisible barrier around his mind.

Crox could feel a newfound mental barrier as if a solid wall had been erected within his consciousness.

Once Crox was confident that the mind guard spell was protecting him, he began scouring the grimoire for any other useful spells against the evil in the forest. Deep within the book's pages, he discovered a spell that called upon one's ancestors. It was similar to the one he had used to summon his mother's spirit, but it could bring a deceased blood relative back from the grave to live once more.

Crox hesitated, thinking of the potential consequences of casting such a spell. Bringing someone back from the dead could unleash dangerous karma into the world. We all have a destiny, and when it is your time to go, it is your time. Death is a part of life and the universe may not act kindly to messing with the order of things.

The only person Crox could consider resurrecting, and tempting fate was his mother, who the Shadow had consumed. She could be an ally or just another creature intent on killing him. Either way, he felt that it had to be done, and he would deal with the consequences later.

The potential benefit of returning his mother from the dead would be discovering her true intentions toward him. His strange dreams left him unsure whether she wanted to help or harm him. But despite his fear of her being against him, Pittapat had been a powerful witch, and he felt compelled to take the risk and cast the spell to bring her back to the land of the living, just not at this moment.

The sound of cats scratching at the door reminded Crox that it was time to feed them.

He got up from his chair and opened the door, and Jax quickly darted inside. But instead of expressing gratitude, Jax bit Crox on the leg. "Ouch! Why did you do that?" Crox cried out, rubbing his injured limb. Jax stared back at him with an intense gaze as he communicated telepathically. "You need to stop messing with spells you don't fully understand," Jax said, but the voice faded away. Jax began meowing loudly and seemed distressed. "What? Speak up. I don't understand you, cat." Crox scolded.

Jax's became crazed. He spun around in a circle like a cat possessed, his eyes darting in all directions. Crox finally realized that the Mind-Guard spell may have severed the telepathic connection with Jax. A heavy sigh escaped Crox's lips as he recognized the unintended consequence of his actions. He had cast the spell to protect himself from mental intrusion, but now he felt a pang of regret for losing his bond with Jax. Karma was a bitch.

His mind swirled with doubt as he carefully poured kibble into the cat's food bowl. Was this indeed the best thing to do? With each insistent meow from Jax, he felt a pang of guilt for cutting off their telepathic connection. But he couldn't risk being attacked in his dreams. He kneeled and looked into Jax's bright green eyes, trying to convey his thoughts without words.

"I'm sorry, my brother," Crox whispered, "For now, we can not communicate. Once I am free of the Shadow, I will reverse the spell."

Jax continued to meow in protest, but Crox paid no mind to his familiar. There was a more pressing matter at hand: speaking with his mother. Returning to the home office and shutting the door behind him, he retrieved the grimoire from the safe again. Taking a deep breath, Crox prepared himself for the dangerous spell he was about to perform – one that would bring his deceased mother back from the grave.

As a precaution, he slid his .38 Smith & Wesson pistol into his waistband. Bringing his mother back from the dead carried risks, especially considering her past attempts to have him killed for her selfish gain.

He would not hesitate to send her back to the grave if she posed the tiniest threat to him. The spell required him to kill someone from the living and spirit worlds. The thought of harming another living being for his personal gain made him sick.

He couldn't bring himself to do it, even if it meant bringing back his mother, who could potentially stop the wolves and the evil magick controlling them. Crox weighed his options. Suddenly, the grimoire pages began turning on their own again, revealing the section on astral projection.

Crox remembered how he had visited Janice in spirit form using this spell before, and a realization dawned on him. During his previous astral projection, Janice had stabbed him, causing a fatal wound that would have killed him if he hadn't returned to his body. But if he stayed in the spirit realm and performed the spell to bring back the dead, perhaps it would work as he would be making a sacrificial death himself.

Crox took the gamble and attempted the spell on the astral plane without consulting the grimoire. He was able to recite the spell flawlessly from memory. As he spoke the words, he felt the lightness come over him as if his spirit was being lifted out of his body.

Crox slowly opened his eyes, and the world shifted and blurred around him. His body remained slumped in the office chair while his astral self stood beside it in spirit form. The pain from the knife wound flared up, a sharp reminder of his urgent task to resurrect a dead person and not become one.

There was frantic banging at his study door and loud meowing from the other side. Jax must have been trying to stop him. But Crox could no longer hear or see anything except for the swirling colors and energy that enveloped him. He pushed aside the distraction of Jax and focused all his energy on bringing Pittapat back from the depths of the hell where she resided.

CHAPTER TWENTY-SIX

MOTHER IS BACK

Jax slammed his head against the heavy wooden door of the study, desperate to stop Crox from attempting to resurrect their mother. Since Crox had cast the Mind-Guard spell, Jax's telepathic pleas fell upon deaf ears. They were ignoring the commotion on the other side of the door.

Crox gazed upon his own lifeless body sitting in the chair before him. He could feel the pain in his stomach as if he was being stabbed again and the knife was being twisted. He had little time to do the spell to call on a blood relative from the grave. He needed to return to his body soon or risk dying and his spirit being lost in this realm.

He began to recite the spell's words aloud, hoping it would work in the spirit world since, in the living realm, he would have to kill an innocent to make it work. "In the depths of darkness where spirits sleep, Where tortured souls forever weep, by the light of the moon and stars above, I cast this spell to summon thee. My long-departed mother, Pittapat, tortured soul and spirit trapped, I bid you rise from your grave and return to life. Walk once more among us."

Despite feeling his strength waning, Crox focused on returning to his physical body. The astral plane was blurring, and a strong force was pulling him back. The pain from the knife wound was excruciating, and he clenched his teeth in an attempt to endure it. With every ounce of determination within him, he fought to return to his physical body. The spirit realm distorted as he felt himself being pulled toward the realm of the living while the pain in his stomach continued to intensify.

In a split second, he was back in his physical form. He was still exhausted, but the stomach ache had vanished. Crox took a moment to gather himself. When he looked up, he was taken aback by the sight of his mother standing there with a smile on her face. Pittapat had come back to life. "My son, it brings me great joy to see you alive and well again. Thank you for bringing me back. I am no longer trapped in that dark place," Pittapat said with a smile full of warmth.

Crox could hardly believe it; the spell had actually worked. "Mother, what have I done?" he asked, his voice trembling.

With the grace of a dancer, Pittapat approached him, her movements fluid despite having been dead for years. "You have brought me back, my dear. You have saved your mother from the Shadow's grasp. The spell from my grimoire has allowed me to return and live once more. I am impressed you were able to decipher it. Well done," Pittapat's voice echoed hauntingly. She then asked, "Why did you bring me back? What troubles you so deeply that you would risk the delicate balance between life and death?"

Crox's face furrowed as he asked, "Why have you been appearing in my dreams?"

Pittapat's gaze was filled with sorrow as she answered, "Yes, I have, but it wasn't my choice. The Shadow used its power to forcibly enter your subconscious while you slept, to weaken you. I've been trapped in its realm, tormented by its darkness." She paused before continuing, "It manipulated my spirit to deceive and confuse you. But now, thanks to your spell, or should I say my spell, you were able to decipher, I am free from its grasp."

Crox looked at his mother, pleading, "Mother, I need your help. The Shadow has released wolves that were once human into the forest, and they have been attacking and killing innocent people. There's also a witch who claims to have been resurrected and is seeking to control the remaining members of the Circle of the Eternal Shadow."

Pittapat's eyes darkened as she listened to her son's words. In a firm voice, she replied, "You don't need the Circle of the Eternal Shadow. They are just tools of the Shadow. Your power is much stronger than theirs, as proven by the protection spell you have cast and the Mind Guard spell."

Crox was confused as his mother's words sunk in. "How do you know about the spells I've cast?" he asked. But Pittapat ignored his question and spoke calmly as if talking to a simple-minded child. "The wolves are lost souls controlled by the Shadow. They were released back into the land of the living to do the Shadow's bidding with a promise to make them human again. We must sever their connection with it to break its hold on them. However, it won't be easy."

Attempting to Comfort her son, Pittapat placed a hand on Crox's shoulder. "We'll need to gather allies; a small group of trusted members from my old coven should suffice. Together, we can break the Shadow's link to this world."

Crox pushed his mother's hand away and stood up. "I want to trust you since I have no other choice. Just know that the power you took away from me has returned, and I have learned to control it. If you betray me again, I will put you back in the ground."

"Relax, I could break your neck with my mind if I wanted to. Don't get so hostile," Pittapat spat back, her tone dripping with venom.

Just as Crox was about to respond, the study door burst open with a loud noise. Jax and Slick came running in. Jax was taken aback by seeing their mother seemingly risen from the grave. The black cat jumped nearly a foot in shock.

Meanwhile, Slick came to an abrupt halt, his hair standing on end as he let out a long hiss. Crox struggled to decipher whether this reaction was fueled by hatred or fear toward Pittapat.

Pittapat let out a chuckle, thoroughly amused by the feline's reactions. "Looks like I have quite an audience here. It's been a while, Jax and Slick," she said, addressing the two cats. Jax growled and narrowed his eyes while Slick continued to hiss in response.

The room was tense as the three of them faced each other. Crox stepped in between them, trying to defuse the tension. "Everyone, calm down! What's gotten into you all?"

Pittapat stood there with a mischievous grin while Jax and Slick meowed nonstop, circling around her. Crox shouted, "Jax, be quiet! I can't understand you!"

"I can," Pittapat replied with an evil laugh.

"What? Can you understand Jax and Slick? Crox asked cautiously.

"You mean your brother and dead lover, Sean. It appears I am not the only one who has escaped death and the Shadow's torture." Pittapat explained.

Crox was in shock, unable to process his mother's words. His thoughts were jumbled and chaotic as he tried to understand what she was saying. "Sean? Are you saying the Shadow killed him? I thought Sean left town." Crox's voice shook as he spoke.

"Silly child, even in death, I watched over you. As a powerful witch, my abilities remain intact whether I am alive or not," his mother replied calmly.

Crox felt mixed emotions overwhelm him - anger, confusion, and a deep sense of betrayal.

He looked at Slick, the cat sitting before him. "Is it true, Slick? Are you really Sean trapped in this body?"

The orange cat let out a long "meow" in response. Crox scooped up the orange cat and held him close, tears streaming down his cheeks. But his mother's stern voice snapped him back to reality. "Stop the waterworks. We have work to do," she ordered.

Crox wiped away his tears and gently placed Slick back on the floor, taking a deep breath to calm himself. Under his breath, he muttered, "You're still as heartless as ever, you hateful bitch." After composing himself, Crox stood tall in front of Pittapat and made his demand. "If you can understand them, give me that power without breaking my Mind Guard spell."

Pittapat raised an eyebrow, considering Crox's request. "Alright, my son. I can grant you the ability to understand them without compromising the spell. But remember, everything comes with consequences."

Whispering an incantation so low that Crox could barely hear, Pittapat called upon the elements and her ancestors to grant her offspring the power to hear those who had been taken by the dark realm and returned.

As Pittapat completed the spell, a tingling sensation washed over Crox, spreading from his head down to his toes. He could feel the connection between himself and Jax strengthen, their minds merging together as one. At the same time, he became acutely aware of Slick's presence in his mind, like an extra layer of consciousness.

"Do you think it worked?" Slick asked Jax.

Crox glanced at the orange cat and confirmed, "Yes, it was successful."

Jax and Slick exchanged glances before Jax turned back to Crox with anger in his eyes. "I warned you not to meddle with magick you don't understand. Look at the evil you released back into the world."

Slick chimed in. "Why, of all people, did you bring that murderous witch back?" he demanded, his telepathic voice shrill and frantic. "She'll probably kill us all,"

Pittapat, not paying attention to the cats, stated, "We need to reach out to the remaining loyal members of my coven. They hold the key to breaking the link between the wolves and the Shadow. Slick, I know I made a mistake by having you killed. Please let me make it right. I will do everything possible to restore you and Jax's souls to human form."

Slick hissed back at Pittapat in response. Jax was still mistrustful but seemed less hostile toward her. He muttered, "We'll have to see about that, Mother. I am keeping a cautious eye on you."

Crox interjected, his voice sharp and commanding, "Enough bickering. Do you have a plan, Mother?

Pittapat nodded. "I can sense my old coven who abandoned this place after the Shadow killed me. They have no leader and are being called back for some reason. But they hold the key to breaking the link controlling the wolves. I must regain control of them before the Shadow does."

Slick couldn't help but voice his disdain, "Wasn't it- your desire for complete control over the Coven that got us into this situation in the first place, WITCH?"

Pittapat let out a bored sigh, contempt evident in her voice as she replied, "Yes, I craved power, but now I understand the consequences of my actions. My goal now is to undo the harm I caused. The Shadow's influence is far greater than you realize; we must join forces against it."

Jax sat across from his mother. His feline features showed visible hurt and distrust. "I suppose we have no choice but to work with you now that you've been brought back to life, but I still have reservations about trusting you. Proceed with caution, mother."

"I understand, my child. I will do my best to earn back your love and trust, but I need rest to regain my strength. Crox, is there a spare room I can use?" Pittapat answered back.

Crox led Pittapat upstairs to the bedroom above the garage, which had remained unused since he built the house.

It was as if Crox had always known this room would belong to his mother. He nicknamed it the 'Marilyn room' because its walls were adorned with photos of the iconic actress Marilyn Monroe, whom his mother had dearly loved.

Pittapat asked him to go shopping for clothes and toiletries for her as she closed the bedroom door in his face. Crox stood in shock. "Damn, she still has the balls of a truck driver," he thought to himself. With a shake of his head, Crox descended the stairs to prepare a list of essential items for his mother.

Crox wanted to chat with Slick (aka Sean) before he headed out to Target, now that he could communicate with him telepathically like Jax.

However, as Crox searched through each room on the main floor, he couldn't find either of the cats. Finally, he spotted Jax sitting on the back deck railing outside, gazing into the surrounding woods.

"Hey there, little one. What are you up to? Where's Slick?" Crox asked.

Without taking his eyes off the forest, Jax replied, "Slick was worried about what to say now that you can hear him. He's not as comfortable in his cat form as I am. He's off roaming the woods to see if he can gather any useful information for us."

Crox exclaimed in concern, "What? Why did you allow him to do that? It's far too dangerous outside; he could easily become a meal for those wolves!"

"He knows the woods well and has been able to avoid the wolves since they arrived. I'm sure he'll be fine and will bring back valuable information. Besides, I think he needs some time alone now that mother is back from the dead. You realize she had him killed to get him away from you," Jax stated, twitching his tail back and forth.

Crox lowered his head and said a silent prayer. "May the gods have mercy on our souls and protect us in this hour of darkness. Blessed Be,"

CHAPTER TWENTY-SEVEN

THREE QUEENS

While Crox was distracted by dealing with his resurrected mother, Slick had silently sneaked in through the small cat door in the back of the house. The sight of her, the one who had betrayed and caused his tragic death, filled the orange cat with a mix of anger and sorrow. Trapped in this feline form, there was little Slick could do to seek revenge against Pittapat.

Feeling frustrated and powerless, Slick retreated to the dense forest that had become his home since his return from death. It was a place of peace and solitude for him now.

Slick had a new purpose: to observe and gather information that could aid Crox in defeating the wolves and closing the portal that had allowed the Shadow to unleash them into the living realm.

As much as he wanted to stay by Crox's side, Slick knew that his current form would only add more emotional strain for both of them.

Slick carefully navigated through the thick underbrush, his senses heightened and alert for the wolves and Victoria. The forest was unusually quiet, and there were no sounds of the other felines or animals that called the forest home. Moving with the grace and agility that only a cat possesses, Slick made his way deeper into the forest, taking note of the wolves' movements through their tracks in the soft ground and remnants of their prey scattered across the forest floor.

A low, menacing growl rumbled through the air, causing Slick's fur to stand on end. He immediately crouched down in an attempt to blend into his surroundings, but with his bright orange coat, it was nearly impossible. Peering from behind a fallen tree, Slick observed two wolves feasting on a long-haired gray cat.

The stench of death filled the air, making Slick's stomach turn. This poor cat's once-living human soul now joined the ranks of the other souls still trapped by the Shadow. As Slick watched the two wolves tear apart the dead cat, Victoria stood in the forest's clearing, commanding the attention of her loyal followers from the Circle of the Eternal Shadow, who had answered her summons and returned to the forest.

Standing tall and confident, Victoria exuded power and authority over her coven. Her eyes gleamed like hot coals, fueled by the Shadow's dark power.

The other group members stood around her in a tight circle, their bodies tense and faces strained as they tried to hide their fear of the resurrected witch. But Victoria could sense the collective terror hanging heavy in the air like an ominous presence.

She couldn't help but smirk, reveling in the power she now possessed over them. Amara and Mortimer finished their meal and approached Victoria with reverence, bowing to their queen. The rest of the coven watched in awe as this display solidified Victoria's dominance over them once again.

In a chilling tone, Victoria addressed her devoted followers, "The time has arrived for the Circle of the Eternal Shadow to rise again, with me as your high priestess. The Shadow's power flows through me and extends to each of you. Together, we will amplify its strength, releasing its darkness from the realm of the dead into the living world. No one shall impede our path; the wolves are just the start. We will unleash forces that will blanket this region in eternal night."

The words that escaped Victoria's lips sent a chill down Slick's spine, causing his fur to stand on end. He waited for the perfect opportunity to escape and return to Crox's house unnoticed. When the chance finally presented itself, he darted through the forest with lightning speed, skillfully maneuvering past the wolves and coven members as they made their way toward the clearing. Among them was Charlotte, the powerful witch who couldn't shield her thoughts from Victoria's telepathic message.

As Charlotte neared the clearing, she couldn't shake off the ominous feeling in her gut. She had sensed the dark energy radiating from the forest, but nothing could have prepared her for what lay ahead. From the edge of the clearing, Charlotte caught sight of Victoria standing amid a group of coven members flanked by two menacing wolves.

Her heart sank as she realized that Victoria had indeed been brought back from the dead. Despite desperately holding onto hope that it was all just an illusion created by the Shadow, Charlotte now faced undeniable proof of Victoria's resurrection.

Charlotte was well aware of the danger that came with Victoria's return. She knew she had to act fast to safeguard herself. Drawing on her powers, Charlotte tried to cast a spell to hide herself from Victoria. Sadly, it didn't work.

A low, sultry chuckle escaped Victoria's lips as she spoke. "Well, well, it seems we have an old soul in our midst," she taunted, her voice dripping with sarcasm and power. Her piercing gaze locked onto the newcomer. "Could it be my dear friend Charlotte?

Come closer now and kneel before your queen Charolette, you old witch." she commanded, her tone playful yet commanding.

Charlotte stepped into the clearing and faced Victoria without bowing. She stood tall and spoke firmly, "You are not a queen. You are merely a pawn of the Shadow. I will not submit to you or allow you to spread your darkness further."

Victoria's eyes widened in anger as she declared, "How dare you! Who are you to dictate what I can or cannot do? You disobeyed me once and now look at the consequences of those actions. Cursed to wander the earth for eternity, unable to die or escape from your pain and suffering. Kneel before me, heathen."

Charlotte refused, not allowing Victoria to dominate her. Summoning all her strength, she met Victoria's gaze and proclaimed, "Return to the hell from whence you came; your reign has long ended. Back to the grave with you, witch."

Victoria's eyes blazed with anger as she began to cast a pain spell on Charlotte. But then, a voice echoed through the trees. It was the Shadow. "Hold your hand, Victoria. This one could be valuable," it said. I gave you the gift of eternal life, yet you used it on Charlotte as a curse. What a waste."

The Shadow then instructed Victoria to restrain Charlotte without causing her harm, as he wanted to deal with her himself when he returned. Reluctantly, Victoria obeyed and signaled for two members of her coven to bind Charlotte's wrists with sturdy ropes, rendering her powerless. Charlotte tried to resist, but it was no use. She needed to find a way out before it was too late.

Slick slinked out of the clearing without drawing any attention to himself. He sprinted towards Crox's house, his heart racing from the unaccustomed burst of physical activity. As a cat, he had become accustomed to lounging around all day and found this sudden exercise quite challenging.

Slick's top priority was to locate Crox and Jax and inform them about what he had seen in the woods - Victoria and her coven posed a serious danger that needed to be addressed immediately.

The once peaceful forest was now filled with crazed witches. As Slick emerged from the woods and entered the backyard, he saw Pittapat approaching him on the deck's stairs. The orange cat froze. He didn't know what to expect from Crox's mother. She had already killed him once, and he couldn't put it past her to do it again.

Pittapat halted her steps when she spotted Slick looming in front of her. Curiosity danced across her face as she crouched down to meet his gaze, studying him intently. Slick braced himself, unsure of how to react.

"Don't worry, you orange buffoon. I won't hurt you unless you try me. I'm not the same person I once was. I want both of my sons to be safe. I know what's been happening in this forest and needs to be stopped. That's why Crox brought me back from the dead." With those words, Pittapat patted Slick on the head before continuing into the woods.

Slick remained motionless for a moment, stunned by Pittapat's bold statement. How did she know about everything going on? The only explanation was that she had been working with the Shadow and Victoria all along.

Crox returned home from running errands for his mother to find Jax perched on the back of the couch. "Has Slick come back yet?" Crox glanced around the room, but there was no sign of the orange cat.

"Nope, not yet. Did you pick up any treats for me while you were out?" Jax asked with a sly grin.

"You can be such an annoying little shit sometimes," Crox quipped.

After unpacking the supplies he had bought at Target and laying them on the kitchen table, Crox stepped onto the back deck and spotted Slick sprinting towards him. He also noticed Pittapat slipping between the trees in the distance, disappearing into the woods. It suddenly dawned on him that she may have planned this all along - asking him to leave the house so he wouldn't be able to stop her.

"Shit, Fly in a Monkey Suit!" Crox screamed out.

Slick bounded up the stairs, panting heavily, and collapsed onto the deck. Crox picked up Slick and checked for injuries. After not seeing any, he asked, "What happened? Are you okay?"

Slick took a moment to catch his breath before recounting what he had seen in the forest: the gathering of the Circle of the Eternal Shadow members and the return of Victoria, the first witch of Stafford County.

"We now have two of the most powerful witches ever known in this region, both of whom ruled with an iron fist as queen and high priestess. Do you think this is going to go well? We must kill them both before they kill us all over a power struggle as Queen of the Shadow." Jax hissed out.

Crox's voice quivered with sadness as he took a deep breath. His gaze fell on Slick, ignoring Jax's outburst. He asked, "What have you learned about their plans?"

Slick nodded, "Victoria plans to strengthen the Shadow's power by shattering the seal between the dark realm and the living world. She aims to undo your protection spell that has kept the Shadow at bay for so long and bring the creature back into our realm. The coven members blindly follow her lead, and even the wolves have fallen under her control."

Crox inquired of Slick, "What was Pittapat's reason for entering the woods?"

"Pittapat claims she wants to protect us. Perhaps she has gone to fight Victoria, but who knows what her true intentions are? We cannot fully trust her." Slick answered,

"How many allies does Victoria have?" Crox demanded, his eyes narrowing in suspicion. "Slick, you mentioned members from the old coven."

Slick chimed in, "I spotted a group of about twenty individuals. Most appeared to be frightened, as if they were being held against their will. Victoria seemed ready to confront someone named Charlotte, but instead, she bound her to a nearby tree."

"Interesting," Crox mused. "Perhaps we can convince those who fear the return of the Shadow to join us in defeating it, including this Charlotte. I'm unfamiliar with this person; her name doesn't ring a bell."

Jax telepathically said, "Charlotte was among the first to join the coven during the early days. She opposed Victoria's authoritarian ways. That's why she was cursed with immorality and banished to wander the earth for all time. She's a powerful witch and could become a valuable ally against Victoria."

"What do you mean immortal? How do you know all of this?" Crox inquired, surprised by the black cat's knowledge.

The black cat sat on his hind legs and puffed out his chest before answering confidently," Charlotte was the high priestess of the Circle of the Eternal Shadow when our mother joined the coven. She allowed Pittapat to take over when she left to travel the world. Charlotte also played a significant role in creating Mother's grimoire; many of its powerful spells are hers."

"Well, now we have three witches who used to lead the same coven together, with two returning from the grave and one who may be immortal. This is not going to end well," Crox muttered quietly under his breath.

CHAPTER TWENTY-EIGHT

THE BATTLE

Crox was overwhelmed with the thought of facing The Shadow, Victoria, and his mother alone. Not to mention confronting Charlotte, an immortal witch, and the twenty or more coven members. The odds seemed impossible for him and his two small feline companions. He knew his only chance was to seek assistance from Relda, but he couldn't bring himself to put her in danger. However, she was the only one he could turn to.

As a decorated police officer and skilled sharpshooter, Relda could defend herself if the situation turned violent. Crox also had a gut feeling that she possessed some supernatural abilities, but he couldn't gauge their strength.

Relda didn't believe in her abilities when it came to witchcraft. With no other options left, Crox reached out to his friend, knowing she would have his back.

After four rings, Relda finally answered with a slightly slurred voice. "Hello, what's going on?"

Crox took a deep breath, trying to gather his thoughts before speaking. "Relda, I need your help. Can you come over to my place right away?"

"I'll have to take an Uber; I stayed home from work today and have been enjoying some nice Hawaiian haze, if you get my drift."

"Great, now stop smoking that grass and get your head clear. I'll order the Uber for you; a car should pick you up in fifteen minutes; be ready." Crox stated.

"Damn boy, who do you think you are ordering around? What the hell is going on now?" Relda said, clearly annoyed.

"Please, just come and bring your shotgun. I'll explain everything when you get here." Crox hung up the phone; he did not need Relda's reply. He trusted her enough to know she would come as requested.

As Crox waited for Relda to arrive, he gathered Jax and Slick on the couch.

"Were there any indications that Victoria's influence over the coven members was weakening?" Crox asked the orange cat

Slick nodded in acknowledgment, "There seemed to be an underlying sense of fear among the people. It was as if they were being forced to obey her commands. But perhaps her hold over them is not as strong as it appears.

If we can discover a way to break that hold, we may gain allies within the group who want nothing more than to see Victoria and your mother put back into their grave permanently. I know that is something I want to see." Once Slick was finished, he jumped off the couch and headed to the kitchen for some kibble.

Crox shifted his attention to Jax and inquired, "Tell me more about this, Charlotte. How could someone who lived during Victoria's reign as a high priestess still be alive today? I've never heard of her.

Jax responded, "Based on my estimations, she is almost one hundred thirty years old."

Crox was shocked, "How is that even possible?"

Jax explained, "As far as I can remember from mother's stories when Victoria first arrived in Stafford County from Kentucky, she and her family purchased the land where you now reside. They hired Charlotte as a caretaker for their four children while they built their church, which they named Circle of Eternal Faith."

Jax continued, "In addition to being a healer, Charlotte possessed the gift of foresight, a useful tool that Victoria took advantage of when rumors of her doing witchcraft began circulating in town. According to Pittapat, Charlotte kept her abilities hidden from the townspeople, who never suspected her of wrongdoing. However, Victoria had bigger ambitions than just controlling the narrow-minded residents of a small town through religion; she wanted total domination over them. Victoria repeatedly revealed her true nature as a witch while attempting to achieve her goals and was eventually ostracized by the town."

Crox broke in, "But how does this relate to Charlotte still being alive?"

"Please, let me finish," Jax scolded.

Crox leaned back with his arms crossed and instructed sarcastically, "Go on."

"Thank you," the black cat said crossly. So when Victoria was exiled from the town and left to survive in the woods with her family, she turned to black magick and transformed the Circle of Faith into the Circle of the Eternal Shadow—a coven of witches. Charlotte first introduced Victoria to the dark realm and its black magick, thanks to her gift of second sight. Some witches possess the ability to see into other dimensions and call upon entities that some may refer to as demons."

Jax continued, "With Charlotte's assistance, Victoria beseeched the Shadow for aid in surviving the frigid winter in the forest. However, Victoria's greed led her to desire more than just sustenance; she sought revenge against the townspeople of Stafford County for rejecting her."-

"Charlotte was born and raised in Stafford and had strong connections to its people, couldn't bear the thought of bloodshed. But the Shadow had its agenda, using the women's desperation to deceive them. They were unaware that it fed on the souls of those it killed, and our realm provided an endless supply of nourishment for it. It manipulated Victoria by telling her whatever she wanted to hear to get her help to enter our realm. Eventually, Charlotte saw through its lies and tried to send it back to the dark realm. However, Victoria intervened and stopped her. To punish Charlotte for her betrayal, Victoria used a spell given to her by the Shadow to curse her with eternal life. She would have to watch all of her loved ones die and suffer but never be able to escape her pain by death. That's the story of Charlotte," Jax finished with a sigh.

Crox could only manage to exclaim, "Well, shit in a bucket."

Slick added, "Eww gross, I hate that saying."

As Crox tried to make sense of this bizarre story, the doorbell chimed, indicating Relda's arrival. He quickly opened the door and let her in. Relda walked in, clutching a shotgun in her hands.

"What's happening? Why did you have to interrupt my relaxation time?" Relda demanded, scanning the room. "And why did you ask me to bring my shotgun?"

Crox grinned mischievously as he led Relda towards the couch, where Jax and Slick waited patiently. He took a deep breath and proceeded to explain everything, from Pittapat's miraculous resurrection to Sean being trapped inside Slick's body and the sudden appearance of two witches who were over a century old, along with other members of the Circle of the Eternal Shadow who had also returned. "The shit is about to hit the fan," Crox concluded after filling in Relda.

"You've got witches and zombies in your backyard!" Relda exclaimed, sighing. All I wanted to do tonight was relax and smoke a bowl, not fight off supernatural creatures and religious zealots."

"Victoria and Pittapat are not zombies; their souls have been restored, and their bodies have been rejuvenated," Slick clarified.

Relda glanced down at Slick and sternly said, "Will you please quiet down? You're making too much noise." She could not hear the cat speaking. All she heard was yowling.

While Jax was telling Charlotte's story, Pittapat was making her way to the forest's center to confront the first and potentially strongest witch of Stafford County. Pittapat moved gracefully through the dense woods, seemingly knowing each tree and fallen branch. Her long hair was tied up tightly in a bun, giving her the appearance of a warrior from Japan.

The moon's glow filtered through the leaves, creating a white aura around her small but muscular frame as she approached the clearing where Victoria held court with the coven members. Pittapat could see Charlotte bound to a tree guarded by members of her former coven.

Pittapat moved stealthily towards the clearing, her gaze fixed on Victoria. Mortimer, smelling a new presence, let out a low growl and bared its teeth at the intruder. The coven turned toward the sound of the small wolf's growls to see another resurrected high priestess. Taken aback by the unexpected appearance of someone new, Victoria's eyes narrowed when she recognized the newcomer.

"Pittapat," she sneered, "you have the nerve to show your face? You were supposed to be dead. Did your son bring you back so you can watch him die and lose his soul to the Shadow?"

Pittapat retorted sarcastically, "Who brought you back from the grave? I'm surprised the Shadow allowed you to return to the land of the living."

Victoria let out a dark chuckle, her voice carrying through the dense forest. "My return is none of your concern. You've always been weak, Pittapat. I brought this coven together and summoned the Shadow, who has granted me powers beyond your under-standing. I have returned to finish what you failed to do - claim Crox's soul and rule as high priestess once more."

Charlotte then began to scream in defiance, struggling against the ropes that bound her.

Pittapat paid no attention to Victoria's taunts or Charlotte's screams of anger. She focused on the other coven members, scanning their faces with her eyes. Fear and uncertainty emanated from them, and she could sense it, which pleased her. Just like Victoria, Pittapat reveled in others' fears.

Pittapat's voice boomed with authority as he addressed the coven. "I understand that some of you may have been forced to come here against your will," she stated firmly. "But we must band together and resist both Victoria and the Shadow, who is limited in its powers while trapped in the dark realm. We must combine our strength and fight against this darkness."

The coven members exchanged uncertain glances, unsure of what to do. Still bound to a tree, Charlotte shouted, "These are just empty words from someone who also fell prey to the Shadow's seduction! I trusted you, Pittapat, when I passed on my role as high priestess to you. But did I not warn you about getting too close to the Shadow?"

Charlotte continued per pleas, "Didn't I teach you how to keep it trapped within these woods? And yet, you betrayed us all by offering up your own son's soul! How can we trust you to protect us now?"

Pittapat's eyes blazed with fury. "I'm willing to admit my mistakes, Charlotte, and I've returned to fix them. Crox is my son, and I won't let him become a victim of the Shadow or anything else. I'm here to end this madness."

Victoria addressed Amara and Mortimer. "Get rid of her. Send her back to hell where she belongs."

The two wolves let out synchronized howls as they closed in on Pittapat. However, she stood firm, focused on the approaching animals. With a quick gesture of her left hand, she retrieved a small vial from her back pocket and hurled it to the ground. A dense smoke, the color of dark amber, billowed out from the shattered container.

Amara froze in shock as Mortimer, who was walking a few feet ahead of her, walked into the smoke and then dropped to the ground, lifeless.

The large wolf growled fiercely as it bared its teeth and released a menacing howl. "I'll rip you apart slowly so that I can savor every moment of your pain, you foul bitch."

Pittapat's lips curled into a small, tight smile, making her look like she had fangs for teeth. "Come and try you mangy mutt."

The two faced off with dancer-like stances. Amara lunged and tried to attack, but Pittapat's movements were incredibly swift; she gracefully evaded the wolf's advances. In one smooth motion, Pittapat pulled out another small vial from her pocket and threw it toward the wolf as Amara was in mid-air.

As the vial shattered against the wolf's body, it emitted a brilliant orange light that covered Amara. The wolf yelped and stumbled back, temporarily blinded.

Seizing the opportunity, Pittapat recited the incantation to bind Amara's movements. "I bind you, wolf, as the roots of a tree hold firm in the earth. You will remain frozen, able only to watch but not to move. I also bind your tongue for your own safety. Be still and live to fight another day. By the power of my ancestors, you are bound to obey my commands. Now stay boo boo, stay."

As soon as Pittapat uttered the words, Amara's body was instantly immobilized. She tried to resist the magical hold, but it was too strong. Victoria screamed a fierce frustration as she watched her pet being controlled.

While Pittapat battled the wolves and Victoria, Charlotte took advantage of the commotion to break free from her restraints.

Once liberated from the ropes, Charolette used telepathy to communicate with her fellow coven members. "My friends, this is not our fight. These witches have caused nothing but harm and torment. We must unite against them and defeat them, or else we face the possibility of eternal enslavement. Join me."

CHAPTER TWENTY-NINE

FIGHT ANOTHER DAY

Crox, Relda, and the two cats entered the backyard and entered the dense woods beyond. Crox was confident that the protection spell he had cast earlier would extend to Relda while Jax and Slick could take care of themselves with the help of the forest cats.

As they ventured deeper into the forest, Crox silently prayed to the goddess of the crossroads, Hecate, for her protection from the witches who had lost their way. He felt apprehensive about what may lie ahead of them but did not let on. Crox wanted to appear stronger than he felt.

Relda marched by his side, her shotgun at the ready, scanning their surroundings for potential threats. She was prepared to take down anything that dared come near them.

Jax and Slick were on high alert, using their heightened senses as they trailed behind. The only sound in the forest was the crunching of leaves beneath their feet.

The radiant light of the full moon filtered through the thick trees, casting a faint glow on their path toward danger. Jax and Slick could see shadows of the forest cats lurking behind the trunks, observing their journey with curious interest. The cats' emerald eyes sparkled in the moon's rays as they trailed Crox and his companions.

When they reached the clearing, chaos awaited them. Pittapat was in the center of it all, locked in a standoff with Victoria and her followers. The large black & white stood still, looking at the smaller gray wolf's lifeless body lying on the ground. Dark fumes from Pittapat's vial lingered around the animal.

Victoria's eyes widened in surprise as she spotted Crox and Relda entering the clearing. "Well, well, look who has decided to join the party," she sneered, her lips curling into a sinister grin.

Crox paid no attention to Victoria's taunts; he was focused on Pittapat and the group of people surrounding her. He also noticed a woman standing at the edge of the forest who seemed ignored by everyone else. She was dressed in fashionable but loose dark pants and a tight white top stained with dirt. Her untidy blonde hair was cut in a bob, similar to a 1920s flapper.

"Be careful with Charlotte," Jax warned Crox through their telepathic communication. "She's just as dangerous as Victoria and Pittapat."

Crox nodded silently, taking Jax's warning seriously. He couldn't afford to let his guard down around her. Meanwhile, Relda prepared her Shotgun and the sound caught the attention of the coven members, causing them to turn toward her.

Crox's voice was composed and steady as he addressed the group of coven members gathered before him. "Listen to me. You don't have to follow these power-hungry women. Their path leads only to darkness and destruction. But if we work together, we can defeat the Shadow and restore peace to this forest. Join forces with me."

"What makes you think you're worthy of ruling over the Circle of the Eternal Shadow?" Victoria sneered, amused by Crox's bold words. "It's a shame you won't live long enough to see your plans fail. Although I admire your ambition, it seems your balls have finally dropped."

Relda aimed her shotgun at Victoria, loading a bullet into the chamber while Victoria continued to taunt her. But Relda remained steadfast; Victoria sneered as she looked down the gun barrel; she knew she held all the cards. "You think that little gun can kill me, you simpleton? My powers are far beyond mortal weapons."

Relda remained frozen with the gun aimed at Victoira's chest, refusing to give in to the witch's manipulations. "I am a law enforcement officer, and I will not allow you to cause any further damage." Her tone was unwavering and determined.

As Victoria raised her left hand, conjuring a deadly spell with her dark magick to snap Relda's neck in one swift motion, Pittapat sprang into action.

The small woman moved with astonishing speed, her small body fluid and agile as she launched herself at Victoria. She forcefully brought the larger woman down to the ground in a powerful display of strength. With animalistic ferocity, Pittapat sank her sharp teeth into Victoria's exposed throat, tearing out a large chunk of flesh and spitting it out onto the ground like a discarded bone.

Crimson blood gushed from the wound, staining the earth beneath them and filling the air with its metallic scent.

Pittapat's attack disrupted Amara's binding spell, causing the wolf to howl and struggle until it could move again. From the edge of the clearing, Charlotte yelled, "Be careful of the wolf! It's breaking free. Shoot it!"

Relda's finger tightened on the trigger of her shotgun. She aimed at Amara with deadly precision, pulling the trigger and unleashing a barrage of buckshot pellets that struck both the wolf and Pittapat.

The force of the impact sent them both flying; Pittapat writhed in agony as blood gushed from the wounds in her back and right legs. Victoria lay motionless, her throat slashed by Pittapat's teeth, whose mouth was still dripping blood. Relda stood victorious, her shotgun smoking in her hands as she surveyed the scene with cold satisfaction.

Despite the searing pain of its wounds, Amara let out a guttural howl. In a human voice filled with pure hatred, the wolf screamed at Crox, "The Shadow will have you!" Amara's body then began to writhe and convulse from the gunshot wounds inflicted by Relda.

Crox's eyes scanned the clearing and saw the coven members had remained frozen in shock. Their faces twisted in horror at the scene unfolding before them. He ran over to his mother to assist with her injuries when Victoria sat up, blood spilling out of the hole in her neck; the damage Pittapat caused would have killed a normal person, but Victoria was far from Normal.

Pittapat's eyes bulged with fear. As she saw Victoria stand up, she yelled, "Don't worry about me. Just kill Victoria and send her back to the grave!"

Victoria's eyes were filled with searing hatred as she locked eyes with Crox. "You and your cowardly alliance will pay for this. The power of the Shadow cannot be stopped," she spat, her voice hoarse and strained from the wound in her throat.

Relda aimed her shotgun at Victoria, but before she could pull the trigger, Victoria let out a bloodcurdling scream and threw up a hand in a quick motion. A blast of energy shot from her fingertips, sending Relda flying backward with a sickening thud against a tree.

Crox summoned every ounce of his willpower, drawing upon the deep well of magick within him. Focusing on the old grimoire spell he had carefully transcribed, he willed the spell to come alive and flow through his body. He could feel the weight of Victoria's magic pressing down on him, but he refused to falter.

He channeled his energy into the spell, unleashing a surge of magical force that crackled and glowed around him like a blazing fire. It was a gamble, but one that had to be taken.

With a booming voice that echoed through the clearing, Crox began to chant, "By the power of earth, wind, fire, water, and spirit, I bind thee, witch Victoria! You are banished from this realm! Never again shall you be seen or heard; leave this land of the living and let darkness consume you for eternity!"

His voice grew louder and more vibrant with each repetition of the chant until it seemed to shake the ground beneath their feet. A sudden and cold wind roared through the clearing, swirling around Victoria with the force of a tornado. The coven onlookers could only watch in horror as she was lifted off her feet by the cyclonic vortex, screaming in fury and pain. Amidst the chaotic winds and thunderous screams, Crox channeled all of his power to keep Victoria trapped within the powerful twister.

Everyone scrambled for cover as debris flew through the air. But Crox never wavered. His eyes locked onto Victoria as she thrashed about within the turbulent storm. The wind's force escalated to a deafening roar, shredding and ripping at Victoria's clothes and hair as she fought against Crox's powerful banishing spell.

Victoria felt the magick engulfing her with its overwhelming power. In a final act of desperation, she let out a bloodcurdling scream before vanishing into the vortex of wind, leaving behind only echoes of her terror. As the hurricane winds died down to a gentle breeze, Crox collapsed to his knees, drained physically from the intense spell. The toll it took on him was evident in the sweat on his forehead and the blood trickling from his nose.

Relda rushed to his side, helping him stand. "Are you alright?" she asked, noting his bleeding nose. Without hesitation, she tore off a piece of her shirt and pressed it into his nose. "Hold this tight," she instructed.

Crox nodded weakly, struggling to breathe after exerting so much magical energy. But he knew he couldn't rest for long.

Victoria may be gone for now, but he felt she could come back stronger and more determined than ever before.

"I'll be fine," he replied, his voice strained. "But we're not out of danger yet. Please check on my mother."

The sudden disappearance of Victoria left behind a haunting emptiness. Crox's mind raced with doubts as he struggled to catch his breath, wondering if the powerful spell cast had truly banished Victoria. If she had been dragged into the Shadow's realm, She could have been returned to the land of the living. The unease gnawed at him like a hungry beast, threatening to consume his sanity.

Relda rushed to check on Pittapat without hesitation, leaving Crox to face the mysterious Charlotte alone.

"So you're the one they call Charlotte... What is your true intention in all of this?" he asked, his words laced with a newfound sense of urgency.

Charlotte stepped forward, her expression unreadable as she stared back at him with unnerving calmness.

Charlotte smiled. "I never would have guessed you had the power to banish Victoria. You've grown considerably since I last saw you as a child."

Crox glared fiercely at her words. "You know nothing about me," he snapped. "Why are you here? What do you want?"

Charlotte sighed heavily before answering, "I am here for the same reason as everyone else. Victoria summoned me, and I didn't have a choice. But I also have my reasons for wanting to end this chaos, send the Shadow back where it belongs, and seal the portal."

Meanwhile, as Relda was tending to Pittapat's wounds, she cautiously asked Charlotte,

"Are you sure? You haven't been much help so far."

Charlotte gazed at Relda with a disdainful expression. "I know it's hard to believe, but I genuinely want to help. I have no loyalty to Victoria or her plans to revive the Shadow and the Circle of the Eternal Shadow.

Once, I cared for this town and its people, and I do not wish to see it consumed by darkness again. I can be an asset to you, but you must trust me."

Relda narrowed her eyes in suspicion, but eventually, she nodded. "Alright, we need all the help we can get. Just know that if you betray us, there will be dire consequences. Now, what about these people? They seem drugged. How can we safely remove them from here?"

Charlotte scanned the faces of her fellow coven members, noting their confusion and disorientation. "I can undo Victoria's spell on them, but it will take all of us working together. And with your mother here, our combined powers will be even stronger."

She walked over to Pittapat, who was still bleeding from her wounds but not as severely, thanks to Relda's quick-thinking tourniquet. Charlotte, Crox, and Relda placed their hands on Pittapat's shoulders. The forest cats, brought over by Jax and Slick, also joined them. Charlotte then took hold of Pittapat's hand in both hers and began to chant with a commanding tone.

"By the will of my spirit, the earth's foundation, the breath from the air, the fire that burns bright, and the water that flows freely, break the bonds that bind these souls. Release them and let them awaken to a free mind."

Soft orange light radiated from their clasped hands as she spoke, illuminating the clearing and its inhabitants. The coven members, still dazed, slowly snapped out of their trance and took in their surroundings.

Charlotte addressed the group, "I understand that some of you were brought back here against your will while others came willingly. I ask for your assistance for those who comprehend the necessity of destroying the Shadow's portal to our world. If you do not wish to help, now is your chance to leave. I won't warn you again. You can leave this place and never return, or it will cost your life. There are no other choices."

The coven members exchanged wary looks, unsure of what to do. The forest cats formed a line, almost appearing to guide them towards the exit out of the forest. Their bright green eyes glowed, lighting the way. Meanwhile, Pittapat leaned on Relda for support as she could not stand on her own due to the gunshot wounds.

After a brief moment of contemplation, some of the coven members decided to leave, following the guardian cats as they led them through the thick forest. They were grateful to be free from the nightmare that had held them captive. However, there were still a few who remained behind, unsure of what to do next.

Charlotte walked up to Crox with a faint smile and gently reminded him, "The bond between Victoria and the coven has been broken. Each member is now able to make their own choices. The power of the Shadow may tempt some, while others will choose a different path. It is not our place to dictate their fate."

Relda joined in the conversation. "What should we do next?"

Crox replied, "First, we must close the portal to the Shadow's realm. After that, we can focus on getting my mother to the hospital. It looks like we live to fight another day."

CHAPTER THIRTY

IMMORTAL ONE

The forest cats blended seamlessly into the shadows as the ex-coven members dispersed into the night. Crox and Relda carried Pittapat back to Crox's house, guided by the faint light of the moon filtering through the thick canopy of trees. Charlotte remained behind, informing Crox that she would join him when the forest was free of coven members. Despite his reservations about her, Crox was too exhausted to argue.

After arriving at Crox's house, Relda wasted no time calling for a rescue squad to transport Pittapat to the nearest hospital.

The shotgun wounds on her back had stopped bleeding, but she needed urgent medical attention. Thankfully, it appeared that the bullets had not hit her spine, and there would be no permanent damage.

Relda suggested she go with Crox's mother to the hospital and come up with a believable story for her gunshot wound. She told Crox to hide the shotgun and advised him to say that he had called Relda when he heard gunshots in the woods behind his house. They went to investigate, and his mother was accidentally shot in the process. The shooter, who they assumed was a hunter, quickly ran off into the woods and vanished without a trace.

Crox nodded gratefully at Relda's quick thinking. As Pittapat was whisked away in the ambulance with Relda by her side, Crox was left alone in the eerily silent house, his mind racing with thoughts and questions about the battle that had just transpired. "Is it over?" He thought. Jax and Slick stayed behind in the forest, keeping a watchful eye on Charlotte. They were determined to uncover her reasons for staying and understand her intentions. It was still a mystery why she hadn't left with the rest of the coven.

Crox poured himself a large glass of bourbon and collapsed onto the couch, trying to drown out his thoughts of Victoria's vicious death at the hands of his mother. However, he couldn't shake the feeling that the real battle had yet to come. As he drank more, he drifted into a deep slumber.

Meanwhile, Relda spun a tale for the doctors at Mary Washington Hospital about an unknown hunter lurking in the woods on the other side of Crox's property, diverting their attention from the clearing where the witch's showdown had occurred. The police department would surely be called, as was protocol for all gunshot wounds. Pittapat, still in pain from her wounds as well as a little drowsy from the pain medication, stayed on point and told everyone her name was Billysue Parham. She had been visiting the forest as a pilgrimage since her great-great-grandmother Victoria had lived and died there. Relda was quite impressed with her tall tale.

Back in the forest, Charlotte had taken charge of the forest cats, speaking to them with authority and reverence. My loyal guardians of these woods, it is time to rid our sacred sanctuary of the looming darkness of the Shadow. Crox's bloodline makes him vulnerable to the Shadow's influence, and we must guide and protect him from it." The cats' emerald eyes glowed as they listened intently to Charlotte's instructions.

They seemed to comprehend her words as she continued, "We must be watchful and alert at all times. The Shadow may seek another way into our world. We must prevent this from ever happening. Crox will require my guidance, and with your special gifts, we will shield him from the impending darkness together." Jax and Slick observed as the forest cats encircled Charlotte, obeying her respectfully as if she were an old friend.

"It seems she has a hold on the guardians," Jax murmured, glaring at Slick.

With a glint in his eyes, Slick replied, "She must have gained their trust somehow. There may be more to Charlotte than meets the eye. We should keep a close watch on her, but for now, it seems she is an ally."

In the hospital room, machines beeped rhythmically as Pittapat lay in a sterile bed, her life hanging by a thread. Relda sat silently by her side, contemplating whether it would be best to smother the resurrected witch while she slept.

Fortunately, the bullets had missed any major organs or bones in Pittapats' body. The emergency surgery was a success without any complications. Relda had messaged Crox to update him on the situation, but he had not responded yet. She hoped he was asleep and not out in the woods.

Crox woke up with a jolt back at the house. Despite the lingering effects of the bourbon, memories of last night flooded his mind. He checked his phone and saw Relda's messages about Pittapat's condition. A wave of relief washed over him, but he couldn't shake off the lingering anxiety.

As Crox got ready to go to the hospital, he sensed a strange energy in the air, causing the hairs on his neck to stand on end.

He glanced at his phone and saw it was seven a.m. He had slept for over six hours. He called out for Jax and Slick, but there was no response. The cats still had not returned home.

Crox raced to the hospital, his heart pounding with worry, hoping his mother was still alive. As he drove, he noticed the sun rising in a stunning display of oranges and pinks. Usually, such a beautiful sight would inspire Crox, but today, it only made him feel small in this enormous world.

In Pittapat's room, Relda greeted Crox with exhaustion and relief. Pittapat was asleep, heavily medicated by the nurses after her surgery. The doctor assured Relda that she would recover with rest and time. Crox sat beside his sleeping mother. He began questioning whether bringing her back to life was worth it. So far, she had not been much help in defeating the Shadow. Now that she was confined to a hospital bed, how could she aid in their mission?

The doctor who had done the surgery to remove the bullets came into the hospital room and assured Crox that the patient would recover without complications from her gunshot wounds. Since Pittapat still had not come around, and the doctor stated it could take some time for her to regain consciousness, Crox decided to leave and go back home to check on the cats.

He gestured for Relda to follow him into the hallway and said, "There's no need for us to stay here. I'll leave my contact information at the nurse's station if they need to reach me when Pittapat wakes up. Now that I've rested and feel more energized, I want to return to the woods and talk with Charlotte."

After Crox and Relda departed from the hospital, a surprise visitor appeared at Pittapat's bedside. A faint gray mist shimmered above her, floating in mid-air. Pittapat heard a telepathic voice in her deep slumber, "Awaken, you wretched traitor. Wake up and fulfill your promise to me. You have yet to pay with the soul of your son." The Shadow had exerted its last ounce of energy to reach out from the dark realm and communicate with its final remaining high priestess, who could still release it into the living world.

The voice of the dark entity reverberated through her mind, but she fought against it with all her might. Despite the pain and exhaustion from the drugs, Pittapat used her well-honed magical abilities to create a mental barrier, preventing the Shadow from fully infiltrating her thoughts. She imagined a shield of protection around her consciousness, attempting to block out the entity's influence.

Crox and Relda returned to the house, exhausted and needing rest. While Relda retreated to the spare bedroom for a few hours of sleep, Crox searched every room for their missing cats, Jax and Slick. But they were nowhere to be found. Growing increasingly worried, Crox grabbed his .38 Smith & Wesson before heading into the woods to search for them.

Crox entered the forest depths and was greeted with a sense of calm. The trail seemed different as if the events of last night had drained the energy from every tree and shrub on its path. Calling out for Jax and Slick, Crox's voice only echoed through the thick foliage.

As he reached the clearing, Crox saw Jax and Slick huddled together, watching Charlotte sitting in the rock circle. A group of forest cats stood guard around her. They all turned to face him as he approached. Charlotte stood up and stepped out of the circle of rocks, and the cats parted to let her pass. Her eyes bore into him with a menacing intensity.

"You have finally returned," she inquired, "I knew you would. We must talk about your mother and her ties to the Shadow."

Crox's face contorted in anger at the mention of his mother. "What about her?" he demanded.

The witch's eyes narrowed into slits as she paused, her calculating gaze sweeping over him before she spoke again with a voice as sweet as southern ice tea. "Darling, Your mother was unlike any witch of her time, bless her heart. She was a cunning and powerful force consumed by the allure of the Shadow and its promise of eternal life. This is the only reason she sought to join the Circle of the Eternal Shadow, and I unknowingly welcomed her into my coven. But she was not alone in her ambitions.

The infamous Amara and her mate Mortimer also coveted the power of immortality long ago and were willing to do anything to achieve it. And now, they are nothing but two dead wolves — casualties of their greed." Her lips twisted into a smirk.

Crox listened intently, his mind racing with thoughts and questions. "What happened to Amara and Mortimer that turned them into wolves?"

"They were killed before they could join the coven," Charlotte explained, reading Crox's thoughts. "But the Shadow offered them a deal. If they helped it collect souls, they would be allowed to cross over to the living world in a new form, as long as they remained loyal to the Shadow."

"What does this have to do with my mother?" Crox asked

"Your mother's desire for immortality and power drew her closer to the Shadow than she realized. When she failed to bring you to it, the Shadow killed her and then sought revenge on her by whispering lies and manipulating her into making a pact with her in death, ensuring she would come back and be immortal. There is a reason you found the spell to bring her back from the dead; it was foreseen. The Shadow's influence over her is still strong, demanding payment of your soul." Charlotte explained.

Crox's face contorted with a mixture of disbelief and anger. "So, everything that's been happening—the return of Victoria, the witches from the coven, and the wolves—is all because of my mother's pact with the Shadow?"

"Victoria's return was unplanned; I could sense the confusion in the Shadow. Why did the Shadow not kill her on sight? Well, this was most likely due to it wanting to use her to get to you in case you could not rise Pittapat from her dark grave," Charlotte stated absently.

"So, what do I do now?" Crox asked, his voice trembling with anger.

"We must find a way to break your mother's deal with the Shadow and prevent it from taking your soul. Your mother's grimoire may be the key to stopping this, but it must be destroyed after the Shadow is completely banished from this realm.

Death is the Begining must not find its way into the wrong hands. If it did, the portal could be reopened. Be warned, this won't be easy. The Shadow will do everything in its power to stop us," Charlotte replied

Charlotte raised her hands as if in prayer, and the forest cats gathered closely to her. After a few moments, the cats took off through the woods, fast as lightning.

"What the hell was that all about?" Crox said in shock.

"I am utilizing the forest cats' agility and stealth to sneak into your house and retrieve the grimoire from your study. Do not worry; they will not disturb your cop friend."

"How are they going to be able to do that? The house is locked, and the grimoire is in a safe. Also, how do you know Relda is asleep in my house?"

"My second sight sees far and wide; I know more than you could comprehend. Do not worry. My little guardians will succeed in the task I gave them. I am their queen, the immortal one."

Chapter Thirty-One

CLOSE THE PORTAL

Jax was concerned that the forest cats would cause chaos in the house, so he wanted to track them. Slick placed his paw on Jax's shoulder, signaling they needed to watch Crox. They couldn't predict what Charlotte might do.

After a few anxious minutes, the forest cats returned, two of them carrying the grimoire in their teeth. Crox was amazed. He had never expected them to retrieve it so quickly.

He turned to Charlotte in disbelief. "How did they break into my house, unlock my safe, take the book, and return so fast? Cats don't even have thumbs."

Charlotte laughed in a carefree, to hell with the devil tone and then replied. "My dear man, these are no ordinary felines. And besides, I helped ease their entry into your home. Trust me, my powers extend beyond the few hundred yards to your house. And the protection spell around your home won't stop me or my guardians."

Charlotte picked up the grimoire the cats had dropped at her feet. "My Pittapat did well in creating this grimoire. It contains all of my best spells and those of other powerful witches I knew. How she obtained them makes me wonder if she stole them or killed for them."

Charlotte opened the book and flipped through its pages while mumbling under her breath. The forest cats surrounded her with their emerald eyes reflecting the moonlight peeking through the trees. Crox watched intently as Charlotte seemed to search for a particular spell.

"What exactly are you looking for? The grimoire pages change on its own," Crox asked impatiently.

"We need to perform a separation spell to sever the connection between your mother and the Shadow. This will weaken its grip on her and prevent it from using her to reach you," Charlotte explained without taking her eyes off the book.

She continued turning pages, occasionally pausing to study one before moving on to another. After what felt like an eternity of flipping back and forth, Charlotte finally stopped and tore out a page.

Crox objected, "What are you up to? That book belongs to me. You can't simply tear pages out of it."

In a stern yet maternal tone, Charlotte responded, "Be quiet and show some respect for your elders. This may be your book, or rather, Pittapat's book, but this spell is mine. I had to tear it out because your mother placed a spell on the grimoire that changes the pages, making it difficult for you to complete the spell before the page changes. We need This spell to close the portal between the dimensions for good."

Crox nodded in frustration, though understanding that tearing the page was necessary. He had also felt the book's spells affect him. Charlotte placed the torn page on the ground and motioned for Crox to join her within the circle of rocks.

The forest cats gathered around them while Slick attempted to join the other cats. However, Jax stopped him, insisting he stay put. Slick's heart raced as he fought the overwhelming urge to rush to Crox's side, but Jax commanded that he stay put and prepare for whatever danger may come about. Slick's tail twitched with pent-up energy as he sat and watched.

Charlotte's voice began reverberating through the air, each syllable ringing out with a power that seemed to shake the ground beneath her feet. Her hands trembled as she chanted the words from the torn page of the spell book, her desperation evident in every breath. But just as her incantation reached its climax, a voice shattered the stillness of the woods.

"So, the whole gang is here, huh? Don't make any rash decisions, Sweet Charlotte." The visitor's face was shrouded in darkness, but Crox could feel his mother's presence. Her voice sends chills down his spine, a warning of impending danger.

Pittapat emerged from the dense trees and entered the clearing, still dressed in her hospital gown. The IV had been removed or torn out, as there was blood trickling down her arm from where it had been inserted.

"Mom, why did you leave the hospital? How did you even manage to get here like that? You're not even wearing shoes," Crox exclaimed as he crossed over the ring of rocks towards his mother.

Charlotte grabbed his arm and pulled him back into the circle. "No, stay here where you'll be safe. The Shadow cannot pass through my protective spell around this circle."

"What are you talking about? That's my mother, and she's hurt. I need to help her," Crox pleaded urgently.

"No!" Charlotte shouted, "That is the Shadow; it has taken over Pittapat's body."

Crox stood in shock and disbelief. "That is not possible. My mother would never allow such a thing."

"Your mother was weakened by being shot and is now able to be easily manipulated," the Shadow hissed through Pittapat's lips. "But thanks to her, I now have a new form in this realm, and I will now claim your soul."

Charlotte continued her incantation without faltering, ignoring the Shadow's threats. The forest cats growled and hissed in response. Pittapat's body thrashed and spasmed as the Shadow struggled against the protective barrier of the rock circle, determined to capture Crox's soul.

The Shadow's laughter echoed through the forest as it taunted them, "You are such foolish mortals to even try to stop me. I will claim what was promised to me, and no one will stand in my way."

The Shadow's evil laughter continued to echo through the trees, and Charlotte's chanting grew in intensity and volume, overpowering the evil sound coming out of Pittapats mouth.

With the Shadow struggling against the protective barrier, Pittapat's body twisted in impossible ways. Her arms contorted and broke while her fingers clawed at her face, leaving bloody marks on her cheeks.

Crox's heart ached as he watched this horrifying creature use his mother's form as its vessel. But he knew he couldn't let his emotions distract him or put himself within the Shadow's reach, so he stayed within Charlotte's protective circle.

"Stay focused, Crox. Help me complete the spell before the Shadow breaks through the portal; it can only possess Pittapat's body for so long," urged Charlotte.

Crox and Charlotte joined forces, reciting the incantation to seal the interdimensional portal and sever the connection between the Shadow and Pittapat, thereby forcing the entity out of her body.

"I summon the elements of earth, wind, fire, water, and spirit; hear my call. Close this gateway of darkness forevermore. Banish this Shadow of evil from our realm. Silence its whispers of fear and hate. Invoke the power of light and peace. Drive this creature away. Sever its ties to our world."

The forest trembled, causing the trees to sway rhythmically as if they were dancing to a disco beat. A deep rumbling sound filled the air as the ground split open beside Charlotte and Crox, revealing the opening to a dark cavern below. The wind picked up speed, howling through the trees and swirling around them. Suddenly, a vivid lime-green light burst from the center of the stone circle. It moved swiftly, engulfing the Shadow in its radiance.

The furious creature let out a deafening roar, attempting to break free from the luminous light's hold. Yet, it seemed to be trapped by the green glow. In a fit of rage, the Shadow, still inhabiting Pittapat's body, bit off her index finger and spat it onto the ground. As blood spilled from the wound, the Shadow used it to draw a mystical symbol on Pittapat's forehead, which was then chanted in a strange foreign tongue.

The Shadow's chanting grew more fervent as if it were a counter-spell fighting against the light that held it captive. The forest cats circled around Pittapat's body, their eyes blazing in fury as they hissed and spat at the Shadow that resided in the witch's body, adding their own layer of power to maintain Charlotte's spell.

Relda emerged from behind a large tree, shotgun in hand. "Looks like you could use some backup," she said as she positioned herself on the opposite side of the rock circle, gun aimed at the once-Pittapat creature. The forest cats intensified their efforts, growling and hissing louder, while Crox and Charlotte continued their chant.

The Shadow's voice grew more desperate, its chanting reverberating louder through the clearing. The ground continued to tremble under Crox's feet as he focused all his mental energy on maintaining the spell that held the Shadow in place. Sweat dripped down his forehead as he struggled to keep control.

Suddenly, a blinding flash of light engulfed the entire area, followed by a powerful burst of electric energy that knocked everyone off their feet, including the forest cats.

Crox shielded his eyes but could feel an immense surge of strength begin to course through his body.

When the blinding light faded, there was no sign of the Shadow. Only a pile of ash remained, along with the fading echoes of its furious screams. With the destruction of the Shadow came Pitta-pats' demise as well. It was as if the brilliant light had incinerated her physical form completely.

The ground stopped trembling, and the wind died down. Crox could see that the open cavern entrance was now sealed shut as if it had never been there. The forest cats returned to their original positions around the rock circle, their eyes losing their ferocity and their fur flattening back down. Crox and Charlotte stood there, trying to catch their breath after the intense physical exertion.

"Is it truly gone?" Crox asked, still struggling to believe what just happened.

"Yes, for now. By closing off its portal to this dimension, we have ensured that it will never harm anyone again," Charlotte replied with a sense of relief in her voice.

"Thank you for your help. You have some powerful magick in you," Crox said respectfully.

"Don't thank me just yet. There is still one final step to guarantee that the Shadow will never return," Charlotte said gravely.

Crox was determined to protect his home and community at all costs. "What do we need to do?" he asked.

"Our only option is to destroy your mother's grimoire. If even one trace of the spell that summoned the Shadow remains, it could find its way back into the wrong hands," Charlotte explained.

Crox furrowed his brow in confusion. "Why does the whole book have to be destroyed? Can't you eliminate this specific spell and others related to the Shadow?"

Charlotte shook her head. "Your mother placed powerful protection spells on her book. Removing one page won't erase the spell from the rest of the book. It constantly changes with each use, so tearing out a page won't get rid of it permanently. The only way is through a blood fire.

Crox turned to Slick and Jax for confirmation as they finally joined him. "Wait, did you just say a blood fire?" he asked.

Relda interjected, walking over with her shotgun at the ready. "Can someone please explain what's going on here?"

Charlotte turned to Relda, frustration evident on her face. "You were there hiding in the woods, and you saw everything. I banished the Shadow back to its realm and closed the portal it used to enter our world."

"Actually," Crox said with a hint of attitude, "we both closed the portal."

Relda couldn't help but smirk at Crox's remark. She then turned back to Charlotte. "Okay, okay. So you both closed the portal and now you must destroy the entire book? And what's this about a blood fire?"

Charlotte's eyes narrowed as she glared at Relda, her voice dripping with disdain. "How many times do I have to explain this to you? Pay attention. A blood fire is a force of pure destruction that can annihilate any spell book created by one's flesh and blood. It requires a fire fueled by the blood of someone directly connected to the book through their bloodline. And since Pittapat was your mother, Crox, your very blood holds the key."

Charlotte's harsh tone caused Relda to flinch, but her curiosity was stronger than her fear. "Let me get this straight," Relda said bitterly. "In order to destroy Pittapat's spell book, we have to use Crox's blood to ignite this blood fire spell? How are we supposed to do that?" Charlotte smiled at Relda and replied, "You shall see.

CHAPTER THIRTY-TWO

FOREST WITCH

In the pale moonlight, Charlotte's eyes shone as she described the intricacies of the blood-fire spell. Crox found himself entranced by her gaze. Without warning, she seized his arm with a viselike grip and dug her sharp nails into his bicep, drawing forth droplets of crimson blood that trickled down his arm.

Jax and Slick lunged at Charlotte's legs, their teeth sinking into her flesh, but she barely flinched as she held onto Crox with one hand and swatted the cats away with the other. A sinister smile spread across her face as she reveled in Crox's pain.

Relda Screamed, "STOP YOU DAMN BITCH!"

Relda swung the shotgun, connecting with Charlotte's face and causing her to stumble backward. As a result, Crox was released from Charlotte's grasp, his arm bleeding profusely onto the ground.

"That was uncalled for," Charlotte snapped, wiping away the blood from her split lip. "I need his blood to complete the spell to destroy the grimoire."

"Well, you could have asked politely," Relda retorted, still gripping the shotgun like a bat.

Crox's fists were clenched so tightly that his knuckles turned white. The scowl on his face could have melted steel. "Just get this over with," he spat at Charlotte, his voice dripping with disdain. "But if you touch me again, I swear I will knock you into next week."

Charlotte could see the anger simmering just below the surface. She then laughed in his face, paying no attention to Relda's or Crox's threats. She picked up the grimoire with her blood-stained hands and stepped back into the rock circle, standing atop the pentagram that had been burned into the ground.

Charlotte carefully opened the leather spellbook, its pages yellowed and frayed with age. She wiped her hands on the pages, which were covered in Crox's blood. A thick, pungent scent of iron filled the air from Crox's drying blood.

Closing her eyes, Charlotte raised her arms toward the sky, palms facing upward as if reaching for the power of the heavens. Her lips moved with practiced ease as she chanted the incantation that would destroy this cursed grimoire once and for all.

As she recited the spell of blood fire, her voice grew stronger with each word. "From blood of blood, ignite this book in flames. Burn as hot as the sun. Destroy the evil of *Death Is the Beginning*, made from kindred blood. Turn it to ashes and scatter it to the four winds. Leave no trace of the secrets held within." The spell took hold, and a low hum resonated from the center of the rock circle where Charlotte stood.

The forest cats gathered around her, their eyes glowing with a bright white light as they bore witness to this magick. The felines' purring seemed to merge with Charlotte's chanting, creating a symphony of mystical energy that reverberated through the clearing. Slowly but surely, a faint red glow emanated from the grimoire as if responding to the spell. It was a sign that the spell was working—soon, this book would be nothing but ashes and dust, unable to harm anyone ever again.

Relda, her fingers tight around the cold metal of the shotgun, stood ready. Her eyes were laser-focused on Charlotte, never breaking her gaze as she prepared for what may come next. Crox, now a silent spectator, watched with bated breath as the grimoire began to emit thick smoke. The air grew heavy with the acrid scent of burning paper.

The flames erupted from the grimoire's pages, turning them into blackened ash and destroying the dark magick within its binding; Charlotte's voice rose in volume. Her words carried a commanding power, directing the fire to purify the book completely.

A warm wind swept through the forest, carrying the faint scent of charred paper and remnants of the powerful magick that once resided within its pages. The fiery embers danced and swirled in the air before floating upwards towards the treetops, their glow casting a red aura over the forest.

As the last remnants of the spellbook dissolved into nothing but black smoke, a surge of energy erupted from the rock circle, spreading across the forest. The feline inhabitants of the forest let out a collective cry as the wind carried away the remaining ashes like fiery snowflakes, leaving behind nothing but empty space.

Charlotte's arms dropped to her sides, and the purple glow within the circle faded. The forest's quiet enveloped them once more, only interrupted by the faint rustling of leaves.

Relda lowered her shotgun and let out a deep breath. The cats retreated into the woods, seemingly satisfied with their job. Jax and Slick approached Crox, rubbing against his legs as if to offer comfort as he tended to his wounded arm.

After a few moments of silence, Relda finally spoke up. "That was quite a show. Is it over now? Are there no more Shadows or evil witches to worry about, apart from our esteemed company?"

Charlotte turned towards them with a serious expression. "For the time being, yes. The portal has been closed, and our realm is no longer linked to the Shadows. But we must stay vigilant. The Shadow is devious; some still seek to harness its power for their own gain."

Crox nodded in understanding. "What do we do next?"

Charlotte glanced between Relda and Crox before gesturing towards the forest cats that had remained and gathered around her.

"You two don't have to worry about anything else. My friends and I will take care of the forest and keep it safe from any evil that attempts to cross its border," she stated confidently.

Relda wasn't satisfied with this vague response. "That doesn't answer anything," she snapped.

With a mysterious smile, Charlotte replied, "Maybe it's better if you don't know." Then she turned on her heel and walked away, following the forest cats, disappearing into the trees. Relda and Crox stood in shock, their mouths hanging open.

"That was less climactic than I anticipated," Relda commented, finally breaking the silence between them.

Crox chuckled, "I was expecting more dramatic theatrics, especially from a powerful and immortal witch."

Their laughter filled the air as they walked back toward the house. Crox called out for Jax and Slick, but the cats seemed too comfortable to move. Jax communicated through telepathy that they would join them for dinner later and asked for it to be prepared when they returned home.

As Crox and Relda made their way back to the house, Slick pulled Jax aside and shared his worries, "I don't think the portal has been securely closed. It would be wise for me to stay here and keep watch, just in case. The forest is not only home to cats that need protecting, but now Charlotte as well. I want to assist her."

Jax nodded in agreement, "We'll handle whatever comes our way in the future. With Crox fully in control of his magick, he can defend himself. But he still needs both of us. Now that he knows you are Sean trapped in this form, you need to reconnect."

Slick's expression was sad as he replied, "Crox will never be able to live his life fully if I am around this form. It wouldn't be fair to him. If Charlotte can find a way to restore me back to my human self, I will return home. Until then, I'll stay in the forest and keep watch over him from afar."

"I understand. I'll always be here for you if you need me. I can't leave my brother alone." Jax replied before rushing off to meet Relda and Crox.

The forest was once again safe, and the cats who guarded its border could roam freely without worry. They now had an immortal guardian—Charlotte, now known as the Forest Witch, who would watch over the woods and the animals that called them home.

While the threat of the Shadow still lingered, Crox and Relda were satisfied, knowing that, for now, they were safe. As they walked among the trees toward Crox's house, they were confident their bond would only grow stronger after this ordeal, making them an unbreakable duo for any future danger threatening the Fredericksburg, Virginia, Region.

Crox, Jax, Relda, and Slick would remain vigilant and strike down any evil that dared to enter these woods. The story was far from over, and the battle for the forest may rage on until their dying breaths. United, they will stand firm and face any obstacles that come their way. This battle had only been the start of an unending war against darkness and black magick, not the end.

ABOUT THE AUTHOR

David Cropper owns and manages Cropper Home Sales LLC., an esteemed real estate brokerage. Renowned for his unwavering reliability and trustworthiness, David has solidified his position as the go-to figure in the Fredericksburg Region for buying and selling homes. Beyond his professional pursuits, David finds fulfillment in his personal life alongside his beloved husband, Sean. Together, they share their home with a lively bunch comprising four feline familiars and a spoiled German Shepherd mix.

Motivate and encourage others to join in creating a harmonious world where everyone has the opportunity to find solace and security within their own home—a place where each person's voice is heard and their personal experiences are valued and shared. Together, let us build a community where all can find a sense of belonging.